A Woman of the Iron People

"At last, a non-predictable,
thought-through-can't-stop-reading-it-story,
full of complicated and irresistible people,
some of them human.
This fascinating novel asks
some big, serious questions,
and it gives no easy answers–
but some very wise and funny ones.
ENJOY, ENJOY!"
URSULA K. LE GUIN,
author of *The Dispossessed* and
The Left Hand of Darkness

"MONUMENTAL . . .
Arnason's well-knit storyline and subplots
resonate with insight . . .
A WORLD BUILT TO GET LOST IN"
Houston Post

"A SUPERB STORYTELLER . . .
Eleanor Arnason promises to be
as important as Ursula K. Le Guin . . .
A gentle but moving parable
about the nature of human society
and sexuality."
CHARLES PLATT, author of *The Silicon Man*

"A REAL PLEASURE,
like a long, cool drink of water
full of unusual and diverse flavors,
flashes of the unexpected, and
delightful glints of humor."
SUZY MCKEE CHARNAS,
author of *The Vampire Tapestry*

"A MASTERPIECE . . .
An excellent and worthy book"
Mythprint

"EXCELLENT . . .
Strong prose, meticulously detailed cultures
and commanding characterization . . .
AN INTELLIGENT, PROVOCATIVE BOOK"
Publishers Weekly

"I LOVED THIS NOVEL . . .
A work of genuine science fiction
in which attention is paid to extrapolation
and true scientific detail.
Eleanor Arnason tells her story
with grace, elegance and wit,
enticing the reader from the very first page
and not letting go until the last."
PAMELA SARGENT, editor of *Women of Wonder*

"A NOVEL WORTHY OF COMPARISON
TO URSULA LE GUIN"
Denver Post

"ARNASON DOES A FIRST CLASS JOB . . .
An engaging piece of
anthropological science fiction"
The Pioneer Press

"A COZY AND DISTURBING BOOK,
FULL OF GOOD STORIES,
ENGAGING CHARACTERS,
AND DANGEROUS IDEAS"
M.J. ENGH, author of *Arslan*

"SHE WRITES WITH AN EASY,
INFECTIOUS CHARM . . .
Keeps exceeding the reader's expectations–
which is surely the most we can ask
of any science fiction novel."
Washington Post Book World

"WELL ABOVE THE HERD OF
ANTHROPOLOGICAL SF NOVELS . . .
She has undertaken an immense task here–
nothing less than describing
the collision of cultures–
and manages to do it in fascinating detail . . .
Jonathan Swift would have understood
and approved."
JOHN SLADEK, author of *Tik-Tok*

"A CELEBRATION . . .
A truly exciting development in our genre"
GWYNETH JONES, author of *Divine Endurance*

Look for Part 2 of
A WOMAN OF THE IRON PEOPLE *by*
Eleanor Arnason
Coming Soon from Avon Books

CHANGING WOMEN

A Woman of the Iron People

Part One

In The Light of Sigma Draconis

ELEANOR ARNASON

AVON BOOKS • NEW YORK

In the Light of Sigma Draconis originally appeared as "Part One" and comprised the first half of the hardcover A WOMAN OF THE IRON PEOPLE by Eleanor Arnason, published by William Morrow and Company, Inc., in 1991.

AVON BOOKS
A division of
The Hearst Corporation
1350 Avenue of the Americas
New York, New York 10019

Map by P. C. Hodgell
Cover illustration by Gary Ruddell
Published by arrangement with the author
Library of Congress Catalog Card Number: 91-92419
ISBN: 0-380-75637-4

Published in hardcover by William Morrow and Company, Inc.; for information address Avon Books.

First AvoNova Printing: June 1992

Printed in the U.S.A.

RA 10 9 8 7 6 5 4 3 2 1

For the Members of the Aardvarks,
the oldest established SF writing workshop
in Minneapolis and/or St. Paul

(We also do mysteries
and doctoral dissertations.)

ACKNOWLEDGMENTS

My thanks to the following people who read this novel in manuscript and gave me advice on changes:

Ruth Berman, John Douglas, David G. Hartwell, Eric M. Heideman, Albert W. Kuhfeld, Mike Levy, Sandra Lindow, and Shoshona Pederson.

Al Kuhfeld designed the wonderful starship and read the novel with an eye for errors in science. The manuscript went through three revisions after he saw it, and he is in no way responsible for any new errors that may have been introduced. Susan Pederson helped me design the culture of the Iron People. Ruth Berman came up with my favorite name for the starship. P. C. Hodgell drew the map.

My special thanks to Bill Gober, who heard me talk about the novel years ago at Minicon. Every year since then he has come up to me at Minicon and loomed over me and said, "Have you finished the novel about the furry people *yet?*"

Here it is, Bill. I hope it's worth the wait.

CONTENTS

The water says:
I remember.
I came first of all.
There was nothing before me.

In the time of rain
rain fell on the water.
In the time of dryness
the water reflected the sky.

I came first of all.
There was nothing before me.

Vapor rose.
It became
the tree of heaven.

Vapor rose.
It became
the bird of the sun.

A seed fell.
The earth began growing.
Animals sprang up.
The vegetation was thick.

Then came the people.
Then came the spirits
and the powerful demons
who live under the earth.

Let me tell you:
I will outlast them.

Even the demons
will disappear in time.

I have no shape.
No one can divide me.
No one can say
what I really am.

FROM: *The Committee on the First Contact Problem*
TO: *The Members of the First Interstellar Expedition*

The problem, as we see it, divides in three. (1) You may meet people who have a technology more advanced than ours. (2) You may meet people with an equal technology. (3) You may meet people with a less advanced technology.

(We will leave aside, for the time being, the problem of what is meant by "more" and "less" advanced. We will also leave aside the possibility that the aliens may have a technology so different from ours that there is no way to compare the two.)

We think you are most likely to encounter problem number three: the aliens with a less advanced technology. But we'll discuss all the possibilities, just in case.

The aliens with an equal technology present the least problem. We certainly cannot hurt them, not at a distance of 18.2 light-years. If their technology is more or less the same as ours, they won't be able to hurt us, either. There is the possibility of considerable gain for both cultures without much risk. You can probably go ahead with confidence.

If you meet aliens with a really advanced technology (with FTL travel, for example) you will have to stop and think.

According to current social theory, any species that is able to travel to the stars is also able to destroy itself, and any species that can destroy itself will, unless it learns very quickly how to deal with its own less pleasant aspects.

We think it's unlikely that you will meet a star-faring species that is aggressive, violent, bigoted, or crazy with greed. But all our theories are based on a sample of one, and we may not be as nice as we think we are.

If you meet a species with a superior technology, be cautious. You may want to keep your distance, at least at first. You may not want to tell them where you come from.

If they are decent and peaceful, they will respect your caution. If they do not, remember that your ship has been provided with the means for self-destruction. If necessary, you can wipe the computer system clean and kill everyone on board.

This capability has been provided with extreme reluctance. (See Appendix D.) It may be evidence that we, as a species, have not outgrown our own terrible past.

The problem when dealing with a more advanced species is self-protection.

(Remember, when we talk about advancement here, we are speaking only about technology.)

The problem when dealing with a less advanced species is karma. We don't want to hurt them. Our species has done a lot of hurting over time.

Be *very* careful if you encounter people whose technology is not equal to ours. Remember all the cultures destroyed over the past seven centuries. Remember all the millions of people who have died on Earth: entire tribes and nations, language groups, religions—vanished, murdered. Remember the other hominids who are no longer with us. Remember Homo sapiens neanderthalensis.

We think we understand the process now. We think we will not do these things again. But we are not certain.

Go very slowly. Think about what you are doing.

Lao Zi and Zhuang Zi remind us of the dangers of action.

The masters of Chan and Zen warn us that when we discriminate, when we divide "good" from "evil" and "high" from "low," we are moving away from true understanding.

Karl Marx tells us that action is inevitable and that we have to discriminate in order to understand.

You have your choice of sages.

However, remember that—according to Marx—the goal of socialism is *mindful* action, history made conscious, people who know what they are doing.

Remember, also, that categories are not fixed. "Good" and "evil" change their meaning. "High" and "low" are relative. The distinctions—the discriminations—you take with you on your journey may not be useful when you arrive.

Good luck.

Copies of this memo have been input to the Open Access Information System (OASIS), the Archives of the Alliance of Human Communities (ANKH), and the Archives of the Fifth, Sixth, and Eighth Internationals.

Appendix A: On the possible meaning(s) of "more" and "less" advanced.

Appendix B: Why we think you are more likely to meet people with a less advanced technology.

Appendix C: Minority report on the dangers of cultural chauvinism.

Appendix D: Minority report on the dangers of fear.

Appendix E: Minority report on the relevance of Daoist and Buddhist concepts.

Appendix F: Minority report on the relevance of Karl Marx.

Appendix G: *Dao De Jing* (Complete.)

Appendix H: *The German Ideology*. (Selections.)

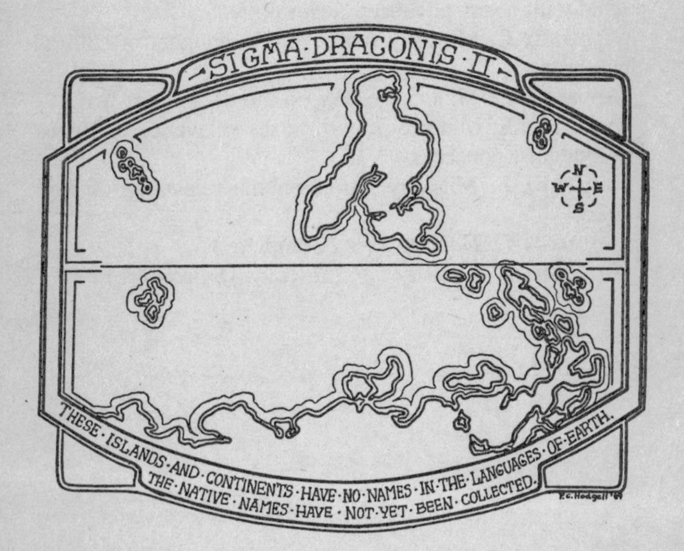
SIGMA·DRACONIS·II
N
W
E
S
THESE·ISLANDS·AND·CONTINENTS·HAVE·NO·NAMES·IN·THE·LANGUAGES·OF·EARTH.
THE·NATIVE·NAMES·HAVE·NOT·YET·BEEN·COLLECTED.

ANASU

Her mother had been a metal worker, a follower of the Mistress of the Forge. But she died young, one spring in the mating season. This sometimes happened. A woman left the village and never returned.

The old crones said, “A crazy man got her. Hu! The lot of women is difficult!”

In any case, Nia and her brother were alone. Suhai, who was one of her mother’s sisters, took them in. She was a large gruff woman with a pelt so dark that it looked more black than brown.

Besides taking them, she took their mother’s belongings: the tent, the cart, the six bowhorn geldings, and all the tools of iron, bronze, and stone.

“A just payment,” Suhai told them. “You will cost me a lot in the winters to come. I have children of my own to care for, too.”

Her brother Anasu, who was eight then, said, “You have always been a grasping person.”

Suhai glowered. “Go outside. I don’t want to look at you.”

Anasu made the gesture of assent, then stood. The flap of the tent was up. She could see her brother clearly. He was slender and graceful. His pelt was reddish brown. It shone like copper in the sunlight. He wore that day—she thought she remembered later—a kilt of dark blue cloth, high boots, and a belt with a silver buckle.

Anasu left. Nia looked at Suhai, sitting hunched by the fire, which was out.

"Thank the Mother of Mothers I have no sons. Well, I intend to do that which is right. I'll raise him, though I don't expect to enjoy a moment. You, Nia, will be less trouble, I am sure. The women of our family have always been even-tempered."

Nia made no reply.

Things turned out as Suhai had expected. She got no pleasure from raising Anasu, though he was clever and dexterous. No lad his age did better embroidery. He was good with a bow. He was good-humored, too, except around Suhai. The two of them always quarreled.

Nia stayed out of the quarrels. She was, she discovered, a timid person. Good for little, she told herself. She could not help Anasu, though she felt closer to him than to anyone; and she could not stand up to Suhai. Always and always she did what her aunt wanted.

Like all the people in the world, her people followed the herds. In the spring they went north to the Summer Land: a wide, flat plain. There were many small lakes and shallow rivers. On days when Suhai let her go free, she and Anasu built fish traps out of the branches of a bush that grew at the edges of the rivers. The branches were thin and flexible. They could be woven around one another, then tied with pieces of stringbark.

They put the traps into a river. Then they sat on the bank and talked till a thrashing in the water told them a fish was caught.

When he was in a dreamy mood, Anasu talked of flying. The large clouds of summer looked habitable to him.

"Not the thunderclouds, of course, but the others. I don't think they'd be good for herding. They have too many hills. But I could take my bow up there. We know there is water. Maybe there are fish."

She listened, not saying much. Anasu was two years older than she was. He always had more to say.

In fall the village went south: the herd first, guided by the adult men. Then came the carts, the women and children, and the very old men. Hisu the bow master was one of these.

The Winter Land was a rolling plain dotted with trees. In the south were stony hills. Beyond the hills was an enormous body of water.

"Our salt comes from there," Anasu told her. "Some of the men, the really adventurous ones, stay here alone in the summer. Hisu told me this. He did it when he was young. He waited till the herd was gone, then crossed the hills. On the other side are smaller hills, made of sand, and then the water. It stretches to the horizon, Hisu said, like the plain in the Summer Land; and it tastes salty. Anyway, he made pans out of wood. There is no wood nearby, he said. He had to bring it from the hills of stone. Hu! What a lot of work! Anyway, he filled the pans with water. When the water dried, there was salt in the pans." He looked at her, excited by this bit of information and wanting her to be excited, too.

Nia made the gesture that meant she heard and understood.

Anasu made the gesture that meant "if that's the way you feel about it." Then he said, "I think I'll gather salt when I'm a man."

There was something hard in her throat. She never liked to think of growing up.

The years went by. When she was ten, Suhai began to teach her how to work iron. This made her happy, she told Anasu.

"You ought to have started a year ago or maybe two years back. Suhai is always grudging and slow."

"Nonetheless, I am happy," Nia said. "Suhai is good at what she does."

"In the smithy, maybe. Elsewhere, no."

Anasu grew tall. His body began to thicken. Suhai really hated him now.

"I have never liked men. Even when I was full of the spring lust, I still thought they were awful. I'm tired of coming home and finding you in my tent."

Anasu, who was fourteen by this time, made the gesture of assent. He gathered his belongings—the kilts, the boots, the one long cloak for winter—and left. His bow was in its case over one shoulder, and his knife hung from his belt.

Nia stood up, shaking. "Enough is enough, old woman. I won't tolerate you any longer. I'm going, too."

"Very well." Suhai sat down by the fire. Dinner was cooking in a big pot. She pulled out a hunk of meat and ate it.

Nia began to pack.

She walked out of the tent, feeling proud. For the first time she could remember, she had done something important on her own. What next? She didn't know. She stopped and looked around. It was late summer. The day was hot and still. Smoke rose straight up from the village's cooking fires. In the distance the yellow plain shimmered. She had no idea at all of what to do.

"Nia?"

It was Ti-antai, her cousin: a plump woman with dark brown fur.

"Anasu told me he has left my mother."

Nia made the gesture of affirmation. "So have I."

"That terrible woman! She will end by driving everyone away. My grandmother told me once, Suhai ought to have been a man. She is too quarrelsome to be a woman. Come stay with me, for the time being anyway."

Nia made the gesture of agreement.

She stayed with Ti-antai on the trip south. Then, when they reached the Winter Land, she moved in with Hua, an ancient woman whose children had all died. Her tent was empty, and she needed help at her forge.

"A good exchange. You help. You keep me company. I will teach you the secrets of gold and silver. I know them, you know. There was a time when I was the best smith in the village. I'm not so bad these days, either. My hands have gotten a little stiff, of course, and my eyes aren't what they used to be. But what is, after all? In any case, I will teach you how to inlay silver into iron. And gold, too. Move in whenever you like."

Anasu traded his best piece of embroidery for two pieces of leather. From these he made a tent, a small one. He lived by himself at the edge of the village. That winter Nia saw him little.

In the spring, on the trip north, he rode near Hua's cart and helped with the bowhorns. One of them was a young male, strong but reluctant to pull.

By this time Anasu was full grown. He was quieter than he used to be, though still good-tempered.

One morning, midway through the trip, Nia woke a little earlier than usual. She got up and went outside. They were camped next to a river. Mist drifted on the water. The sun was just beginning to show above a range of hills in the east. She went to the cart. The back panel was fastened with hinges and chains. It could be let down, so that loading and unloading could be done more easily, and it could be fastened halfway down, making a flat place. Anasu slept on it. He had thrown off his cloak sometime in the night. He lay on his back, one arm over his face, shielding his eyes. All at once Nia saw her brother clearly. He was large and solid. He looked shaggy, rough, a little unfamiliar. The change was coming. She felt a terrible grief.

He woke and stretched. "Hu! Am I stiff!"

She thought of hugging him, but decided no. She would have to explain why she did it. Instead, she went to start the fire and make breakfast.

That summer Nia tried to spend more time with Anasu. But he was restless, silent. He liked to hunt and fish alone. When he was in the village, he worked at making arrows or on finishing a large piece of embroidery. It showed a man with large curving horns: the Master of the Herds. On either side of him were bowhorn does. Above him was the sun and a pair of birds.

"Don't bother him," Ti-antai said. "He is getting ready for the change. If you want to do something for him, work on his parting gifts."

Nia made the gesture of assent.

The summer was rainy and unusually short. The sun was still pretty far to the north when the birds began to leave.

"A bad winter," Hua said. "I'll ask the tanner what she wants in exchange for a good fur cloak. Now, we'd better start packing."

Just before they left the Summer Land, the sky cleared. For two days it was bright and warm. Anasu came to her then. "Let's go catch fish."

They made traps and set them in the river. Then they sat on the bank. Already the leaves on the bushes were starting to turn yellow. The sun was hot. A river lizard sat on a nearby rock. Head up, it watched them carefully. Under its chin was a bag of skin, orange in color. Once or twice, it inflated this and croaked.

Anasu picked up a twig and broke it into pieces. "I'm getting more and more irritable. There are days, Nia, when I can barely stand people. I think—the next one that comes near me I will hit."

The change, Nia thought.

"I decided to tell you this. I want you to know, if I leave suddenly or get violent, it is because I cannot keep control any longer."

"We all know this."

He made the gesture of disagreement suddenly, violently. "You cannot know. My bones are on fire. It's like a fire in a peat bog that never goes out. I have never felt worse than this, even when our mother died." He stood up. "I'm not going to stay here, Nia. Good-bye."

He walked away. Nia sat awhile looking at the river. A fish thrashed in the water where they had set one of their traps. She waded out to get it.

On the trip south she barely saw him. Once or twice, through the dust, she got a glimpse of a young man riding. It might have been him. One evening he came to their tent. His fur was rough and dull. His clothes were dirty. He sat down across from them and helped himself to dinner. Old Hua, who was usually talkative, said nothing.

At last Nia said, "How are you?"

He looked at her blankly. His eyes were not pure yellow, she noticed. There was orange around the pupils. She hadn't remembered that.

He made the gesture that meant neither good nor bad. Then he went back to eating. After he was done, he left.

"Finish up your gifts," old Hua said.

She did. The last one was a buckle made of iron, covered with silver. It showed a bowhorn fighting a killer-of-the-mountains.

"Not bad," said Hua. "You will do me proud someday."

Nia made the gesture that meant a polite or modest refusal to agree.

"You have too little self-respect," Hua said.

The trip ended. The people set up their tents next to the Brown River. North of them there was a stone ridge. Its lower slopes were forested. To the south, across the river, was the plain: rolling, tree-dotted, late summer yellow. The herd was pastured there.

There was no sign of Anasu. Nia felt uneasy.

"He will come," Ti-antai said. "No man leaves without his parting gifts—unless, of course, the change drives him crazy. But that rarely happens."

"You are not always a comfort, cousin."

At first the weather was dry. Then it began to rain. Every day there were a few drops at least. Most days it rained or drizzled for hours. The air was cold. Hua said her bones ached. Nonetheless, she kept busy.

One afternoon they were both at the forge. Nia worked the bellows for Hua, who was making a long knife: a parting gift for Gersu, the tanner's son, who was a little younger than Anasu.

When the hammering was done and the blade was in cold water, Nia set down the bellows. She rubbed her neck.

"Nia." It was Anasu. His voice sounded hesitant.

Nia looked around. He stood nearby, holding his bowhorn's reins. He looked worse than ever: shaggy, muddy, confused.

"Anasu?"

"I—" He stopped for a moment. "I have come for the gifts. I am going across the river."

She made the gesture of acknowledgment, then the gesture of regret.

"You stay here," Hua said. "No one will bother you. We'll pack everything."

They went inside. Hua put wood on the fire, then set a pan of milk to heat.

Nia got out the new saddlebags the tanner had made, then the cloth she had gotten from Blind Angai the weaver in return for a new pot. She or Hua or Ti-antai had made most of the rest of the things. She laid them out one by one: the new knife, the kettle, the brass needles, the awl, and the long-handled comb, the kind that men used to comb the hair on their backs.

What else? She was having trouble thinking.

"The new belt, ninny!" Hua was packing food: dried meat, dried berries, bread.

At last they were done. Hua poured the milk into a cup. They took the saddlebags to Anasu. It had begun to rain a little. He was standing where they'd left him, looking nervous. His bowhorn, sensing the nervousness, kept moving, turning its head, flicking its ears, tugging at the reins.

Just as they reached Anasu, he yanked the reins and shouted, "Keep still, you!"

The bowhorn bellowed and reared. Anasu pulled it down. He grabbed the saddlebags from Nia. A moment later he was astride the bowhorn. He bent and slapped the beast on one shoulder. The bowhorn began to run.

"Anasu!" Nia cried.

He was gone.

"Men!" said Hua. "They always make a spectacle. And here I am with this cup of milk. I meant to give it to him. Well, it will do me as much good." She took a swallow.

Nia made a groaning sound, then doubled her hand and began to beat one thigh.

"That is right. Get the grief out of you."

Nia kept hitting her thigh.

As Hua had predicted, it was a bad winter. It was cold, and there was a lot of snow. Nia wondered how Anasu was doing. She prayed to the Master of the Herds, asking him to protect her brother.

At the time of the solstice Gersu went crazy and had to be driven out of the village. Afterward, his mother took his gifts across the river. She hung them from the branches of a big tree.

Maybe he would find them and take them. Most likely, not.

"He always had a bad look in his eyes," said Hua.

Nia made the gesture of agreement.

Spring came early. The plain turned pale blue. The bushes along the river put out yellow blossoms. Nia felt almost happy.

"You see," said Hua. "We get over everything."

"No. I don't believe that."

"You will see."

The mating season came. Ti-antai, who had just finished weaning her last child, felt the spring lust and left. Nia moved into her tent and took care of the children.

Ten days later Ti-antai returned. She looked rumpled and relaxed. "Well, that's over." She stretched and yawned.

"Did you see Anasu?"

"Of course not. Nia, what's wrong with you? He must be far to the south with the other young men. I didn't get down there." Ti-antai rolled a blanket into a pillow, then lay down. She yawned again. "I got a big fellow, half a day's ride from here. He does good carving. He gave me a salt horn full of salt. Hu! Do I need to sleep!"

None of the women had met Anasu, but none of them had gotten very far south. They had all mated with older men, who had their territories close to the village.

"Don't worry," said Hua. "In a year or two or three someone will meet him and tell you."

Nia made the gesture that meant she understood. As she made the gesture, she thought—there was something wrong. Something out of balance. Why were people so often lonely?

They went north to the Summer Land. Once settled there Nia looked around for new friends. She had spent too much time with Anasu. She had relied on him too much.

She picked the younger Angai to be her friend. Angai was the daughter of the shamaness. She was a thin, clever girl, often sarcastic. But she knew many interesting things: the uses of plants, the meaning of flights of birds. Like Nia, she was lonely.

"I have many skills," she told Nia. "But not the skill of friendship. How terrible!"

Nia looked at her. Was she being sarcastic? Yes. Her mouth was twisted down at one corner, a sign that she didn't really mean what she had said.

At midsummer, at the festival, they got drunk together and fell asleep in one another's arms.

In the late summer Nia made a necklace for Angai. Every link was a bird made of silver.

"Wonderful!" Angai said. She hugged Nia, then put the necklace on. "Everyone in the village will envy me!"

"You think too much of other people's opinions."

Angai looked irritated, then said, "That may be."

For a day or two after that Angai was standoffish. Then she came to Hua's forge and brought a gift. It was a salve that made any burn stop hurting.

"It's my mother's own recipe. I made it this time. My mother says it's good."

Nia took the jar. "Thank you."

"Can we stop fighting now?"

Nia laughed. "Yes."

The fall was dry, and the trip south was easy, almost pleasant. Nia and Angai kept together. Sometimes Angai rode in Hua's cart. Sometimes Nia rode beside the cart of the shamaness. She never got into it, of course. It was full of magic.

One day they rode off, away from the caravan. They let their bowhorns run. When the beasts began to tire, they stopped. The land was flat and empty. They saw nothing except the yellow plain and the blue-green sky. Somewhere close by a groundbird sang: *whistle-click-whistle.*

"Hu!" said Nia. She rubbed her bowhorn's neck.

"There are times," Angai said, "when I get tired of people. I think, I would like to be a man and live by myself."

"You have a lot of strange ideas."

Angai made the gesture of agreement. "It comes of living with my mother. Let's spend the night out here, away from everyone."

"Why?"

Angai made the gesture of uncertainty.

"That is not much of a reason," Nia said. "And I have no desire to do the things that men do."

Late in the afternoon they rode back to the caravan. It was still moving. The carts and the animals threw up clouds of dust. As they came near Nia could hear the sound of voices: women and children shouting. For a moment the noise made her angry. She wanted to turn back, into the silence of the plain.

She didn't. Instead, she rode on, looking for Hua's cart.

When they reached the Winter Land, Ti-antai fell sick. Blood came out of her, and she miscarried. The shamaness held a ceremony of purification and a ceremony to avert any further bad occurrences. After that Ti-antai grew better, but very slowly. She was sick well into the winter.

Nothing else important happened, except that Nia found she could get along with Suhai. They took to visiting each other—not often, but once in a while. Suhai was getting old. There were grey hairs in her pelt. Her broad shoulders sagged. She complained of the winter cold and her children's ingratitude.

"They never visit me. After all the years of care they leave me alone. Is this in balance? Is this usual and right?"

Nia said nothing.

"Well?" Suhai asked.

"I will not criticize their behavior. The proverbs say, don't speak badly of kinfolk or anyone else you travel with. The proverbs also say, don't intervene in other people's quarrels."

"Hu! I raised a wise woman, did I?"

Nia didn't answer.

Suhai got up, moving stiffly. "I'm not going to listen to a child spit out wisdom like the fish in the old story that spit out pieces of gold. It's unnatural. Good-bye."

"Good-bye, foster mother. I will visit you in a day or two."

Spring came. It was early again. Nia began to feel restless. At night she was troubled by dreams. Often, in the dreams, she saw her brother or other young men, even crazy Gersu.

When she was up, she was usually tired. She found it difficult to concentrate on anything. She began to make mistakes at the forge.

"Can't you do anything the right way?" Hua asked.

Nia stared at her, bemused.

"Well, that's an answer of a kind. But not a good kind," Hua said.

Finally she picked up a knife blade that was still hot. She burnt her hand badly. Hua took care of the burn, then said, "Enough. Get out. Don't come back until you are able to work."

Angai gave her a potion that reduced the pain. She slept a lot. Her dreams were fragmentary, unclear, disturbing. Always, it seemed, Anasu was in them.

At length her hand stopped hurting. Now, though, it seemed her body was full of eerie sensations: itches and tingles. Often she felt hot, though it was still early spring. The weather wasn't especially warm.

She went to visit Tiantai.

"The spring lust," her cousin said. "I can see it in your face. Well, you're old enough. Pack your bag now. Food and a gift for the man. Something useful. Cloth or a knife. You'll be ready to go in a day or two."

She packed. That night she didn't sleep at all. Her body itched and burned. In the morning she went out. The touch of the wind made her shiver. Time to go, she thought. She got her favorite bowhorn and saddled it. After that she went to get her saddlebag.

"Take care," Hua said.

For a moment she didn't realize who the old woman was. Then she remembered. "Yes." She went out, mounted, and rode away.

She forded the river. The water was shallow. There was a little mist. On the far side was a tree. A couple of rags hung from the branches. There was a knife driven into the wood. The blade and hilt were rusted. She glanced at all this, then forgot it and rode onto the plain.

At midafternoon she came to the edge of the herd. The first animal she saw was a huge male. One horn was broken. The long shaggy hair that covered his neck and chest was silver-brown. He bellowed, then lowered his head, as if about to charge. Then he lifted his head and shook it. A moment later he trotted away.

Good, she thought. She was in no mood for a confrontation.

She rode on. Soon she came upon other animals: yearlings and two-year-olds. They were too old to be mothered and too young to stand their ground against the big males, the guardians of the herd. This time of year they stayed at the edges of the herd, well away from the does and their new fawns. They didn't like it at the edges. Often the yearlings would try to go in and find their mothers. But the big males would drive them away.

Nia stopped at dusk. She found a tree and tethered her bowhorn. Then she built a fire. The night was cold. She had forgotten her cloak. She stayed up and kept the fire going.

In the morning, at sunrise, the man appeared, He looked to be thirty or thirty-five, broad-shouldered, heavy. His pelt was dark brown. He wore a yellow tunic, high boots, a necklace of silver and bronze.

He reined his bowhorn and looked at her a moment. His gaze was steady and calculating. Then he dismounted. She stepped back, all at once uneasy.

"I thought you looked pretty young," he said. "Is this going to be a lot of trouble?"

"I don't know."

His fur was thick and glossy. He had an interesting scar: a streak of white that went down his right arm from the shoulder to the inside of the elbow.

"Who are you?" Nia asked.

He looked irritated. "Inani. Do you mind not talking? Talking makes me edgy."

She made the gesture of assent. He moved closer, then reached out and touched her. She shivered. Gently he put one arm around her. What happened next was not entirely clear to her.

When they were done, Nia got up and rebuilt the fire. She heated milk. Inani dozed with his back against the tree. From time to time he started awake. He glanced around, then relaxed and dozed off again. At last he woke completely. Nia gave him a cup. They sat on opposite sides of the fire and drank.

Inani said, "Who are you?"

"Nia. Suhai's foster daughter. Have you met my brother Anasu?"

"No. I know the men whose territories are next to mine. I keep away from them as much as I can, but during the migrations things get mixed up. People get too close together. Sometimes I think it would be better to go away entirely."

"Who is your mother?"

"The tentmaker. Enwa. Is she alive?"

"Yes."

"Good." Inani stood up. "Stay here, will you?" He mounted his bowhorn. "You're less trouble than I expected. I'll return in the evening."

He rode off. She slept most of the day. In the evening Inani returned. They mated again. He made camp a short distance away. Nia watched his campfire for a while, then went to sleep.

The next day he left again and came back in the late afternoon. They mated. He returned to his camp. The night was cloudy. There were gusts of cold wind. Nia huddled close to her fire and shivered. After a while she looked up and saw Inani. He stood at the edge of the firelight, just barely visible.

"Yes? What is it?"

He stepped forward and held something out. A cloak. It fluttered in the wind.

Nia got up. "Thank you."

She took the cloak. Inani stayed where he was. For a moment Nia thought he was going to speak. He didn't. Instead, he made the gesture that meant "oh, well." He turned and walked into the darkness.

Strange! She wrapped the cloak around her, then lay down.

The next morning he rode off again. Nia stayed by the tree. She was getting restless, but she didn't dare go riding. She didn't know where Inani's territory ended. If she strayed into another man's territory, he would claim her. Inani might follow her. Then there would be an argument. She had heard about such things. Usually, the two men threatened each other until one of them gave up and went away. But sometimes they fought. Old Hua had seen a man die, a knife blade in his chest. How terrible! But also interesting. What would it be like to watch a fight that was really serious?

Inani came back in the evening. They mated. This time he stayed after. He sat on the far side of the fire and asked questions. How was Enwa? And his sisters? Was old Niri still alive?

"No."

Inani scratched his head. "Well, he was old. He taught me carving. Can I stay here tonight?"

Nia made the gesture of assent.

She woke at sunrise. The air was cold and still. Inani was gone. She sat up, stretching and groaning. The fire was out. Beside its ashes lay two objects.

"What?" she said out loud. She went over and examined them: a bag full of salt and a box. The box was made of dark wood and inlaid with pieces of shell. She turned it over, admiring the work. He was a fine craftsman, Inani.

After a moment or two she realized the meaning of the objects. They were mating gifts. Such things were given when the time for mating was over. Inani was done with her.

This soon? She felt embarrassed and insulted. Had she done something wrong? Or had Inani found another woman in his territory? Someone he found more attractive.

Nia sighed, then packed the box and the bag of salt. She laid out her gifts for Inani: a knife, a belt, and a piece of blue cloth. He would come back and find them. She saddled her bowhorn. She felt tired and a little disappointed. But the lust was gone. That was good. She mounted and rode home.

When all the women had returned to the village, Nia asked if anyone had seen Anasu. No one had.

"Don't worry," Hua said. "He will turn up. He isn't one of the unlucky ones."

Nia made the gesture of acknowledgment.

The trip north was difficult. There was rain. The herd, traveling ahead of the village, churned up the wet earth, turning it into mud. Time and time again the carts got mired. Tempers grew short. Several of the old men saddled their bowhorns and took off.

Hisu the bow master was too old to go. He sat in his cart and cursed fate.

Nia, riding close, heard him say, "I should have died years ago." He was talking loudly to no one she could see. "In my prime, alone. The proper way. Now . . . O Master of the Herds, what an end! To live surrounded by women!"

In truth, he looked miserable. He was huddled in a cloak. A wide leather rain hat sheltered his face. His fur, she noticed, was completely grey.

She waved. He cursed. She rode on.

At last they reached the Summer Land. Most of the old men returned and settled down as usual at the edge of the camp. But two never came back.

"Two fools!" said Hua. "Why did they go? They were old. They could behave in a reasonable fashion. Did they? No! They ran off like crazy boys. And now something has gotten them."

Nia said nothing.

The rain stopped. The summer was cool and dry. It became evident to her that she wasn't pregnant.

"Don't worry," said Ti-antai. "This often happens. You will have a child next year or the year after."

Nia made the gesture of acknowledgment. She hadn't been worried. She was happy as she was. In the day she worked at the forge. In the late afternoon she and Angai went riding or sat by the river and talked. Angai did most of the talking. She was very observant and had sharp things to say about the people in the village. Because of the dry weather, there were only a few bugs in the air. It was pleasant to sit and listen while the sky changed color.

Her friend was certainly clever, Nia thought. Almost as clever as Anasu.

That summer there was a scandal in the village. It concerned the bronze smith Nuha and her son.

He was sixteen; and everyone could see that he had gone

through the change. His fur was coarse, his body thick and wide. He acted restless. But he didn't leave the village. Instead, he stayed inside his mother's tent or worked with her at her forge.

The old women grimaced and muttered. Hua said, "This is what happens when a woman has no daughters. She cannot let go of her sons. Look at the way she treats him! She doesn't send him to learn archery or something else that will be useful to him. She lets him work the bellows and even pour the bronze. Aiya! This is terrible."

Nia said nothing. She had always liked Enshi. As a child he had been friendly and talkative, always telling stories and making jokes. Even now he was always polite. He never lost his temper, which was strange in a boy—or a man—of his age.

He was a poor archer, though. Anasu had told her that.

"He rides badly, too," her brother had said. "He won't last on the plain alone."

Fall came. The village made ready to move. Enshi rode off one morning.

"At last!" Hua said. "Now I can talk to his mother again."

He was gone five days. Then he rode back in, looking tired and dirty. The villagers glared. Enshi ignored them. He rode to his mother's tent and dismounted.

Nuha, who was short and fat, ran out and hugged her son.

"Disgusting," Suhai said. "May the Mother of Mothers teach that woman shame."

"Are you cursing the woman?" Nia asked. "If so, I'm going to make the gesture that averts. Who can tell what spirit will hear a curse? Or what it will do about it?"

"Are you planning to become a shamaness, my foster daughter?"

"No."

Suhai glowered, then made the gesture that averts.

"Good," said Nia.

The next morning, early, the old women went to the shamaness. They stood at the entrance to her tent and complained. Nia heard their shrill voices and went out. The day was bright. The air smelled of wood smoke and leather and the dry summer plain.

Nia watched the shamaness walk across the village. She wore a robe covered with red embroidery and a big necklace made of bronze. Hu! What an impressive woman!

The old crones hobbled after her. Nia watched.

They all stopped at the tent of Nuha.

"Enshi!" the shamaness cried.

After a moment Enshi came out. Nia couldn't see his expression.

"Have you no sense of what is right?" the shamaness asked loudly.

Enshi looked down, then up. He mumbled something that Nia couldn't hear.

"It's time you left," the shamaness said.

Enshi made the gesture of assent. His shoulders were sagging now. He looked discouraged.

"Go today. And don't come back. You have become an embarrassment."

Enshi made the gesture of assent a second time. Then he turned and went into his mother's tent.

The shamaness left. But the old women sat down and waited.

Nia went to the forge and worked alone. Late in the afternoon Hua came.

"He is gone," she said. "We told him we would curse him if he ever came back."

"Is that so?" Nia said. She straightened up and rubbed her neck. "How I ache today."

The village went south. The weather remained dry. The herd kicked up a cloud of dust that went most of the way to the sky. Day after day they saw the cloud in front of them. It was dark brown in color. Nia thought, Anasu is there, riding in the dust. And Enshi, too, the poor buffoon.

They reached the Winter Land. Usually they camped to the north of the herd. But this year they went south and east to the Great Rush Lake. Now they were at the eastern edge of their pasturage. Across the lake was the land of the

Amber People. They pitched their tents. The shamaness went to visit the Amber People. Angai went with her, also nine other women. They all led pack animals, laden with gifts.

They were gone thirty days. The weather remained dry, though Hua kept saying that rain was coming. She could feel it in her bones.

When they returned, they brought gifts from the Amber People: amber, of course, colored shells, and copper.

"Hu! What an experience," Angai said. "We had to go around the lake. On the far side are marshes. Beyond the marshes is a river. It is wide and deep. We had to cross it. That was dangerous. Animals live in it. They are like river lizards. But larger. Much larger. They will eat anything, my mother says."

"Hu!" said Nia. "Tell me more."

"We made rafts. That's how we got across the river. I didn't see any of the animals. They are called divers or killers-of-the-deep-water."

"Aiya!" said Nia.

"On the far side of the river is the land of the Amber People." Angai paused and frowned. "They are the same height as we are, but broader; and a lot of them are fat. Their fur is dark. Their shamaness is huge. She wears a hat made of feathers. I could barely understand them. They talk so strangely. They are very hospitable, though. And they drink a kind of beer I've never had before. Nia, I heard a story there I don't believe. But they swear it is true."

Angai paused to drink a little milk. Nia waited.

"They say to the east of them are a people who stay in one place. They never move."

Nia made the gesture of astonishment.

"They live in houses made of wood. The houses can't be folded or taken apart. They are solid like boxes.

"They live next to a forest, the Amber People say. And their men live in the forest. They don't herd animals the way men ought to. Instead they hunt and catch fish. The women don't think much of them. They say, all men are savage and nasty."

"The Amber People say this?"

"No! No! The people who never move. In fact, the Amber People say, some of the women refuse to mate with men."

Nia scratched her head. "How can that be?"

"When the spring lust comes, they go out in pairs, two women together. They mate with one another."

For a moment Nia sat quietly and stared at the fire. "How do they produce children?"

"The usual way. The Amber People say, few of the women mate only with women. Most of them want children. They mate with men until they have as many children as they want."

Nia scratched her head again. "This is a very strange story."

"Yes. I'd like to go and visit those people."

"They are perverts!" Hua said. "And the Amber People are liars. No such people exist. Houses of wood! What a crazy idea!"

Angai looked angry.

"I don't want to talk about this anymore," Nia said. "This story makes me uneasy."

The winter was cold. At night, in the northern sky, lights shone. They were green and white and yellow.

"The winter fire," said Hua. "Up north it fills the sky. We don't often see it down here."

Ti-antai said, "It is bad luck."

Snow fell. There was a coughing sickness in the village. A number of people died. Most were old women or very young children.

Suhai got the sickness. For a while, in the dark time after the solstice, everyone thought she would die. In the end she recovered, though slowly. All the rest of the winter she stayed in her tent. Nia and Ti-antai looked after her. It was hard for Nia to go and see her, hunched by the fire. Her fur was more grey than brown. She looked bony and unhappy.

Why, Nia wondered, did her throat contract at the sight of the old woman? She didn't even like her foster mother.

Spring came at last. It was cold and rainy. Hua's hands became so stiff that she could not work at the forge. "This place is full of bad luck," she cried.

"I think you are right," Nia said.

The trees put out leaves, pale blue in color. Among the dry reeds in the lake, flowers blossomed. They were yellow and orange. Other flowers, tiny and white, appeared at the edge of the plain. Nia began to feel restless. The spring lust, she thought. She began to assemble supplies.

"Why don't I feel the lust?" asked Angai.

"You are younger than I am." Nia crouched and stared at the things she had made in the winter: long knives and needles, brooches, files and awls. What was the right gift?

"I'm half a year younger," Angai said. "That isn't much."

"Why do you ask me? What do I know? Ask your mother."

Angai left. She was angry, Nia realized. Too bad. She reached out and picked up a knife. It had a good blade, made of iron that had been folded and refolded. That would do, she thought. And needles and a brooch, also—maybe—leather from the tanner.

She stood up. Now, food for the trip.

That night she dreamt of Anasu and of riding on the plain. She woke, feeling more restless than before. She pulled up the tent flap and fastened it. Sunlight came in. The air was still and mild. It smelled of the new vegetation. She thought, I will go today, before the lust gets any stronger. I will ride until I forget this terrible winter. She turned and looked at Hua.

"I know," the old woman said. "I sometimes wish I still felt the lust. Then I think, I must be crazy to want a thing like that. In any case, go."

She packed her saddlebags and went to find her favorite bowhorn. By noon she was on her way. Her bowhorn was restless and wanted to run. She let it. After a while it slowed, then stopped. Nia looked around. She was alone. On every side, the plain rolled to the horizon. She took a deep breath, then let it out. Her bowhorn flicked its ears.

Where did she want to go? Not west, she decided. The herd was there and the full-grown men. No. She would go south, toward the hills where the young men were. She glanced at the sun and then at her shadow. Then she turned her bowhorn south.

She traveled for three days. The weather remained clear. She met no people, nor anything, except for birds and the small animals that lived on the plain. Slowly the lust grew stronger. It felt almost pleasant. She began to wonder what kind of man she would meet this year.

The fourth day was cloudy and windy. At noon she reached the southern hills. They were low, with many outcroppings of stone. There were trees on the hills. One kind was in blossom. Here and there on the blue slopes were patches of yellow. She found an animal trail that went along a stream. It led east into the hills. She followed the trail, feeling a bit uneasy. She wasn't used to places where the sky was narrow.

"O Mother of Mothers, take care of me," she whispered.

Overhead the branches moved. Leaves rustled—a loud noise, unlike the soft *whish* of vegetation moving on the plain.

She prayed to the Mistress of the Forge. "Bring me safely home, O holy one."

Late in the afternoon she met a man. He was on top of a small hill, sitting on a boulder. There were no trees nearby, only bushes with small blue-green leaves. His bowhorn grazed on one of these.

Nia reined her animal. Her heart began to beat quickly.

"I thought I saw a woman. What a surprise! Nia, is it you?"

She looked at him. He was dark brown, and his eyes were grey. A very strange color. "Enshi?" His tunic was ragged, she noticed. He looked thin.

"How is my mother? And what are you doing here? The women never get this far south."

She opened her mouth to answer. Enshi stood up, then jumped off the boulder. "Let's talk later. There is a scent coming from you, Nia. I can't tell you what it does to me." He held out a hand. "Come on."

His dark fur gleamed in the sunlight. She realized, all at once, that he was handsome. She dismounted and tethered her bowhorn, then got her cloak.

They went into the bushes and mated there. The ground was stony. The leaves had a fresh spring smell. As for Enshi, he was a little awkward, but perfectly adequate.

When they were done, he rolled over on his back. "Is that what it's like? I expected more. Still . . . " He looked at her. His grey eyes were half-shut. He reached out and touched her gently. "What soft fur!" He made a low *ruh* noise in the back of his throat, then shut his eyes completely and went to sleep.

Nia pulled the cloak up so it covered both of them. She looked at the bowhorns, then at the sky. The sun was gone, but the clouds were still shining, white and pale gold. She felt drowsy and happy.

Enshi the Joker! She had never imagined mating with him. For one thing she'd thought he was dead. Who would have thought he could have survived the bitter winter?

Enshi woke at twilight. He glanced at her. "It wasn't a dream. If the spirits are responsible for this, I thank them." He grabbed her. They mated again. Afterward they went down into the nearest valley and made camp. The night was windy and cold. Ragged clouds filled the sky. The fire flickered. Enshi talked.

"What are you doing this far south? Why didn't one of the big men get you, before you got to Enshi?"

She thought for a moment. "I wanted to get down here. I wanted to find my brother Anasu." She stopped, feeling surprised. Was that right? Had she come to find Anasu?

"You did?" Enshi stared at her. "Why?"

Nia scratched her head. "I don't know. Do you know where he is?"

Enshi made the gesture of affirmation. "I get my salt from him. I used to, anyway. The winter was hard, and I don't think I have anything left to give him."

Nia opened her mouth.

Enshi looked at her. His eyes were half-closed. He looked thoughtful, almost clever. "You want me to tell you where he is. I won't. If you came this far to see him, then you're likely to go farther and leave me here alone, feeling stupid. I don't intend to let go of you, Nia. Not until the time for mating is over."

"You certainly are talkative," Nia said.

Enshi made the gesture of agreement. "Remember, I've had no one to talk to all winter."

"Will you tell me where Anasu is when the time for mating is over?"

"Yes."

Nia made the gesture that meant "so be it."

"Now," Enshi said, "tell me about my mother. Is she well? Does she still grieve for me?"

She spent eight days with Enshi. The weather remained cold and windy. Now and then rain fell. It wasn't heavy. The trees above their camp protected them; and they kept a good fire going. They mated often.

Every morning Enshi went out hunting. In the afternoon he came back with leaves and roots and the tender shoots of spring plants. Twice he brought back game: a winter-thin groundbird and a builder-of-mounds. The builder-of-mounds was small, but fat. Or at least it was not thin.

"He did better than I did this winter," Enshi said.

Nia skinned the animal, gutted and spitted it. They sat side by side and watched it cook.

"Hu! What a smell! I used to dream about the smell of cooking meat. I'd wake up and find nothing except snow. What a disappointment! There were times when the weather was bad, and I couldn't travel. I'd begin to look at my bowhorn and think about him as a roast. But I thought, no, Enshi. You'll die without an animal to ride. Then I prayed to the spirits; and the weather would break. I'd go down to the edge of the herd and look for a bowhorn that was too weak to run from me and kill it. The meat was always stringy, with no fat at all. Well, those days are over. Why think about them?"

Nia turned the spit. While the other side of the animal was cooking, they mated.

The next day Nia made a fish trap and set it in the stream at the bottom of the valley. That evening they ate fish stuffed with herbs.

"What a fine cook you are," Enshi said. "Almost as good as my mother."

Nia felt irritated. It seemed to her that Enshi was always talking about his mother. It wasn't right. A boy who was properly brought up talked about himself or about the old men who taught him how to be a man. He didn't go on and on about his mother.

"What is Anasu like these days?" she asked.

Enshi made the gesture that meant "who can say?" "I've met him two times. The first time I tried to talk with him, he said, 'I don't want a conversation, Enshi. What do you have that you are willing to give me?' He wouldn't say anything else. I got out one of my mother's bronze cups and set it on the ground. He got out a bag of salt, then waved me back. When I was far enough away, he came and took the cup, then put down his bag. That was it. He left. I picked up the salt. The second time I met him, he said nothing at all." Enshi paused a moment, then went on. "He's friendlier than the other men. He never makes faces or waves weapons at me."

This sounded bad. Would Anasu be willing to talk with her? She didn't know.

The time for mating ended. Nia gave Enshi her gifts. He looked uncomfortable. "The winter was hard. I lost most of my parting gifts. First a killer-of-the-forest found my cache and tore it apart. Then I lost most of the rest this spring while crossing a river.

"But I make poems. Can I give them to you?"

"Yes."

He recited nine or ten. Afterward she remembered only one. It was about a tree he had seen a few days before.

"All the branches were bare, and the bark was peeling off. Nonetheless, there were shoots all around the tree, growing from the base of it. They were as long as my arm. They bore leaves and flowers. I thought this must be significant. And I made a poem. It goes:

"If you don't give up,
old tree—

"Then I won't
either."

"That one I like," Nia said.

He recited it again. "Is that enough? Have we made a fair exchange?"

"Where is Anasu?"

"Oh, yes. Follow the trail until it forks. Then go south. You will come to a big stone with markings on it. The stone is magical, and no one ever claims that it is in his territory. People go there to exchange gifts. Wait by the stone. If Anasu is anywhere around, he will come."

"Thank you. We've made a fair exchange."

They said good-bye. Nia saddled her bowhorn, then mounted and rode away. The day was sunny. A light wind blew. Birds whistled. She felt content.

At twilight she came to the stone. It was tall and narrow with lines cut into it. She could barely make them out; and she didn't know what they meant. Had people done this? No one she knew cut lines in stone.

She tethered her bowhorn and made a fire. The night was cloudless. She lay on her back. Above her the Great Moon rose. It was three-quarters full. She watched it for a while, then went to sleep.

In the morning she looked at the stone. The lines represented animals: bowhorns, mostly. But there was another animal that she didn't recognize. It had a thick body and short horns. What was it? Nia scratched her head. There were hunters on the stone: men with bows. They made a circle around the animals. Off to one side was a man by himself. He was bigger than the others, and he had horns. They were short, like the horns on the unfamiliar animal. Who was he? A spirit of some kind, apparently. But no spirit she knew. The Master of the Herds had long curved horns. The Sky Spirit was hornless. She scratched her head again. Then she made breakfast.

At noon Anasu appeared. He rode down the trail into the clearing where the stone was. He reined his bowhorn.

Nia stood up. "Brother!"

He was bigger than she remembered and very broad through the chest. His fur was coarse and dark. He wore a red kilt, a wide belt, high boots, a knife with a silver pommel. "Nia?" he said after a moment. He stared at her. "You are past the lust." His voice sounded harsh and disappointed. "Someone else got to you."

"What kind of thing is that to say? Can men think of nothing except sex?"

He laughed. It was not entirely a friendly sound. "This time of year I think of little else. I think—if I were brave, I'd go north. Then I think, I'm not old enough to confront those men. What are you doing here?"

She made the gesture of uncertainty.

"You have never known your own mind." He dismounted. "Do you want salt? I have it."

"No. I want to talk. How are you?" She took a step toward him.

He held up a hand. "Stay where you are. I'm not used to people."

She stopped.

After a moment Anasu said, "I am fine. Is there nothing you want to give me in exchange for salt?"

She took off her belt. "Do you want this? I made the buckle. It's gold mixed with silver."

He hesitated. "All right." He turned toward his saddlebag.

"I don't want salt. I want a conversation."

He turned back and stared at her. "Why?"

"Brother, when I think of you, I feel lonely."

Anasu scratched the back of his neck. Then he made the gesture that meant "so be it" or "these things happen."

"Is there no way we can talk?"

For a long while he was silent. She waited. At last he said, "I do not think that what you want is words. I could give you words, though it would not be easy. I'm no longer used to talking much or saying what is on my mind. But I think you want something else. I think you are like the woman in the old story, whose children turned into birds. She left her tent and wandered on the plain, trying to find them. But she never did; and in the end she died and became a spirit—a bad one, a hungry one." He paused and frowned.

Nia opened her mouth.

He held up his hand. "No. Wait. I want to follow the track of my own thought." She waited. At last he said, "I think you want something that is gone."

"No."

"I know you, sister. I think I am right. In any case, I don't want to talk anymore." He mounted his bowhorn. "Whatever you are trying to do, I don't want to be a part of it." He made the gesture of farewell, then turned his animal and rode away.

Nia doubled one hand into a fist and hit the magic stone. Aiya! How that hurt! She groaned, opened her hand, and felt it. As far as she could tell, no bones were broken. But the skin was scraped along the side of her hand where there was no fur. She licked the scrape, then sat down and rocked and groaned. It did no good. Her hand kept hurting and grief stayed in her, as solid as a stone.

Toward evening she got up and built a fire. All night she sat watching the flames and thinking about her childhood.

In the morning she put out the fire and saddled her bowhorn. There was no point in staying. Anasu wouldn't come back. He had always been stubborn. She rode north. The sky was cloudy. A cold wind blew. Flower petals drifted down onto the trail. They were yellow or greenish white.

In the afternoon it began to rain. She stopped and made camp under an overhang. She went to sleep early. Sometime in the night she woke.

Her fire was still burning. On the other side of it was Enshi. He was plucking a bird.

She lifted her head. He made the gesture of greeting, then held up the bird. It was large and fat.

"I found it on a nest. I have the eggs, if they haven't broken. How was Anasu?"

"He wouldn't talk to me. What are you doing here?"

"You're in my territory; and I thought you might be hungry. Also, I thought I would like to talk some more."

"Why are you so different from other men?"

"I don't know." He looked embarrassed for a moment. Then he went back to plucking the bird.

Nia went to sleep.

In the morning they cooked the bird with its own eggs stuffed inside it. They ate, then Nia got ready to go.

"Can I go with you?" Enshi asked.

"What do you mean?"

"I want to visit my mother. I thought you could show me the way to the village."

"But the old women will curse you."

"Not if you tell me where my mother's tent is, and I sneak in at night. The old women will never know."

"This is wrong."

"Maybe. But I have lost all my parting gifts. I won't last through another winter with what I have. I intend to live, if I possibly can. And I don't care if I do a few things that are shameful. Who knows what the spirits of the dead feel? I'd sooner be alive and a little embarrassed."

Nia looked at him a moment. He was certainly thin, and his tunic was very ragged. She rubbed her hand, which still hurt. Then she sighed. "All right. I'll help you. I expect I'm going to regret this, though."

Enshi saddled his bowhorn. They rode north together.

LIXIA

Eight of us were set down, each one alone: three on the big continent, which sprawled around the south pole of the planet, many fissured and many lobed. The center of the continent was ice. The coasts were green, blue-green, and yellow: prairie and forest and desert, according to the people who analyzed the holograms.

Another four went to the small continent, which lay north of the equator. It had no ice worth mentioning and almost no desert, but plenty of vegetation. There were mountains: a range in the west along the coast and other lesser ranges in the east and south. Nothing impressive, nothing like the Rockies or the Himalayas. But two of the ranges were volcanic, according to the planetologists. One was active. The other might be.

The final person was set down on one of the many islands in the archipelago that stretched in a curve from the big continent past the equator, almost reaching the little continent.

Other islands dotted the rest of the planet-ocean. They were tiny and widely spaced. Interesting to the biologists, of course. There is nothing like an island for studying evolution. But not, we decided, the place for us to begin.

I went to the northeast coast of the northern continent. I was equipped with a denim jacket and a light cotton shirt. My boots were plastic, tough and flexible. In my right forearm, under the skin, was a row of capsules that provided me with vitamins not available on this planet. In my gut were five new kinds of bacteria, designed to break down the local proteins, turning them into amino acids which I could digest.

I had a pack which contained a radio, a medical kit, a poncho, another shirt—exactly like the first one—and a change of underwear. One big compartment was full of trinkets. The trinkets were made from native materials. We didn't want to introduce anything alien except ourselves.

Finally, I had a medallion on a grey metal chain. The medallion was metal, flat and dark, inset with pieces of glass. It was an AV recorder and almost indestructible, I was told. No matter what happened to me, it would survive.

I landed on a beach, next to a row of dunes. They were high and bare, orange-pink in color.

The boat that had brought me turned and started back toward the plane. I went inland, scrambling up a dune. When I reached the top, I heard a roar and glanced around. The plane was moving across the water. Spray flew up, then smoke. It was in the air. Wings shone in the sunlight. The plane kept rising. After a minute or two it was gone.

I looked at the empty sky and felt suddenly very lonely. Then I started down the far side of the dune.

At the bottom I found a trail. It wasn't much to look at. Narrow and sandy, it wound away from the dunes toward a stand of trees.

Had it been made by people? By some kind of intelligent life? We knew the planet was inhabited. Satellite pictures had shown villages and herds whose migrations—the zoologists had told us—were too orderly to be entirely natural.

In any case, I was faced with a trail. I decided to follow it. It led me through the trees and into hills. Often the tops of the hills were bare except for patches of a plant that looked something like tall yellow grass. The leaves or blades were stiff and had sawtooth edges. It wasn't a pleasant-looking organism. Was this planet friendly?

In the hollows between the hills there were more trees. They were small and twisted with little dark leaves. Thorns stuck out of the trunks. The thorns were long and narrow, needlelike. Another unpleasant-looking organism. I began to remember horrifying science fiction stories. Why had I read that stuff? The senior members of my family had warned me: no good would come of science fiction.

There was no point in getting nervous, nor in thinking about the past. I was in a new place, and I had no good idea of what it was like. My job—for the time being—was observation. Later, when I had some information, I could think and remember and compare.

After a kilometer or so I came to an artifact. It was in a hollow at the center of a clearing. The slopes around it were covered with trees. I stopped. The thing was three meters high and made of long narrow pieces of wood. It reminded me of a jungle gym or else of the ritual structures made by the aborigines of southern California. I'd spent time with them. Between my breasts and on my upper arms were the scars of their initiation ceremony. I had never been able to figure out why I had gone through with it. But I kept the scars. I had earned them, and they reminded me—every time I took a shower—not to get too involved with other people's value systems.

I looked the structure over. Now I saw the remains of a fire underneath it. Three grey things hung from one of the lower bars. I knelt and examined them. Fish or something a lot like fish. I rocked back on my heels and felt satisfied. A fish smoking rack. Someone intelligent had made it. I was the first Earth person to see an alien artifact close up—on this planet, anyway, and as far as I knew.

I stayed where I was for several minutes, contemplating the pieces of wood. They were knobby and twisted. Was there no better wood in the area? I glanced around. All the trees in sight had twisted branches. The structure was tied together with strips of fiber. I broke off a piece and rolled it between my fingers. It felt like some kind of vegetable product. Maybe bark.

Something made a noise in back of me. I got up slowly and turned, holding my hands out, the palms forward. The gesture meant "You see? I carry no weapons."

Something stood at the edge of the clearing, maybe twenty

meters away. A biped. It was about my height, stocky and covered with fur. The fur was dark brown, almost black. The creature had two arms, a head, and a face. I was too far away to make out the features. It or he or she wore a kilt and carried—in one hand—a knife.

"I am extremely peaceful." I kept my hands out and my voice low and even. "I mean no harm."

The creature said something which I, of course, could not understand. But I didn't like the tone. It was loud and had a rasping quality.

"I mean no harm."

The creature raised the knife and took a step forward. I stepped back.

"Can't we discuss this?" I concentrated on keeping my tone soft and placating. I didn't meet the creature's eyes. In many species, including my own, a direct stare was a challenge.

The creature took another step toward me. I decided to leave.

"Okay. You win. Good-bye."

I backed across the clearing. The creature followed me halfway, then stopped beside the rack. When I reached the edge of the clearing, I stopped.

"Are you sure about this?"

The creature raised the knife higher and shouted something. I turned and walked quickly away. The skin on my back was prickling. I kept imagining a knife blade going in.

When I reached the top of the next hill, I looked back. The trail was empty. Nothing was following me.

Okay. What next?

Maybe the creature I met was a hermit. Surely there ought to be other members of the species who were friendly or curious.

I walked on, still going inland. I began to notice noises: a low buzz that came, I imagined, from pseudo-insects hidden in the trees. Things like birds flew from branch to branch. When they were at rest, they moaned or whistled. I realized, for the first time, that the day was bright and mild. A light wind blew. Alto-cumuli moved across the sky, which was deep blue-green. The air smelled of salt water.

I thought about my childhood in the Free State of Hawaii, on the island of Kauai. I had lived in a big house, five minutes from the ocean. Nine parents had cared for me, and there had been a dozen siblings to play with. It should have been a happy time. I remembered sunlight, flowers, kind faces, a white beach, blue water, and no undertow. But I had been a sullen kid, always anxious to get away.

By afternoon I was walking through a boggy forest. Here the trees were tall and straight. Their dark foliage shut out sunlight. The air was still and cool and had a new aroma: the scent of the forest. It was strong and distinctive and like nothing I had ever smelled before.

I thought I'd recognize it if I ever smelled it again, though I was not entirely positive of this. It was a lot easier to remember something if it had a name and a description. For the time being, I would call the aroma "different" and "pleasant."

Late in the afternoon I came to a village. First I smelled wood smoke, then saw houses ahead of me among the trees. I couldn't see them clearly. The forest was too full of shadows. Here and there firelight shone through a doorway or a window.

I stopped and considered what to do. There was no point in sneaking around. If they caught me spying, I'd be in real trouble. The best thing—the thing I had done in southern California and New Jersey—was to walk right in.

The technique hadn't worked in New Jersey, of course. The people there had tried to sacrifice me to their god, the Destroyer of Cities. I decided not to think about that incident. I spent another minute or two gathering courage. Then I entered the village.

At the edge were small huts, built of wood. They were widely scattered, as if the people who lived in them were none too friendly. Farther in, the buildings were large and long, set close together. Children, naked except for their fur, ran in the streets. A trio saw me, stopped and stared, their mouths open. They were close enough so I could see their faces: round and flat and covered with fur. Each one had a mouth, a nose, and a pair of yellow eyes.

"Hello," I said gently.

The children screamed and ran.

I went on, between the houses. Several times I passed large people. Adults. They stared at me, but said nothing. They made no threatening gestures.

This was hopeful. I came to an empty place that seemed to be more or less at the center of the village. A square. I hunkered down and waited. By this time the sun was gone. The sky was darkening. People gathered, talking softly, at the edges of the square. I was sweating. If I'd made a mistake, if they were unfriendly, I was going to die here.

Someone walked toward me: a tall, thin person. He or she wore a robe and many necklaces. Someone important. A shaman or a chief.

I was, of course, using labels from Earth.

I stood up slowly, then held out my hands. "I come in peace."

The person looked me over. At last the person spread his or her hands, duplicating my gesture.

Now what? Let the native decide. I waited. He or she took off a necklace and offered it to me. I took it. The beads were copper, little cylinders. There was a pendant: a piece of shell carved in the shape of a fish.

This was almost certainly a friendly act.

"Thank you." I put the necklace on. Now I would have to reciprocate. I let my pack slide off my shoulders, then bent and opened it.

"Here." I straightened, holding out a necklace made of shell. This particular kind of shell—dark blue and lustrous—was found in the planet's northern ocean, around a little archipelago we named the Empty Islands. Harrison Yee and I had gathered the shells and carved them, using techniques that Harrison had learned at Beijing University in the School of Anthropology.

The person took my gift, then gestured to me, turned, and walked away. I followed. We went past a crowd of people who stared. My shirt was wet with sweat.

We reached a house. The person gestured again. I walked in and found myself in a large long room. A fire burned in the center. By its ruddy light I saw log walls and log rafters. The floor was dirt or clay.

I looked around. No furniture. But there were piles of fur in the corners. Along the walls I saw pots. Some were a meter tall. Black and highly polished, they gleamed in the firelight. The air smelled of wood smoke and something else: a spicy aroma. I looked up. Bunches of plants hung from the rafters. Herbs, I thought. Were they wild or cultivated? Did these people farm? Did they have the potter's wheel? What metals did they work, other than copper?

My host followed me in. I looked at him or her. Now, in the firelight, I saw bent shoulders, bony hands, and greying fur. This was an old person, I was almost certain. Orange eyes regarded me. The lids were heavy. The pupils were vertical slits.

After a moment the person spoke.

"I'm sorry. I don't know your language."

My host reached out and very gently touched my face. There was no fur on the inside of the hand. His or her skin felt hard and dry.

"Hu!"

I had my hair pulled back and fastened at the nape of my neck. The person touched the side of my head, feeling the hair there, then touched the hair that flowed down between my shoulder blades.

"Tsa!"

I reached back and took the clip off my hair, shaking my head. The hair flew out.

My host started. He or she took hold of several strands and tugged.

For a moment I stood the pain, then I said, "Hey," and touched—very lightly—the furry hand.

The person let go. He or she spoke again—was it an apology?—and waved me toward the fire.

Other people appeared, wearing kilts or tunics. I saw more necklaces made of copper and belts with metal buckles. The metal was yellow, either brass or bronze.

The new people spread furs on the floor. My host and I

sat down. Someone brought a bowl full of liquid. My host drank, then offered the bowl to me. It was fired clay, black like the pots and polished. A geometric pattern was incised on the outside, below the rim. The liquid within looked dark and smelled pungent.

I remembered what the biochemists told me. I could probably eat what the natives ate.

"There's a lot you won't be able to metabolize, of course, even with the bugs we've given you. If you stay there any period of time, you will develop a lot of deficiencies. But we don't think you'll be poisoned."

I raised the bowl and drank.

The liquid was sour as well as pungent. Rather tasty. I'd consumed things that were a lot worse in New Jersey.

I said, "Thank you," and handed the bowl to my host.

He or she moved one hand quickly and definitely. The gesture meant something. The other people said "ya" and "hu." It seemed to me that they were more relaxed than before.

In any case, they spread more furs. More people sat down till I was surrounded. The air was full of their dusty, furry aroma.

Food came. I wasn't sure what anything was. I ate slowly and carefully and as little as possible. But I did eat. In most of the societies I knew about, it was rude to refuse food. An anthropologist had to have the digestion of a goat.

The people around me began to talk softly. Often they glanced at me. Only my host kept quiet. He or she kept handing me new dishes, watching to make sure I ate.

One dish was made of fish, I was almost certain. Another reminded me of pickled green tomatoes. A third had the texture of kasha and no taste that I could distinguish.

The people around me belched and made little cooing noises. "Hu" and "ya." I did the same.

The meal continued. I began to feel light-headed. Something I had ingested was having a narcotic effect. The people around me grew noisier. Several reached over and touched my clothes or hands or face.

Someone got out an instrument like a flute. Someone else began to beat two hollow sticks together. *Tock-whistle, tock-*

whistle, the music went. I leaned back on one elbow and watched the flute player. He or she wore a yellow tunic and a pair of wide copper bracelets. The bracelets flashed as the flute player swayed, keeping time with the music. I had no trouble hearing the beat. It was almost always regular: a heart with a slight arrhythmia.

The music stopped. My host stood up, and I glanced around.

There was a new person in the room, just inside the open door. Like my host, this one wore a robe. A sign of importance? Or age? Gender or occupation? The person wore a hat, the first one I'd seen. It was tall and pointed, decorated with shells.

I got up, swaying a little. It took me a moment to focus my eyes.

The new person looked grim. I saw trouble in the stiff, upright posture, in the shoulders held back and up, in the narrow, almost-shut eyes that stared at me directly. He or she carried a staff. Feathers hung from the top of it and fluttered—but not in the wind. The person was shaking. I could not tell if the motion was deliberate.

The person said something. It sounded angry.

My host replied curtly.

The people around me began to rise and move back. This was some kind of power conflict. I had a feeling that I was in the middle of it.

The person with the staff spoke some more. My host clenched one hand into a fist and waved it, then pointed at the door. That was clear enough. "You so-and-so, get out!"

The person with the staff glared and departed. One by one the other people followed until there were only three left: my host, the flute player, and a person with red-brown fur that gleamed like copper in the firelight.

"Hu!" my host said.

The others made gestures that probably meant agreement.

I felt tired and dizzy. I'd had too much of something, most likely the liquid. I would have to be careful about drinking it in the future. I rubbed my face.

My host looked at me, then gestured. I picked up my pack. He or she led me to one end of the room. There was a pile of furs there. My host gestured again. I lay down.

"Nice party. Good night."

My host left. I moved my pack so it was between me and the wall and went to sleep.

I woke with a headache and a feeling of disorientation, sat up and looked around and found I was in a large interior space. Light came through a hole above me and through an open door. It was yellow, the color of sunlight in the late afternoon. But I was almost positive that it was morning.

A voice spoke nearby. I looked toward the sound. It was the old person, my host. He or she wore a dark orange robe and wide belt made of copper. One hand held a staff of wood inlaid with pieces of shell. The other hand was held out to me, palm up. I decided this was a greeting. By this time I had remembered my current location.

The old person came closer and sat down. He or she spoke again, softly and courteously.

I laid one hand on my chest and said my name. "Lixia."

After a moment my host said, "Li-sa," and pointed at me.

"Lixia," I repeated.

My host laid a bony hand on his or her chest. "Nahusai."

I pointed. "Nahusai."

The answer was a gesture, a quick flick of one hand. On a hunch it meant "yes."

Well, then. I knew a word. It referred to my host. But what did it mean? Was it a name or a title or a generic term such as "human being"?

Time would tell.

A person came in: the flute player. He or she wore the same tunic as the night before and the same copper bracelets.

"Yohai," my host said and pointed.

The flute player looked at us.

It was a name. I was almost certain.

Yohai made breakfast: a grey-brown mush. It had a sour flavor. I learned the name of it: *atsua*. When we were done eating, Yohai went to the door and gestured. I got my pack, following him or her around the house. There was an open space in back, where vegetation grew. Most of it was blue with a few white or yellow flowers.

Was it a garden? I didn't think so. The plants grew helter-skelter, and they had a ragged look. This was a patch of weeds.

In the middle of the open space was a building about the size of a walk-in closet. As soon as I got close to it, I knew what it was. A privy. It stank to high heaven. I considered for a moment. Then I used the thing. Afterward I asked what it was called.

"*Hana,*" Yohai said. Or maybe *hna*. I wasn't certain I was hearing a vowel in the first syllable.

He or she gestured again. I followed. We went through the village. The streets were full of children. We met only a few adults. The children stopped playing and stared at me. The adults pretended I wasn't there. I had a feeling that Yohai was uneasy. I felt a little uneasy, too. But the day was lovely, sunny and mild. A light erratic wind blew. It carried the smell of the forest and—very faintly—of the ocean. This wasn't a day to worry. I tried not to.

We reached the edge of the village. There were gardens there: long, narrow, rectangular plots that lay between the houses and the forest. Each was surrounded by a fence made of wood, low enough to see over. Inside the fences people worked, one or two in each garden. They moved between rows of plants. Some weeded. Some picked. Some poured water out of jugs that looked like amphorae.

That answered one of my questions. The society was—to some extent, at least—agricultural.

We entered a garden. At one end was a tree. Yohai led me into the shade and pointed at the ground. I sat down.

My companion began to work. I glanced around. Off to the east were ragged cumuli. A storm tonight. In the next garden over was a baby, tiny and furry, sitting under a plant. As I watched, it reached up, trying to grab hold of one of the leaves. But the leaf was too high.

A short distance away an adult was pouring water. He or she emptied the pot, then set it down, straightened, and turned. Under her tunic I saw the bulge of breasts. Two breasts. She was the first person I had seen who wasn't flat-chested. Clearly she was a nursing mother.

The woman looked at me, then made a gesture: a vertical slash. I had a feeling it was hostile. I looked away.

At noon Yohai came over to me. We sat together and ate bread. The bread was flat and sour. Afterward Yohai taught me several words: "bread," "sky," "tree."

We went back to the house. My host was there. Yohai left. I sat down and learned more words. Late in the afternoon I heard the roll of thunder. Rain began to fall—first a sprinkle, then a downpour. My host and I ate dinner. It was the same as breakfast: *atsua*. Grey mush. I didn't eat a lot.

Afterward we sat without talking. The sun was down. The rain glistened, lit by firelight, a silver curtain at the door. I leaned against a post. My host was by the fire. He or she was hunched over, huddled in the orange robe. One hand moved now or then. It twisted a bracelet or tapped on the ground. This was a person with a serious problem, and I had a feeling the problem was me. Yohai had given me the impression of nervous valor, of someone making a point that he or she did not want to make. "See what we have here. See our guest. See the person we are not ashamed of." That had been the message given when he or she took me to the garden. What exactly was going on? I decided not to speculate. I had too little information, and I could not be sure that I understood anything about these people.

There was more rain the next day. My host and I worked on vocabulary: household objects mostly and some common verbs. In the afternoon Yohai got down a small loom that had been hanging on the wall. He or she began to weave a strip of cloth. The yarn was white and blue. I watched. Yohai worked quickly. Soon I made out a pattern. It was geometric, full of sharp angles. It looked hostile to me and far too intricate. What did it mean? Was this culture byzantine? Or was I paranoid?

I stood and began to do yoga exercises. My host looked at me, eyes opened wide.

I stopped. "This is nothing harmful or malevolent," I said

gently. "I do this to keep my back from hurting and to keep my mind reasonably tranquil."

I continued my exercises. My host watched. The rain lightened. It was a drizzle now.

"Excuse me." I took my pack and went to the privy. It smelled as bad as ever. I went in and sat down, then got out my radio and called the ship.

"Yeah?" the radio said. The voice was deep and a little hoarse. I was talking to Edward Antoine Whirlwind, Ph.D., author of *Native American Society on the Reservation* and *Patterns of Survival in the Late Twentieth Century*, formerly the Bellecourt Distinguished Professor at the University of Duluth—he resigned the position when he left Earth—and for many years my colleague in the Department of Cross-cultural Studies.

"This is Lixia," I told him. "I'm calling from an outhouse, so I'm going to be quick."

Eddie laughed.

"I needed someplace private."

"Okay," Eddie said.

I rested the radio on my knees, then took my medallion off its chain and put it in a slot in the radio.

The little computer in the medallion spoke to the slightly larger computer in the radio. That computer spoke to a computer on board the ship. It only took a minute. The radio beeped and I pulled the medallion out. Everything the medallion had recorded—everything that had happened to me in the past two days—was now in the information system on the ship.

Directory: First Interstellar Expedition
Subdirectory: Sigma Draconis II
Sub-subdirectory: Field Reports—Soc. Sci.
File Name: Li Lixia

The radio asked, "Is there anything else?"

"No."

"Okay. Three other people have made contact. No trouble so far. But take care and call again as soon as possible. I ought to have some real information in a couple of days."

I shut off the radio, packed it, and went out. The rain was coming down hard. I ran to the house.

The next day was clear. Yohai and I went to the garden. The ground was still wet. Drops of water sparkled on the leaves. Yohai taught me to weed. We worked all morning. At noon we rested under the tree. In the other gardens people moved around, talking to one another. But no one came to visit us. Interesting. Once again I had a sense that a point was being made, and Yohai did not want to make it. I bit into a yellow vegetable. It was juicy and bittersweet.

In the evening I sat with Nahusai. Yohai went out, I didn't know where. I learned more verbs and a lot of prepositions: the curse of every language, but they held all information together. To. From. At. Of. Between.

The next day was my fifth on the planet. The sky was clear again. Yohai and I worked in the garden. I learned the names of various plants. Yohai told me that she was a woman. She wasn't a mother, though. When she told me this, she seemed unhappy.

"Nahusai?" I asked.

She made the gesture that meant "yes." "Mother," she said, then put her hand on her chest. "Mother me."

Aha. A kinship relationship. My first one. I began to feel I was getting somewhere.

The day after that Yohai took me to the river. It ran between the gardens and the forest. This time of year—midsummer—it was low. The water ran around yellow stones. Yohai waded in and turned over a stone, then grabbed something. "Tsa!"

She handed the thing to me. It was maybe ten centimeters long, green and hard, with eight legs. I held it gingerly. The legs moved. At one end were two long stalks. Were they eyes? Or antennae? They flicked back and forth.

"We eat," said Yohai.

"Oh, yeah?" I made the gesture that meant uncertainty or confusion.

"You see." Yohai took the creature and tossed it into a pot. "You here." She beckoned.

I took off my boots, rolled up my pants, and waded in. She had another creature. It went into the pot. "You."

I reached into the water and rolled over a rock. Something scurried past my fingertips. I grabbed and missed.

"Damnation." I found another rock and tried again.

We spent all morning in the river. Yohai caught twenty or so of the creatures. I caught two.

At last she waded out of the river. She stared at me, looking puzzled.

"What am I good for?" I said in English. "An interesting question. I'm *very* good at learning languages and pretty good at figuring out how other people think. Though I can't always explain how I know what I know. Is that any help?"

Yohai picked up the pot. The green things were still alive. They crawled over one another, trying to get out.

"Come." She beckoned.

I picked up my boots. We walked downstream. After a few minutes the gardens were gone, and there were trees all around us. The air smelled of whatever-it-was: the forest aroma, sharp and distinctive, for which I had no name.

There were rapids in the river. Nothing important. The water rippled down over a series of little drops. Here and there I saw a little foam. At the bottom of the last drop was a pool. The water was quiet, deep, and green.

My companion put down the pot she carried. She kicked off her sandals and pulled her tunic over her head. Her body was lovely, dark and sleek. It reminded me of otters and bears and of my own species as well. She was remarkably humanoid. The only striking difference was the fur. The eyes were a bit unusual, of course. The pupils were vertical slits. The irises, which were pale yellow, filled the eyes. I could see no white. Her hands had three fingers and a thumb. Her feet had four toes. Except for this and her flat chest, she looked like our senior pilot, Ivanova.

She pointed at me. "You. Li-sha."

I undressed.

"Tsa!" She touched my bare shoulder. "What?"

I kept still. She walked around in back of me. "Hu!" I felt the touch of her hand very lightly on one shoulder blade. I shivered. She came around in front and stared at my chest.

For a human woman I was pretty flat. Still, my breasts were far more noticeable than hers.

"Mother? You?" she asked.

"No."

She looked me straight in the eyes. She was frowning. "What you?"

I answered her in English. "I can't explain, Yohai. Not yet. I don't know how you say 'world' or 'star' or 'friend.' But there's nothing wrong with me. I'm not dangerous. I mean no harm."

Yohai stared at me for another minute, then turned and dove into the pool. She was a terrific swimmer. I saw her glide through the green water as gracefully as a seal.

I dove after her. My foot slipped on the bank, and my dive turned into a belly flop. I came up, coughing and embarrassed. Yohai made a barking noise. A laugh?

I swam to the middle of the river, turned over and floated. The water was cool. There was hardly any current. Far above me a bird soared across the sky. Ah!

After a while I swam to shore. I climbed out and washed my clothes, using a couple of stones—I had learned the technique in California from the aborigines—then hung the clothes on a bush to dry.

Yohai joined me, brushing the water out of her fur. We sat together on the riverbank. Her eyes were half-closed, and her fur glistened in the sunlight. She looked so comfortable! Why couldn't I relax like that? Maybe I should take another course in yoga.

Yohai roused herself and told me the name of the creatures in the pot.

That evening I learned how to kill and shell the creatures. I didn't enjoy this. But I did it. Yohai boiled the remains. The result was delicious. I ate too much. Afterward I sat in the doorway. Children played in the street. They seemed to be playing tag. I watched and felt more or less contented, though I could have used an after-dinner drink. Something light and dry. A white wine maybe.

The next morning I paid another long visit to the privy. I called the ship and got Eddie again.

"I have news for you," he said. "But first, transmit your information."

I put the medallion into the radio and waited. There were half a dozen bugs in the privy. A couple buzzed around my head. I waved them away. The radio beeped. I pulled the medallion out.

"Anything else?"

"Yes. I'm staying with two people. Nahusai and Yohai. No one visits them. When Yohai and I work in the garden, no one talks to us. I think the problem is me."

There was a pause. "Do you think the situation is dangerous? Do you want to get out?"

"No. Not yet."

Another pause. "Your instincts are usually excellent. Okay. But I want you to call in more often."

"I'll try. It won't be easy. There isn't much privacy here."

"Do what you can. Now, for your information—Harrison Yee got driven out of his village. They were polite, but firm. It happened after he took a bath. We think he violated a nudity taboo or a taboo against washing in running water or maybe just in that particular river. Try and find out how your people bathe before you take a bath."

"I've already taken one, Eddie."

"Yeah? Where?"

"In the nearest river."

"Alone?"

"With Yohai. The daughter of my host. She looked a little surprised when she saw me naked. Apparently she hadn't realized that I had no fur on me anywhere. Well, almost no fur. In any case, nothing happened."

"That's interesting. Of course, Harrison was nowhere close to you. However, the language you are learning is similar to the one he was learning, before he took his bath."

"He's on the other side of the continent."

"Uh-huh. And your language is almost identical to the one Derek is learning. He's down the coast from you."

A bug landed on my face. I swatted and missed. The radio began to slide off my knees. "Damnation!" I grabbed it before it could go into the hole below me.

"Lixia?"

"Nothing. What does all of this mean?"

"We don't know. But there are theories. You may be learning a trade language, something like pidgin English. Or maybe all the people contacted so far are closely related, part of a recent migration."

"How likely is that?"

"Not very. The trade language is a distinct possibility—or so we think at the moment."

I signed off and left the privy. Outside, a couple of meters away, a person waited. He or she wore a robe and a tall hat. The robe was covered with embroidery. The hat was decorated with shells. After a moment I recognized him or her. It was the person who had broken up Nahusai's party.

"Yes?" I said in the native language.

He or she made a gesture—a vertical slash—then turned and walked away.

I went back to the house feeling a bit nervous. The person had radiated hostility. Who was he or she? I couldn't ask. I didn't know the right words.

For the next half-dozen days the sky remained clear. The weather was hot. Yohai and I worked in the garden. Mostly, we brought water from the river: pot after heavy pot. We poured the water out on the dry ground. Then we returned to the river. We refilled our pots. We went back to the garden.

My arms hurt. My shoulders hurt. There was a terrible ache in the small of my back. I tried to remember how I had gotten into this situation. It had something to do with the romance of interstellar travel. Or was it the quest for knowledge?

In the afternoon we went to the house and rested. In the evening Yohai went out—back to the garden or maybe somewhere else. I stayed with Nahusai. She taught me more of the language. I began to understand complete sentences.

I was never left alone, except when I was in the privy. I wasn't sure why. Did Nahusai and Yohai fear me? Or were they afraid that someone might try to harm me?

I didn't feel especially safe, even in the privy. People might be watching. The person in the hat certainly had been. People might notice if I spent a long time inside. They might decide to creep up on me and listen. They wouldn't understand my conversation, but they would know that I was talking to someone who was not present.

I ended by calling from the house on a night when my companions went to sleep early.

"Where in hell have you been?" asked Eddie.

I turned the volume down and explained.

"Lixia, you have to keep in touch. We've been getting worried. Ivanova has been talking about coming after you. Can you imagine what that would be like? She'd go in like the Seventh Cavalry, and we'd have to figure out how to fix the mess that she made."

"Okay," I said and turned the volume down further. On the other side of the house Yohai and Nahusai snored. They sounded almost entirely human.

Eddie told me the news. Harrison Yee was back on the ship, as was Antonio Nybo. Tony had been in the archipelago. He'd found a number of ceremonial sites—rocks arranged in circles and cliffs with pictographs—but no people. His island was empty.

"Of archaeological interest only," Eddie said. "We pulled him out."

There were five other people from Earth still on the planet. Four of them were in villages more or less like mine. The fifth—Gregory—was staying with an extended family in the western mountains.

"They keep flocks and do fantastic weaving, or so Gregory tells me."

"Uh-huh."

"There don't seem to be any large population centers. We don't know why as yet. We don't even have any theories."

"A desperate situation," I said.

Eddie laughed.

Yohai groaned and rolled over.

I said, "I have to go."

On the fourteenth day of my stay in the village I decided

I had to call again. I waited till after dark, then went to the privy. The planet's one big moon was rising. It hung over the rooftops, bright orange, three-quarters full. I left the door of the privy open. Moonlight shone in. I could see well enough to operate my radio.

This evening Eddie had a new and interesting piece of news.

"Yvonne says there are no mature males in her village. There are a few old men. They live at the edge of the village, she says, each one alone. And there are boys—male children. But in between, nothing."

I thought for a moment. "I know the word for 'boy,' and I've seen boys play in the street. The younger children wear no clothing. Gender is obvious and an interesting example of parallel evolution. But I don't know the word for 'man.'" I chewed on my lip for a moment or two. "Let me check into this."

"Okay," said Eddie.

I signed off and slung the radio over my shoulder, then stepped out of the privy. The moon was directly above me. It was smaller than Luna, but closer to its primary, with a much higher albedo. It lit the area around me: the weed patch, the privy, and half a dozen houses.

I started toward the house of Nahusai. Something moved in the shadow along the wall.

"Yes?" I called. "What is it?"

Something else moved to the right of me, near one of the neighboring houses. I turned. A person stood in the moonlight. He or she wore a robe.

"What is it?" I asked.

"I am Hakht," a voice said harshly. Or maybe the voice said "Akht." I was not certain about the initial aspirate.

Other figures emerged from the shadows. There were half a dozen. Two had sticks. They formed a circle around me—at a good distance. Nonetheless, they blocked my way out of the yard.

"We heard you. You go there—" The figure in the robe pointed at the privy. "You talk. You do . . . " He or she said something I didn't understand. It sounded like an accusation.

"I do nothing bad," I said.

The person made a gesture that meant—I was pretty sure—"no" or "I disagree." "You are a something-something. I tell you, go!"

"I do not understand," I said.

"Go!" the person shouted.

I looked around. No one was coming close. What was I supposed to be? An evil spirit? I walked forward. The people in front of me moved to either side.

"Thank you," I said in English.

Behind me the person in the robe shouted, "Something! Go!"

I walked around the house to the front and then inside. Nahusai had gone to bed. Yohai sat by the fire. She was weaving, using the little hand loom. She looked up.

"A bad thing," I said. "A person named Hakht or Akht."

"Tsa!" Yohai scrambled upright. "What?"

"I was in the privy. I came out. Hakht was there. Hakht said, 'Go.'"

"Hu!" Yohai ran to her mother and shook the old lady awake. They talked softly and rapidly. I bit my thumbnail.

"Nahusai!" a voice said behind me. It was Hakht, of course. He or she stood in the doorway. One hand held a staff. The other hand held a rattle. The rattle was painted white. Black feathers dangled from the handle.

"What is this?" asked Nahusai.

I glanced at the old lady. She was standing now. Yohai held a belt made of silver. The old lady smoothed her robe, then took the belt and put it on. After that she opened a box and pulled out half a dozen necklaces. They were silver, copper, bronze, and shell. She put them on. Yohai handed her a staff. She walked toward us slowly, with dignity, leaning on her staff.

"It is night, daughter of my sister," she said to Hakht. She spoke slowly and clearly. I had an idea that she wanted me to understand. "Why are you here?"

Hakht waved the rattle at me. It made a buzzing sound. "This one will go."

"No," Nahusai answered.

"She is a something!" Hakht said.

"No. What did I teach you, daughter of my sister. How do we know a something?" Nahusai held up a finger. "They do not like to eat." She held up a second finger. "They never sleep." She held up a third finger. "They do not go in the water. Is this not so?"

Hakht frowned, then made the gesture that meant "yes."

Nahusai waved at me. "This one sleeps. She eats—" My host made a wide gesture, indicating that I ate plenty. "She uses the privy. She has been in the water. Yohai saw this. She is not a something. You say a bad thing, daughter of my sister. It is not true."

Hakht frowned. She opened her mouth to answer.

Nahusai pointed at the door. "I will not talk in the night. Go!"

After a moment Hakht turned. She left slowly, with obvious reluctance. Her back looked rigid. The hand that held the rattle moved slightly. I heard a soft erratic buzz.

When she was gone, Yohai began to moan.

"Tsa!" the old lady said.

I discovered I was shaking. I sat down, almost falling as I folded myself up. Nahusai and Yohai began talking. Their voices were full of strain. I couldn't understand a word of the conversation.

What had happened, anyway? Hakht had accused me of being some kind of supernatural creature. A monster, an evil spirit, a ghost. Nahusai had said I didn't have the distinguishing characteristics of whatever it was. She had sounded like a doctor, discussing the symptoms of a disease. She must be a magician or a priestess, and Hakht must be one, too. A rival specialist. In any case Hakht had withdrawn, foiled for the moment. But I was pretty sure that this quarrel wasn't over. Should I ask Eddie to pull me out? I bit a fingernail. Not yet.

My host spoke, her voice calm and definite. Whatever she said sounded final. Yohai made a gesture I didn't entirely understand. But I thought it meant "so be it."

Nahusai sighed. She leaned her staff against the wall, then took off her jewelry. She looked exhausted.

"Li-sha." It was Yohai.

"Yes?"

"Sleep." Yohai pointed at my pile of furs.

I went there, but I didn't get to sleep for hours.

Yohai shook me at dawn. "Wake you. Eat."

I sat up. The fire was burning brightly. A pot hung over it, and my host sat nearby.

"Come," said Yohai. "Now."

I went to the privy first. It was cold outside. There was dew on the ground, and the sky was an indeterminate early morning color. Why was I up at this hour? More trouble, I decided. I used the privy and went back to the house. There was water in a big basin next to the door. I washed and went inside.

Breakfast was mush. It seemed to be their favorite food. When we were done eating, my host looked at me. Her expression was grave. "Li-sha." She paused and frowned. "Hakht says bad things. People listen. They say, 'Yes. Li-sha is a something. She is bad.'" She paused again and stared at the fire, then looked back at me. "I am old. They know I go . . ." She patted the floor. Underground, that gesture meant. "I talk. They do not listen. Go with Yohai."

"Where?"

"A good place. Go."

I packed, then slung my pack over my shoulders. Yohai put on a plain brown tunic and a leather belt. A sheath hung from the belt, and there was a knife in the sheath. It had a handle made of brass and horn.

"Come," Yohai said.

I stopped in front of Nahusai. I didn't know the word for "thank you," but there was a gesture. I touched my chest, then turned my hand so the palm was toward Nahusai.

She returned the gesture.

I held out a gift: a box. It was made of wood from one of the Empty Islands, inset with pieces of shell. They were iridescent pink and green, lovelier than abalone or mother-of-pearl.

Nahusai took the box.

"Good-bye," I said in English. I followed Yohai out the door.

The sun was just appearing. Looking to the east I saw it: a line of orange light above a rooftop. The sky was clear. The street was empty, except for a yellow *ki*—a domestic bird, something like a crane. It was hunting for bugs in the weeds along a house wall. We startled it. It stalked away, and we hurried off in the opposite direction.

By the time the sun was fully up we were in the forest. Trunks rose up on every side of us like pillars in an old-time cathedral. Way above us were the branches. Their dark leaves hid the sun. Now and then we came to a clearing, full of sunlight and flying bugs. There must have been a hatch. Or was I seeing a migration? In any case, the bugs were all the same. Their bodies were electric blue. Their wings were transparent and colorless, except for two large red spots.

There was one clearing where the bugs were especially numerous. They floated around us. One landed on my arm. I stopped, enchanted. It fanned its wings. I counted eight legs and two antennae.

"Come," said Yohai.

I hurried on. The bug flew away.

At noon we came to a building standing in a larger-than-usual clearing. Weeds grew around it, and a stream ran in the back. I heard the rushing water.

"This is the place," my companion told me.

The building was small and old. A log propped up one wall. The roof was leather. I was pretty sure that it wasn't the original roof, but rather a makeshift repair, done by someone who was no carpenter. Off to one side was a second structure. A lean-to. Smoke came out of it. What was it? I got my answer a moment later: the sound of a hammer. A smithy.

My companion walked toward the sound. I followed. We stopped at the entrance to the lean-to and looked in. A fire burned in a stone forge. A person bent over an anvil made of iron. There was metal on the anvil, glowing bright yellow. The person lifted a hammer, then brought it down, lifted it and brought it down again.

Yohai raised one hand in warning. "Wait" that gesture meant. I waited.

After a while the person put down the hammer. He or she straightened up, stretched, groaned, then turned and saw us. "Hu!"

Yohai said something I didn't understand.

The smith made a gesture.

Yohai talked some more. I studied the smith. He or she wore a leather apron and sandals. Nothing more. I got a good look at him or her: broad shoulders, a deep chest, and powerful-looking arms. This was a formidable creature. The fur that covered him or her was reddish brown. An unusual color. Hadn't there been someone like this at the party on the night I arrived?

Yohai stopped talking.

The smith made another gesture, then looked at me. "I am Nia. You will stay here."

I made the gesture of assent.

Yohai said something to me. Was it good-bye? She turned and walked away, moving quickly. In a minute or two she was gone.

"Sit down," said Nia. "I—" He or she waved at the fire.

"I understand."

I settled in a corner. Nia added charcoal to the fire, then began to pump the bellows: a large bag, made of leather, with a stick attached to it. Nia raised and lowered the stick. The bag filled and emptied. The fire brightened. After a while Nia picked up tongs and laid the metal in the fire.

"What is that?" I asked and pointed.

Nia told me the word for iron, then went back to work. He or she beat the piece of iron till it was flat, then heated it and folded it, then beat it flat again. This was done over and over. I got tired watching.

Sometime in the afternoon Nia stopped working. He or she sighed and stretched. "Food."

"Yes." I stood up.

We went to the other building. Inside it was empty except for a pile of furs and a couple of jars. Nia took off the apron, then rummaged among the furs and found a tunic. She put it on.

"Here." She pulled bread out of one jar. The other jar was full of a liquid: the pungent narcotic I'd drunk at the party.

We sat down in the doorway and ate and drank.

"Where are you from?" asked Nia. Her mouth was full of food. I didn't understand her, and she had to repeat the question.

"Not around here," I answered.

"I am of the Iron People," she said. "They are far away. There." She pointed toward the sun. "You?"

I waved in the opposite direction, eastward.

"Ya." She drank more of the liquid. "These people are hard to understand." She got up and went to the smithy.

I stayed where I was until I heard the sound of Nia's hammer. Then I got out my radio and called Eddie.

After he heard what had happened, he said, "I ought to pull you out."

"No."

"Why not?"

"I don't think I'm in any danger, and if I am . . . Eddie, we all knew how dangerous this might be. We could have sent down robots. We sent down people because we wanted whatever it is that people bring to a situation. The human perspective. We voted to take the risk. It got a clear majority."

Eddie was silent.

"I want to stay. That's *my* human perspective. This is the reason I left Earth—not to sit in a room in the goddamn ship. I'm finally able to carry on a conversation, and I'm starting to learn how the natives work iron. You know I'm interested in technology."

There was more silence, then a sigh. "I opposed using robots because I thought they'd be more disruptive than people. Okay. Stay. But I think you're wrong."

"About what? The situation?"

"No. Technology. It's a typical Western bias. You think a tool is more important than a dream because a tool can be measured and a dream cannot."

I made a noncommittal noise.

"The Greeks are to blame," he said.

"What?"

"They were the ones who decided that reality was mathematical. A crazy idea! An ethical value isn't like a triangle. A religious vision can't be reduced to a formula. Yet both are real. Both are important."

"You have no fight with me. I don't know enough about Western philosophy to defend it. And I have to get off the air."

"Give me a call tomorrow."

"Okay."

At twilight Nia came back. She divided her pile of furs in two. "You sleep there." She pointed at one pile.

I woke at sunrise. Nia was up and putting on her apron. "Yohai says you can learn. Come."

We went to the smithy. Nia got the fire going, then taught me how to work the bellows. That morning she made the blade for a hoe. The blade was pointed and had two barbs at the back—for weeding, I decided, though it looked as if it could be used as a weapon.

I had not seen any real weapons. No swords. No pikes. No battle axes or battle clubs. Nothing that was clearly designed to harm another person.

That was interesting. Maybe the men—wherever they were—had the tools for killing.

At noon we stopped and ate. I asked Nia the names of several things: the hoe blade, the hammer, and so on. She frowned and told me. I had a feeling that she wasn't going to be a very good teacher. She seemed laconic by nature.

We went back to work. My arms started to ache, then my back, and finally my legs. The smoke was bothering my eyes, and I wasn't too crazy about the clouds of steam produced when Nia dropped the glowing blade into a bucket of water. She did this twice. Finally she took the blade outside. She examined it in the sunlight, then made the gesture that meant "yes."

"Is it good?" I asked.

"Yes. I will make another one."

Damn her. She did. By the time she was finished, I was exhausted. I went outside and lay on the ground, while she banked the fire and put her tools away. She was meticulously neat in her work. Her house was a shambles, though. The day—I noticed for the first time—was bright and cool. A lovely day, now almost over. I decided not to call Eddie. It was too much effort. Instead I went to bed.

The next day Nia made wire. I worked the bellows and learned a new phrase. "Pump evenly, you idiot."

In the evening we sat in Nia's house and drank the pungent liquid. We both got a little drunk. Nia began chanting to herself, slapping one hand against her thigh to keep time. Her eyes were half-shut. She looked dreamy.

I leaned against the wall and watched smoke rise from the fire. This was a change for the better, I decided. Nia was taciturn and short-tempered, but she wasn't melancholy. Nahusai had spent a lot of time sitting and brooding, and Yohai had almost always been busy. I found that unrestful.

Nia stopped chanting. I looked at her. She was lying down. A minute later she began to snore. A very restful companion, I told myself.

Nothing much happened in the next ten days. I helped Nia in the smithy. At night I talked to Eddie.

"There's no question about your language," he said one evening. "It's pidgin, which explains why it's so easy to learn.

"The big continent has a trade language, too—a different one, in no way related to yours. Yvonne and Santha are learning it. Meiling is learning something else. A local language, horrifying in its complexity."

"And Gregory?" I asked.

"Another local language, but less difficult. Oh, an interesting thing happened to Gregory—"

I waited expectantly. Eddie, I had learned, tended to save the really important information till the end of a conversation.

"His people found out he was male. They told him to leave. He asked why? The question was a stunner, apparently. They couldn't believe he was asking it. But in the end they told him. In their society the men live alone, up in the high mountains. They take care of the flocks, and they never come to the houses where the women live. The idea is shameful. Gregory says, he couldn't think of a polite way to ask about procreation."

"Did they throw him out?"

"No. He told them he didn't know how to stay alive alone in the mountains. They had a long argument, then decided to let him stay in one of the outbuildings—a barn of some kind. And there he remains. *J'y suis, j'y reste,* he says."

"The men live entirely alone?"

"According to Gregory, yes. The women say the men are bad-tempered. They don't like company."

"Oh, yeah? It explains what happened to Harrison."

"Uh-huh. I warned Derek and Santha. Yvonne is going to talk to her hostess. She's the ideal informant: a tribal historian who never stops talking."

I made the gesture of agreement, then grinned and said, "Yes."

"You talk to Nia. Ask her about the men in her society."

I said I would, but I didn't. Nia was never easy to talk with. Often she would stop in the middle of a sentence and stare off into space or else change the subject. I got the impression she had lived alone for a long time. She had forgotten how to carry on a conversation. I concentrated on prying information about grammar out of her. Questions about folkways could wait until later.

One morning Nia reached into the rafters of her house. She pulled down two axes.

"Come," she told me. "We are going to get wood."

We spent all morning in the forest. Nia felled a tree, maybe ten meters tall. The trunk was straight. The branches were bare, except for a few shriveled leaves. The tree was obviously dead and had been for some time.

When it was down, Nia said, "Make it into pieces."

"I'll do my best."

I started chopping. Nia went off. When I paused to rub my hands, I heard her axe a short distance away. She was felling another tree.

At noon we rested.

"What is this for?" I asked.

"Charcoal." She chewed on a piece of bread. "This wood is dry already. Tomorrow we put it underground. It will burn for nine days, ten days, slowly, underground. Then it will be charcoal." She got up, stretched, and rubbed her palms along her thighs. "Time to work."

I groaned and got my axe.

A few minutes later the blister on my right hand broke. I put down my axe and looked at the blister. There was blood. I was going to have to spray it. I walked back to Nia's house and opened my pack. Should I wash the wound? I decided not to. It looked clean, and I didn't know what kind of microbe lived in the streams, especially the streams close to a village. In theory nothing on this planet could live off me. Our genetic material was too different. No local virusoid could use my DNA for replication. No local bacteroid could use my cells for food. Still and all—

I got out the bandage can and sprayed on a small thin bandage. It stung. That would be the disinfectant. I sat down and waited for the bandage to dry. It was shiny and dark brown: flesh-colored, according to the label on the can, and made in the South African Confederation.

"Nia!" a voice cried.

I looked up. Yohai came out of the forest, walking quickly. "Where is Nia?"

"There." I pointed. "You can hear the sound of her axe."

"Bad news! I must tell her." Yohai ran off.

I thought about following her, but decided no, put the can of bandages away and did a little housework. The mess was beginning to drive me crazy. I hung up Nia's clothes and arranged the furs we slept on in two neat piles. When I was done, I went outside. I couldn't hear the sound of chopping or anything except the rustle of leaves. The sun blazed overhead, almost as bright as Sol. The air was hot. I sat down in the shadow of a wall and waited. After half an hour Nia and Yohai came.

"It is time to tell you what is going on," Nia said.

"I would like that."

They squatted down. Nia laid her two axes on the ground, then scratched her nose. "Nahusai lies in bed. She cannot get up. She cannot eat. Hakht says, you have done this. Hakht says, you must be driven away. If not, Nahusai will die and then other people. You will make songs. The songs will do harm. They will steal breath out of the mouth. They will make the blood in the belly get hard like a stone." Nia glanced at Yohai. "This is what you said."

Yohai made the gesture of agreement. "I think Hakht made the songs. She is the one doing harm. My mother is old. She cannot defend herself. I have no power. The people who are no longer here do not talk to me. I cannot defend my mother."

Well, this was pretty clear. Nahusai was ill. Hakht was accusing me of putting a spell on the old lady. I was a witch—according to Hakht, anyway.

"Why is Hakht doing this?"

Nia answered me. "She cannot wait. She wants to be the most important woman in the village. She will be, when Nahusai goes . . . " Nia paused, then patted the ground. "Nahusai taught her. Nahusai said, this is the one who will come after me. But she cannot wait." Nia frowned. After a moment she said, "There are people like this."

I made the gesture of agreement.

"She tries to put herself in the middle of everything. If Nahusai says 'yes' to anything, this woman says 'no.' Nahusai made you welcome. Because of this, Hakht says you are a demon."

"This is true," Yohai said.

"What do we do?" I asked.

"I can think of only one thing," Nia said. "We must wait. If Nahusai gets better, she will make Hakht be quiet. If she does not . . . " Nia made a gesture I did not recognize.

"What does that mean?"

"Who can say?"

I was going to repeat my question, then I realized Nia had answered it. The gesture—the hand held out, then tilted from side to side—meant "who can say?"

Nia stood. "Yohai, you go home. Lisa and I will be careful. Thank you for the warning."

Yohai made the gesture of acknowledgment. She left. I waited till she was out of sight, then looked at Nia. "Do you think she is right?"

"In what way?"

"Did Hakht make this happen? Did she harm Nahusai?"

Nia frowned. "I do not know if songs do anything. Or if the people who are no longer here listen to anyone. But a woman like Hakht knows things to put in food. This is a bad situation." She clenched one hand and hit the wall above me. "I hate this place! I am tired of the dark trees. I am tired of the people. They are always telling stories about one another. They are always making plans to do one another harm." She bent and grabbed an axe, then walked away. A bit later I heard the sound of the axe. Nia was chopping down another tree.

I thought of calling Eddie, then decided no. Ten to one, he'd want to pull me back up to the ship. I didn't think the situation was dangerous, and I wanted to see what would happen next.

I went to the bank of the stream and did my yoga exercises. Then I meditated, watching the rushing water. At twilight bugs appeared—little ones, like gnats. They didn't sting, but they got in my nose and eyes. I got up and went back to the house, feeling relaxed. My mind, usually busy and a bit anxious, seemed as empty and clear as the sky above me. I stopped outside the door and looked up. There was a moon above the forest: a narrow sickle, less than a quarter full. It was pale yellow, bright with the light of vanished sun. All at once I was full of an intense joy. At any moment things were going to make sense. I would see the pattern in—or beyond—observable phenomena. I would understand the mystery of life, the secret of the universe.

Then the feeling was gone. The moon was only a moon. I shrugged. Once again I hadn't gotten through. To what, anyway? I wasn't really sure these moments of almost revelation meant anything.

I went inside and found Nia making dinner: a thin gruel with berries mixed in. Her movements were abrupt, and her body looked tense. She was still angry. I decided to keep quiet. We ate and went to sleep.

I woke, hearing a noise: a soft *tum-ta-tum.* It came from outside. A drum.

"Nia?" I called.

She scrambled out of bed. A moment later she was at the door, pulling it open. Grey light shone in. Nia stood in the doorway. She was naked, and she held an axe.

I got up and moved in back of her.

It was a little before sunrise. There was light in the east. In the clearing in front of the house five torches burned. They looked impressive, streaming in the wind, but they didn't do much in the way of illumination. I saw dark shapes and knew they had to be people. But I didn't know who they were or even how many stood there. Twenty-five? Thirty? Maybe more.

Nia muttered something and stepped through the door. I followed. A person came toward us. She held a rattle, and she kept it moving continuously. It made a noise like a rattlesnake gone nuts.

"Stop that noise," Nia said. She sounded angry.

"Very well." The noise stopped. "We have come for the demon." I recognized the voice. Loud, harsh, and arrogant, it belonged to Hakht.

Nia glanced around. "What does this mean? Is Nahusai dead?"

"She died last night. I was in my house, making a song to drive away bad luck. I heard Yohai shout. I knew the old woman was gone."

"And Yohai?" Nia asked. "Is Yohai here?"

The sky was getting brighter. I saw the gesture that the sorceress made. It meant "no."

"There are ceremonies that must be performed. She has begun them." Hakht raised her voice. She sounded triumphant. "She will not help you. I told her, she has caused bad luck. She has caused anger among the people who are no longer here. I have said, this must stop. She listened, O woman of the Iron People. She will do what I say. Now—" Hakht raised a hand and pointed. "The demon. Give her to me."

"No."

Hakht took a step forward. Nia lifted up the axe. "Listen to me, sorceress. I have no respect for you. I do not fear your power." Nia paused. Usually her shoulders were rounded. But now she drew herself upright. "All of you, listen! I have done something that few women ever do. I have killed a person."

The villagers shifted around a little. No one spoke.

"West of here, on the plain, are the bones of a person who made me angry. I did not even bury him." She glanced around. "I am willing to do this again."

Hakht opened her mouth.

"Be quiet! Let me finish!"

Hakht closed her mouth. She was frowning.

Nia went on. "I do not want to stay here. I am tired of the darkness under the trees. I want to see the sky again. I will go and take the demon with me. There will be no one left to stand up to you, Hakht. You can be happy then." The contempt in her voice was obvious. "Give me one day, O sorceress. Go away and come back tomorrow morning. I will be gone with the demon, and no one will be hurt."

There was a long silence. Nia kept her pose, standing very straight, her axe raised. Hakht stared at her and frowned. At last Hakht said, "Very well. We will come back tomorrow." She turned and walked away. The rest of the villagers followed. In a minute or two they were gone—out of sight in the forest.

Nia sighed. Her shoulders went down. She took a step back and leaned against the wall of the house.

"Did you really kill a person?"

She made the gesture of assent. "I was very angry." She looked out at the forest. "I would like to kill Hakht, but I am not angry enough." She dropped the axe. "Go in. Get ready to leave. I will come in as soon as I stop trembling."

I went inside and packed. After a while Nia came in. She reheated the remains of dinner. We ate.

"Maybe this is good," she said. "I might have stayed here till I was an old woman. Now I will see the plain again." She got up and pulled a bag out of the rafters. "I'll have to leave my anvil and most of my tools. Aiya!"

She went to the smithy. I went to the stream to wash. When I got back, she was dressing. The bag lay at her feet. It was half-full and lumpy.

"What did you pack?"

"As little as possible. And nothing really big. The kinds of tools I use are not light. The bag is going to seem very heavy, after I carry it for a while." She paused, then made the gesture that meant "so be it." "I am not willing to leave everything behind."

She finished dressing and folded up a cloak made of leather. It went into the bag, followed by all the bread in the house. Ten pieces. "Let's go. Hakht might change her mind." She handed me one of the axes, then picked up the other and slung the bag over her shoulder. I put on my backpack. We left the house.

The sun was up. The sky was cloudless. A strong wind blew.

"A good day," Nia said.

"What will happen to Yohai?" I asked.

"She will listen to Hakht. It will be hard for a while. Then she will get used to it. And Hakht will become friendly when she sees that Yohai does nothing against her wishes. In the end they will get along. The fight was never between the two of them. It was between Hakht and Nahusai. This is my opinion, anyway."

We took the path that went toward the village, walking quickly, and reached the river before noon. I looked around. On the far side of the river was a fence, a low one made of wood. Beyond it was a garden. Blue leaves glistened in the sunlight. I saw no gardener. That was odd. The people of the village seemed to spend a good part of every morning in their gardens.

In the distance something honked. A musical instrument. Maybe a horn. I heard voices, wailing and shrieking.

"The ceremonies," Nia said. "They are going around the outside of the village, making noise to drive Nahusai away, into the far land." Nia frowned. "My people are not like this. We do not fear the dead—only death, which is unlucky. There must be ceremonies, of course—"

The horn honked again. It sounded closer. Nia paused and listened, then went on.

"The ceremonies drive away bad luck. They make the village clean. But we do not fear our friends and relations simply because this bad thing had happened to them. They are—they must be—the same people they were before." She resettled her bag on her shoulder, then walked off.

I thought of asking her for more information about the funeral ceremonies, but she was moving quickly. I had to hurry to catch up, and I had no breath to spare.

ENSHI

We followed a new path that went upstream along the river. The sun went on ahead of us—or seemed to, anyway. We were traveling west.

Midway through the afternoon we turned onto another trail. It led north into an area of low hills. The soil was sandy. The trees were small and scrubby. Here and there we came upon outcroppings of a sandy rock, yellow or dull orange. The trail was barely visible: a faint line that wound among the rocks and trees. It led finally—in the late afternoon—to a shack, made of long branches leaning against rock. Skins were stretched over the branches. Smoke came out of a hole. What a sad little dwelling place!

Nia stopped. "We bring gifts," she called.

A deep voice answered, "Go away."

"I am Nia the iron smith. Do you want a knife? It has a sharp blade. The handle is bone. Very handsome, I think."

There was a long silence. "What gift do you want?"

"I need food. Smoked fish, if you have it."

"Yes." There was another long silence. "Put the knife down. Go away. When the sun is out of sight, come back."

"Yes," said Nia. She rummaged in her bag and pulled out a knife, which she laid on the ground. Then she turned and walked off. I followed.

We went only a short distance. Nia put down her bag. "This is far enough. He can't see us here."

I sat down. "Who was that?"

"I don't know his name."

"It is a . . ." I paused. I didn't know the word for man. "It is what a boy becomes?"

"A man. Yes. Who else would live out here alone? I have met him before. He is friendlier than most men."

"You call that friendly?"

"Yes. The men around here have no manners. Their mothers raise them badly, and the old men who ought to teach them to behave when they leave the village—the old men are surly and mean. They lack self-respect. This is my opinion, anyway."

"Why do the men leave the village?"

Nia stared at me. "What kind of question is that?"

"Do all men leave the village?"

"Yes. Of course." Nia frowned. "What kind of person are you? Why do you ask something like that?"

I thought for a moment. "I come from a long distance away. My people are different from yours. How different, I don't know. Maybe the differences are small—things on the surface, like the fur that you have and I don't. Maybe the differences are big. In any case, among my people men and women live together."

Nia frowned again. "How can that be? After the change no man can bear to be with other people—except at the time of mating, of course, and except for Enshi."

"Enshi?" I asked.

Nia stared at the sky. "The sun is almost gone. We can go back."

We returned to the shack. Firelight shone through gaps between the skins. I didn't see anyone, either inside or out. The knife was gone. In its place was a basket, full of smoked fish.

"This is good!" Nia said. "Now we won't starve."

The basket had a top. She put it on and fastened it, then put the whole thing in her bag. "Come on. We'll go back toward the river and find a place to camp. This fellow won't like it if we stay here."

"That is true," the deep voice said. "It is a good knife, Nia."

Nia glanced at the shack. "The fish smells good. Thank you."

We walked off. The sky darkened and stars appeared along with a moon: a point of light that moved rapidly up from the eastern horizon. We stopped in a hollow. Nia made a fire, and we ate a couple of pieces of fish. It was bony and oily with a strong smoky taste. I did not especially like it.

"Who is Enshi?" I asked.

Nia stared at the fire. There was a brooding expression on her face. At length she glanced up. "I made up a poem about Enshi after I had been in this place a year. It goes like this:

"I am in this dark place,
this forest.

"He is in that dark place,
that grave."

"He is dead?"

Nia made the gesture of affirmation. "I will not talk about him. Do your men really live with the women?"

"Yes."

"That's very strange. Is it right?"

The word she used had several meanings: "usual," "well made," "moral."

"We think so. We've always lived this way."

Nia made a barking noise. "If Hakht knew this, she would be certain that you are a demon. Of course, her people do many things that are not right."

"What?" I asked.

Nia frowned, then scratched her nose. "They do not like men, not even their sons. 'A son is a mouth,' they say. They mean a son is something that eats food and makes noise and does nothing useful."

"Hu!" I said.

Nia made the gesture of agreement. "It is very badly done. There is something else—" She paused. "They do not like to mate with men. Often in the spring they go out, two women together. They stay in the forest. They do things with their hands." Nia shivered. "Do your people do anything like this?"

"Some of us do. I don't."

"Do you think it's right?"

I thought for a moment. "It is common. I don't think that it is wrong." I used a word which meant "unusual," "immoral," "badly made," or "done in a seriously inept fashion."

Nia shivered again. "I did it once. Yohai kept asking me. One spring I went with her. I do not know why. I didn't like it. I felt ashamed. Aiya!" She paused for a moment. "I wish we had something to drink."

The next day we went back to the river. We continued west along it. The land was flat and covered with forest. The sky was cloudless, and the river shone. Birdlike creatures glided from tree to tree, and other things—invisible to me—moved through the underbrush. I saw one as it crossed our path: a bronze shell about half a meter long with many quick-moving little feet beneath it. Two huge faceted eyes stuck out on top.

"What?" I asked as the animal vanished.

"It's called a *wahakh,*" Nia said. "It can live in water and out of it. The people here say that it carries messages from the spirits, and sometimes it acts as a guide for women who go on spirit-journeys. They never eat it, though it is delicious when roasted." She paused. "We'll leave it alone."

Toward evening we came to a lake. The water was clear and dark green. Rushes grew at the edges.

Nia looked around. "I have been here before—when I came east, after I left my people. I remember this place reminded me of a lake in my country. The Great Rush Lake. This is smaller, of course. Aiya! How the years go by!"

We made camp. Nia spent the evening staring into the fire. I went off and called Eddie and told him what had happened in the last few days.

"You take chances, don't you?" he said.

"A few. Not many."

"That crazy shamaness might have decided to kill you."

"I don't think that's likely. I get the impression these people aren't violent."

"Uh-huh. Tell that to Derek."

"What happened?"

"He decided he had to tell the people in his village that he was a man—to see what would happen. He is, as you remember, extremely curious. They tried to stone him. He grabbed his radio and ran."

"Is he all right?"

"Yes. But what would've happened to someone else, someone who couldn't run the way he can?"

I thought about that for a while. Derek was a tall blond from southern California, an aborigine who'd spent his childhood traveling on foot in the desert. When he was fifteen there had been a drought. He walked up to a trading station on the coast and said, "I'm tired of living like this. Teach me something else."

They sent him to school, and he took up running as a sport. Over short distances he was good. Over long distances he was unbeatable.

"Where is he? On the ship?"

"No. He's traveling west. The country is pleasant, he says. Rolling hills, forest, and some prairie. There's a lot of game, much more than in California. He is going to make a bow."

A bug flitted past me. I batted at it and missed. "How is Gregory?"

"Fine. But he says his people are treating him differently. They talk to him slowly and firmly, and they give a lot of orders. Very simple orders. He thinks they've decided he is not very bright. What other explanation is there? He doesn't know the right behavior, and he can't take care of himself."

I grinned.

"One other thing," Eddie said.

Aha, I thought. The zinger for today. "What is it?"

"Gregory says there must be gold in the mountains. His people wear a lot of jewelry, and most of it is gold."

"What's so interesting about that?"

"The planetologists think it may be significant. The planet is denser than Earth, and there's plenty of evidence of volcanic activity. There's a good chance, they say, of finding metal close to the surface. Not just gold—silver, copper, platinum, tin, iridium, chromium, you name it." His voice sounded peculiar: flat and careful.

"What's going on?"

"People up here are getting interested. Members of the crew, mostly. I don't think they have enough to do. They are talking about possibilities. If the metal is here, and if it's high quality, and if it's close to the surface, maybe even on the surface, then it could be mined."

I rocked back on my heels and looked at the radio. I couldn't really see it, of course. The night was too dark. "A mining colony? Eighteen light-years from home? Do they have any idea of the transportation costs?"

"They are thinking of a manufacturing center. A colony to build ships."

"No one is ever going to build a ship at the bottom of a gravity well, unless you are talking about the kind of ship that goes through water, and I don't think you are."

"Final assembly would be done in space."

"Huh," I said.

"There are problems," Eddie said. "Everyone admits there are a lot of problems, but they won't stop talking. They are absolutely fascinated by the idea of all that metal."

Hardly surprising. Our ancestors had done a job on Earth. Most of the metal and coal and oil that was easy to reach was gone, along with other resources. Much of the water. Much of the soil. Hundreds—no, thousands—of species of plants and animals.

Eddie went on. "I've been thinking about Cortez and what happened when he found gold in Mexico."

"You worry too much."

"Uh-huh. I'll bet that's what Montezuma said to his councilors."

I rubbed my eyes and tried to think. I was exhausted. "Eddie, I have to sleep."

"Is it night down there? I guess it is. Sweet dreams, Lixia."

I went back to camp and lay down. Above me the stars shone. Somewhere up there was a relay satellite and a long way to the south—over the middle of the ocean—was the I.S.S. *Number One*. I imagined it, turning in the light of this system's primary, gleaming just a little: an enormous hunk of lithium hydride, shaped like a cigar. The surface was pitted and discolored. More than half the mass was gone. The lithium hydride had been our fuel as well as our main protection against radiation.

At one end of the cigar was a series of metal and ceramic coils. These were the magnets that contained and controlled the fusion reaction that drove the ship. The other end was bare. When we left Earth there had been an umbrella made of cermet, additional protection against the tiny amount of matter between the stars. We had dropped the umbrella at turn around. From that point on, the engine acted as protection, burning whatever bits of space debris might lie ahead of us into ionic vapors, which the magnets guided away.

That was it: a dirty white cigar and a series of rings, black and tan and grey. The living quarters were invisible, hidden in the middle of the cigar: a cylinder made of ceramic, encased in salt.

That was the part of the ship I knew: the rooms and corridors lined with tile. They gave the ship one of its many nicknames—my favorite, the China Clipper.

It had no sails, of course. That idea had been abandoned early on. And there wasn't a lot of porcelain on board. The wall material reminded me of earthenware. It was dull and a bit rough, light orange in color. In places it was glazed, usually white or blue.

It was a lovely material: light and hard and durable, immune to corrosion, resistant to heat, excellent insulation. Eddie was nuts. We hadn't gone to the stars in a tin can. We had gone in something made of clay and salt. There was plenty of both where we came from. We didn't need the metal on this planet.

For the next three days Nia and I continued west. The land rose. We entered a canyon. At the bottom was a narrow shallow stream. In the spring it must have been an impressive river, for it ran through the middle of a wide bed. Even now the water moved quickly. Here and there it was streaked with foam.

Cliffs rose on either side of us. They were dark grey and flecked with something that glittered in the sunlight. Mica?

I saw a new kind of animal. It was tiny and dark grey, the color of the cliffs. Its skin—or shell—glittered as if it were flecked with mica. In most parts of the canyon the animal seemed to be uncommon. But one section had hundreds of the little things. Motionless, they were invisible. I saw them when they moved, flashing out from under my feet, running up a rock away from me. It seemed as if pieces of stone were coming alive, changing into what? Lizards? Not exactly. For one thing they had six legs. On Earth that would have made them insects. But they didn't look like bugs, and the bugs on this planet seemed to have at least eight legs.

"I don't know what they are," said Nia. "And I don't know why there are so many of them. This isn't my country. Ask me questions when we come out onto the plain."

I made the gesture of acknowledgment.

Late on the third day she said, "A person is following us."

"What?" I looked back.

The canyon was shadowy, and I couldn't see far, but as far as I could see, the trail was empty.

Nia grabbed my arm and tugged. "Keep going. Don't let him know that we know."

We trudged on.

"I saw him twice today, this morning and a short time ago. If he means to do harm, he'll do it tonight."

"Harm?" I said.

"There are men who go crazy. They become violent. They attack other people."

"Why?"

"I don't know. But some men—when they go through the change—become like animals. They cannot control themselves. And there are other men who are fine till they get old. They grow weak. They cannot get women. This makes them angry. I have met one like that. They do not attack large groups of women, but if a person travels alone or in a small group, a twosome or a threesome—that is asking for trouble!" She glanced at me. "We have to find a place to camp."

We kept going until we came to a place where the canyon floor was wider than usual. The stream spread out. On the far side the canyon wall was broken. There were fissures and huge black boulders. A waterfall tumbled down between the rocks and there was vegetation, bushes, and a few small trees.

"We'll camp on the other side of the river," Nia said, took off her sandals and picked them up.

I followed her to the edge of the stream. Casually she glanced back. "He's close now. He thinks the dark will hide him. But I have good eyes."

She waded in. I followed. As promised by the people in supply, my boots were waterproof.

Halfway across the water deepened. Nia went up to her knees. I stopped and considered what to do. I couldn't take off my boots where I was, and I didn't like the idea of going back the way I had come. The sun was gone. It was twilight in the canyon. Somewhere in the shadows was the man. I had no wish to meet him, especially alone. I waded on. My boots filled with water.

By this time Nia was on the far bank. She bent and brushed the fur on her legs, then stamped her feet. I climbed up beside her and took off my boots, turning them over. Water poured out.

Nia jumped. "Not on me, you idiot! I just dried my fur!"

"I'm sorry." I took off my socks and squeezed them. "What now?"

"We'll make camp there." She waved at the tumbled boulders. "The man will have to come close in order to see us. I intend to be waiting."

There was a hollow—an empty space—among the rocks. We set our baggage down. In the last light of day we gathered wood.

"Now," said Nia softly. "You build the fire. But do not light it until I speak."

As I worked I heard her moving close to me, invisible in the shadows among the rocks. The noise she made stopped. I listened. A bird whistled, and I could hear the stream. Nothing else.

In back of me a voice spoke: "Light the fire."

I got out my lighter. The dry leaves caught at once. Yellow flames licked up around the branches. I was able to see. On the other side of the hollow was Nia's bag and something that looked like a person lying full length on the ground, wrapped in a cloak or a blanket. But Nia had spoken from in back of me. I was sure of that. Whatever was under the cloak, it was not my companion.

"Going to sleep already?" I said. "All right. Good night." I put another branch on the fire. I was thirsty but afraid to go to the stream. I thought about eating. The bread was dry, and the fish was salty. If I ate either one I'd get even thirstier. Anyway, my stomach was queasy.

The fire dimmed. I added more branches. I had the feeling that someone was watching me. The skin on my back prickled, and I was beginning to sweat. I stood up and stretched, then casually looked around. There was nothing visible except a heap of rocks. I sat down. A pebble rattled. I stood again. What had that been? I listened but heard nothing.

I sat back down. After a moment I began to do my breathing exercises. I inhaled and thought the syllable *so*. I exhaled and thought the syllable *hum*. Gradually I relaxed. It was, I realized, a pleasant night. The air was cool and dry. The sky was clear. Stars shone brightly. A moon was rising over the canyon's rim: a reddish point of light. I kept on breathing slowly and deeply. *So. Hum. So. Hum.*

A scream! I scrambled to my feet, looking around. Something moved behind a boulder. I grabbed my axe and ran.

Two bodies struggled in the shadows. They were both dark, both furry. I couldn't tell them apart. They rolled out of shadow into firelight. A hand went up, holding a knife. Around the wrist was a wide copper bracelet. Nia wore no jewelry. I turned the axe and swung it, bringing the flat side down against the fellow's arm. There was a groan. The hand opened. The knife fell. I stepped back.

They rolled again—almost into the fire. Nia was on top. She had a hammer in one hand. Her other hand reached for the fellow's throat. He grabbed her tunic with both hands. Then he arched his back and heaved. Nia went up. She was in midair. I couldn't believe it. How could he be that strong? She came down in the fire. Sparks flew. Burning branches scattered across the ground. Nia screamed.

The man scrambled upright and grabbed a branch. It was burning from one end to the other. How could he hold it? Was he crazy? He started for me. He certainly looked crazy. His eyes stared and his mouth was wide open. He was howling.

I raised my axe. He swung. I blocked the blow. I could feel the shock along my arm from the wrist to the shoulder. He stepped back and raised the branch again. It was still burning. He was still howling.

The branch came down. I blocked it again. He let go. The branch fell blazing, and he grabbed the handle of my axe, twisting and yanking. I lost my grip.

He turned the axe around—it was a single rapid motion—and raised it over his head. He was making a noise like an evacuation signal, a high even scream.

There was no time to get out. He had reached the top of his swing. The axe blade glinted. I tasted bile.

The screaming stopped, and the man grunted, then looked surprised and fell.

Nia stood on the other side of him: a silhouette against the light of the scattered fire. She was still holding the hammer.

I took a deep breath.

She asked, "How is he? I hit as hard as I could."

I knelt and felt his throat. There was no pulse. Was that normal? I had no idea. I put my hand over his mouth. There was no breath. "Where did you hit him?"

"The head. With this." She lifted the hammer.

I felt the back of his head and found a spot where the skull went in. I pulled my hand away. There was blood on my fingers and something else as well: an object, stuck to the tip of my middle finger. It was hard and triangular. The edges felt rough. I couldn't see the color, but I was pretty certain I knew what the object was. A piece of bone. I wiped my hand on the man's kilt, then looked at Nia. "I think you killed him."

"Aiya! Another one." She dropped the hammer and rubbed her face. "I have to sit down."

I stood up, holding out a hand. She tumbled toward me. I caught her, but she was too heavy. I couldn't keep her upright. I fell, landing on the dead man, and Nia came down on top of me.

Damn!

"Nia?" She didn't answer. I pushed and wriggled out from between the two furry bodies, stood up and rolled Nia over. It wasn't easy. She was limp. A dead weight.

I felt her throat. Ah! There was a pulse, strong and regular, maybe a little rapid. I couldn't be sure. I went to the fire and found a branch that was still burning and carried it back. What was wrong? Her tunic was torn, and one of the torn edges was smoldering. But I saw no other evidence of burning. I crouched and looked at her hands. One palm was puffy. Maybe that was a burn. I touched the palm. Nia winced and groaned.

"Are you awake?"

She blinked.

"Where does it hurt?"

She frowned. "My hand and my leg."

I felt along her legs. There was no blood. I found no wounds.

"The ankle," she told me.

I touched her left ankle. She winced again. I pressed in. Nia groaned. Something was wrong there. But what? How could I tell if anything was broken or out of place? I didn't know how an ankle was supposed to feel. Not on this planet. Not an ankle belonging to an alien. I thought for a moment. There was always bilateral symmetry. I checked her right ankle, then went back and rechecked the left.

"They feel the same."

Nia frowned. "To you. Not to me. What am I lying on?"

"The man."

"Aiya!" She got up on one elbow. "Help me."

"I don't want you to move."

"I will not lie on a corpse."

I frowned, trying to remember my first aid. Would it be okay to move her? I was having trouble concentrating, maybe because I had just helped to kill someone and the body was right in front of me.

Nia struggled into a sitting position. I laid down my torch and helped her off the dead man. "Is your back all right?" I asked. "Are you hurt anywhere else? Do you feel any other pain?"

"I told you. My hand and my leg. Nothing else. I think I will lie down."

I eased her onto the ground. She lay full length next to the dead man. I got up and grabbed hold of his arms. He was heavy, much heavier than Nia, and entirely limp. I managed to pull him a meter or so, then gave up and let go. His arms hit the ground with a thump. "That's it. He stays here."

"I do not feel good," said Nia.

I didn't think her leg was broken, but I wasn't positive. I'd better put on a splint. And get cold water for the hand. And get a cloak. She might well be in shock.

"I am going to need your cooking pot."

"Take it. What a strong man! I made a mistake. I thought he'd be old or very young. I am not as clever as I think I am."

I got her cloak and covered her, then took the cooking pot to the stream, filled it with water, and brought it back. "Put your hand in. It will help the burn. I'm going to rebuild the fire."

She made the gesture of assent. I went to gather wood. When the fire was burning brightly, I made a splint. I had an elastic bandage in my first-aid kit. For padding I used my undershirt and a spare pair of socks.

"I hope this is temporary," I said. "I need those socks. How is the hand?"

"Better, but now my shoulder hurts."

I pulled the cloak down. The fur on one shoulder was matted. I touched it and looked at my hand. The fingers were red. "Another wound. He did a good job on you."

"I knew when I saw him I was in trouble. But it was too late to change the plan. Is the wound bad?"

I got a piece of gauze and wiped the blood away. "It's a nick. He must have got you with the point of his knife." I looked at the contents of my medical kit. What was safe to use? She wasn't human. I had no idea of how she would react to any human medication.

I had brief, horrible fantasies about allergic reactions, toxic reactions, shock, and death.

But the wound ought to be covered. I didn't think any harm could come from a bandage.

I got out the can. "This is going to sting just a little." I hit the button.

"Aiya!" Nia said.

The wound vanished. In its place was a small dark patch of plastic. The patch was lumpy, and clumps of hair stuck out of it, coated with plastic. Idiot! I told myself. I should have shaved the area around the wound. Well, I hadn't and the best thing to do now was leave the wound alone. I rocked back on my heels. "Anything else?"

"No." She took her hand out of the pot, then grimaced. "This still hurts."

"I'll get more water."

I went to the stream and filled the pot again and brought it back. Nia put her hand in. Her eyes were almost shut. I had the impression she was exhausted. I tucked the cloak around her.

"Thank you." Her voice was drowsy. She closed her eyes.

I put more wood on the fire, then got the poncho out of my pack. It was light and waterproof with a removable thermal lining. I did not remove the lining. Instead I wrapped the poncho around me, lay down, and went to sleep.

I woke later, feeling cold. The fire was almost out. I got up and laid branches on the coals. Flames appeared. How silent the canyon was! I could hear water, but nothing else. Above me stars shone. I recognized the Big Dipper. It looked the way I remembered it—maybe a little brighter. That would be the air in the canyon. It was dry and extremely clear.

I went over to Nia. Her hand was still in the pot. On her face was an expression of pain. But she was sleeping, breathing slowly and evenly.

I checked her leg. It had stopped swelling. The bandage wasn't tight. She groaned when I touched her, but she didn't wake. I went to my pack and got out the radio.

This time I got Antonio Nybo. Another North American. There were a lot of them on the sociology team, maybe because there were so many different societies in North America. Tony was from somewhere in the Confederation of Spanish States. I couldn't—at the moment—remember exactly where. Not Florida. Texas maybe. Or Chicago. Most of his work had been done in southern California, studying the Hispanic farmers who were moving back into the California desert and interacting—not always easily—with the aborigines.

"Lixia! How are you?" His voice was light and pleasant with a slight accent.

"I had an interesting day—" I told him about it, then said, "Now for the problem. I don't think the leg is broken, but I'm not sure. Is there any way to tell without doing a scan?"

"I'll ask the medical team. Is it okay to call you back?"

"Yes."

He signed off. I got up and stretched, then touched my toes five times. My stomach gurgled and I remembered that I hadn't eaten dinner. I got a piece of bread. It was stale. I enjoyed it, anyway.

The radio rang. I turned it on.

"First of all they say they need more information." I could hear amusement in Antonio's voice. "They also say there ought to be more hemorrhaging with a fracture—than with a sprain, I mean. And hemorrhaging produces bruises—usually. Or did they say often? Anyway, if her foot turns black and blue in the next three days, she may have a fracture. But a bad sprain could produce bruising, too."

"What are you telling me?"

"The only way to be certain is to do a scan. The medical people suggest that they come down with the necessary equipment."

"Oh."

"They think," Tony said gently, "they ought to. And they would love—absolutely love—to get hold of a native. It is interesting what one finds out when one asks an apparently simple question. The aliens are not alien enough."

"What?"

"I don't mean at the cellular level. There—we have to assume—they are like the rest of the life on the planet. The biologists say there is no question that the organisms they have examined are alien and belong to a different evolutionary line. That is why they can say—so confidently—that we can't catch the local diseases. Nor can we spread our own diseases to anything on the planet." Antonio paused. "You might be interested in knowing that Eddie asked the medical team to double-check this fact."

"Why?"

"A native died shortly after you arrived at your village."

"I told Eddie what the woman died of. Old age, poison, or magic. There was nothing unnatural about her death."

Antonio laughed. "Eddie was worried about the bugs in your gut. The ones that were designed to metabolize the local food. The biology team said absolutely not. The bugs can't live outside a human. The biology team became offended and spoke about people moving outside their areas of expertise, especially people in the social sciences—which, as everyone knows, are not *real* sciences like biology and chemistry."

"Ouch."

"The problem is not at the cellular level. It's the fact that the natives look like us. They shouldn't, according to all the best theories. We ought to be dealing with intelligent lobsters or talking trees.

"According to the biology team, the natives are an example of parallel evolution—like the marsupial saber-toothed tiger of South America. But no one is really comfortable with this explanation. We need more information. The medical team wants some tissue samples, and they want to know what goes on the intermediate levels—between the entire organism which looks like us and the biochemistry which is almost certainly alien. What are the organs like? The muscles and the skeleton? The endocrine system? The chemistry of the brain? They want—in sum—to get into a native and take a really good look around. I'm going to refer this to the committee for day-to-day administration."

"Okay."

"In the meantime, the medical people say to treat the injury like a fracture."

"Okay." I turned the radio off.

"Li-sa?"

It was Nia. I glanced at her. She was up on one elbow, staring at me. Her eyes reflected the firelight. They shone like gold.

"Yes."

"Is there a demon in the box?"

I tapped the radio. "This?"

Nia made the gesture of affirmation.

"No."

"Then how can it speak?"

"A good question." I thought for a while. "It's a way for people to talk when they're far away from one another. My friend has a box like this. When he speaks into it his voice comes out here." I touched the radio again. "I can answer by talking into my box."

Nia frowned. "Among the Copper People—the people of Nahusai—there are songs of calling. When Nahusai wanted something, rain or sunshine or a ghost, she would draw a design that represented the thing she wanted. Then she sang to the design. The thing she wanted would hear her song and come. This is what she told me, anyway."

I made the gesture of disagreement. "This isn't a ceremony. It's a tool, like your hammer."

"Hakht would not believe that."

"What does she know?"

Nia barked. "That is true. Well, then, the box is a tool—though it's a kind of tool I've never seen before. I've never even heard of a tool like that." She paused. "It sounds useful. I am going back to sleep."

I woke in the morning before Nia did. The sky was clear and there was sunlight on the rim of the canyon. I went in among the rocks and relieved myself, then went to the stream and washed. On the way back I passed the dead man. He lay on his back, his arms stretched above his head. He was large—not tall, but wide and muscular with shaggy fur. His kilt was brown with orange embroidery, and his belt had a copper buckle.

His mouth was open. I could see his teeth, which were yellow, and his tongue, which was thick and dark. His eyes—open also—had orange irises.

I was going to have to bury him, I realized. The bugs were gathering already. Damn it. I had no shovel. I glanced at Nia. Still asleep. I bent and grabbed a rock and laid it next to the body. It—he—stank of urine. Poor sucker. What a way to go. Was there a good way? I went to get more stones.

Bugs hummed around me. Clouds drifted across the narrow sky. They were small and round like balls of cotton. My back started hurting. I scraped one hand on the rough edge of a rock. The injury wasn't serious. It didn't even bleed, but it stung.

Finally the man was out of sight, hidden by pieces of rock. Enough. I didn't have to make him a tumulus. I straightened. By this time the clouds were gone. Sunlight slanted into the canyon. Nia was sitting up.

"Good," she said. "His ghost should have a home. Otherwise, the wind will take him and blow him across the sky. That is no fate for anyone."

"Is there any ceremony that ought to be performed?"

"No. If a shamaness were here, she would sing. That would avert bad luck. I do not know the right words nor what to burn in the fire." She frowned and scratched her nose. "I ought to do something. I will give him a knife. A parting gift."

"All right," I said.

We ate breakfast. I bandaged Nia's hand. We didn't talk much. Nia looked tired, and I found myself thinking about the dead man under his heap of stones.

Midway through the morning my radio rang.

"Your box," Nia said. "It wants to talk with you."

I turned the radio on. "Yes?"

"Lixia? This is Antonio. I talked to the day-to-day committee."

"Uh-huh?"

"They voted 'no.' And then they decided this was not an administrative problem. It was a question of policy. I wasn't at the meeting, but there must have been someone on the committee who got upset with the vote and raised the question of policy in order to get another chance."

I nodded agreement to the radio.

"So the question was referred to the all-ship committee. We had the meeting. An emergency session, but a good turnout nonetheless."

"What happened?" I asked.

"Eddie—of course—is against any kind of intervention. You know his arguments. I won't repeat them. Ivanova went along."

"She did?"

"According to her, we decided not to reveal ourselves to the people here until we knew more about them. There are good reasons for our decision: our own security and the fear of endangering the native culture through ignorance. How do we know what kinds of information they can handle?

"Now—according to Ivanova—we are asked to abandon a carefully thought out, democratically decided, historically important course of action. Because of a hairline fracture. A possible hairline fracture.

"She would have a different opinion if one of our people was in danger. But the person with the injury is a native, and the injury is not in the least bit dangerous."

"Huh," I said.

"As for our friends from the Chinese Republic." Antonio paused for effect.

"Yes?"

"They said this never would have happened if the members of the survey team had been properly trained."

"What does that mean?"

"You ought to have gotten a course in socialist medicine. Acupuncture, herbal lore, and Marxist ideology. As far as I can figure out, you are supposed to stick your companion full of needles and read selected passages from the *Communist Manifesto* to her."

"Who came up with this wonderful line of reasoning?"

"Who do you think? It's a perfectly preserved ancient Chinese argument. It came from a perfectly preserved ancient Chinese. Mr. Fang."

The Chinese had said it was hard to go to the stars without children and crazy to go without people of age and experience. The rest of us had remained firm re children. There were none on the ship. But we had taken a number of people over sixty and a few over seventy. Mr. Fang was close to eighty, a thin man with long white hair and thick grey eyebrows. He was from Zhendu in Sichuan, a master wicker worker and a master gardener, in charge of the main room in the ship's garden. Bamboo grew there, a dozen or more varieties. Along the walls were trellises covered with climbing palms. These were the raw materials for furniture. Most of the furniture on the ship was bamboo or rattan. Mr. Fang repaired it when it broke and made new furniture when needed.

I liked him. I had spent hours in his shop watching him work. From time to time we talked about philosophy. He especially liked the ancient Daoists and Karl Marx.

"They respected—at least in theory—the wisdom of the people. That is what matters, Lixia. A philosopher who fears or despises the people will come up with monstrous ideas."

"How did the vote come out?" I asked Tony.

"What do you expect? We talked for hours and ended up where we started. For the time being we will stick to our original decision. We won't go down to the planet—except maybe to help our own people. You are on your own. The medical team is not happy."

"Ah, well." I scratched my head. "What do I do now?"

"Continue to treat the injury as if it were a fracture. Keep it in a splint. Keep your friend off that foot. Time heals all wounds."

"Wonderful. If that's all the advice you have to offer, I'm going to sign off."

"Good luck."

I turned the radio off, then glanced at Nia.

"What did your box say?"

"You're supposed to stay put till the ankle heals."

She grimaced. "How can I do that? We are almost out of food, and there's nothing to eat here. We have to get to a village."

"Is there one nearby?"

"Yes. A day from here. Less than a day. The Copper People of the Plain live there." Nia clenched one hand into a fist. "What bad luck!" She hit her thigh, then winced. "I could walk a short distance if I had a stick to lean on. But I will not be able to walk to the village. And there is climbing. The path goes up in the place where the water falls." She frowned. "You go, Li-sa. Tell the people of the village what has happened. Ask their shamaness to come and bring medicine. I will give her a fine gift. Tell her I am a smith. A good one, from the Iron People. I can make a knife that will cut anything except stone." She thought a moment. "It won't cut iron, either. But anything else."

"Okay."

"What?" she asked.

"I'll go."

"What is that word? Ok . . . ?"

"Okay. It means 'yes' or 'I agree.'"

"Okay," Nia said. "Go now. If you walk quickly, you'll be at the village before dark. Come back tomorrow. I'll be all right till then."

I got my pack and left. On the other side of the river I stopped to dry my feet. I couldn't see Nia, but I saw smoke rising from our fire, and I saw the grave of the crazy man. I thought I saw it. Maybe it was some other heap of stones.

I put on my socks and boots. Then I turned and walked away.

A curious thing about the canyon. From a distance the walls looked bare, and the canyon floor was stone grey. But close up I saw flowers and brightly colored bugs. The six-legged animals had vanished. Now I saw creatures that looked like birds or maybe tiny dinosaurs. They stood on their hind legs, and they were covered with feathers. But they had arms instead of wings. I saw one catch a bug. It grabbed the bug with little clawed hands and opened its mouth. I saw rows of teeth. A moment later—crunch! The bug was gone.

The hunter tilted its head and looked at me. I returned the gaze. The creature had blue feathers except on its belly and throat. The belly was white. The throat was sulphur-yellow.

The creature hissed at me.

"Oh, yeah?" I said.

The creature ran away.

At noon I stopped and ate. Above me birds soared on the wind. A fish jumped in the river. I rested for a while, then went on. The river got more turbulent. The trail began to go up and down, twisting around great rough lumps of a greyish-black stone. Ahead of me I saw the end of the canyon: a wall of stone, badly broken, full of crevices. Water ran down through the crevices, appearing and disappearing. At the top the water was in sunlight. It glittered like silver. Farther down, in shadow, it was grey. At the bottom of the cliff was a pool, half-hidden by mist.

Even at a distance I could hear the sound of the water. It was a continuous low roar.

I kept going. The trail went along one side of the pool. The canyon wall was next to me. Designs had been cut in the rock: spirals and triangles and the figures of animals.

Aha! I thought. A sacred place. But sacred to what? The spirals might represent the sun. Back on Earth the triangle was often a symbol of fertility or female sexuality. The animals were local species, or so I assumed. A quadruped with horns. A biped with a neck like an ostrich and long narrow arms. Were they worshipped or hunted? Or both?

The wind blew spray toward me from the waterfall. The trail became slippery. I decided to concentrate on my footing.

The trail went around a tall rock covered with pictographs. On the other side was a man. No question about his gender. He was naked, and his male member was large enough to be conspicuous. He was dancing, hopping from one foot to the other. He carried a pole. On top was a pair of metal horns, green with corrosion. Copper, almost certainly. The man spun and waved the pole, then spun back so he was facing me. He wore one thing, I realized now. A string of large, round, bright blue beads. They reminded me of faience beads from Egypt.

He stopped dancing and stared at me. I stood without moving, looking back. He was my size, maybe a little wider. His fur was dark brown and shaggy. His eyes were large and pale yellow.

He said something I didn't understand.

"I do not know that language," I said.

"You speak the language of gifts," he said. "You must be a stranger. I thought you were a demon, but a demon would have understood me." He frowned. "I suppose you might be a demon from far away. A demon from far away might not know the language of my people. Are you one?"

"A demon? No. I'm a person. My name is Lixia. Who are you?"

He looked surprised. "The Voice of the Waterfall. Haven't you heard of me?"

"No."

"You must be from very far away."

"Yes."

"I speak for the spirit of the waterfall. It is powerful and knows almost everything." The man sang:

"It knows
what the fish say
in the water.

"It knows
what the birds say
on the wind.

"It knows
what the demons say
deep underground—

"The movers,
the shakers,
the ones who send up fire—

"It knows
what they say
to one another.

"People ask me questions. I tell them what I hear in the sound of the water." He hopped on one foot and turned, still hopping. Then he staggered and came down on both feet. "What do you want? Why are you here?"

"I've been traveling with one of your people. She is hurt, and I'm looking for help."

The man frowned. He waved the pole and shouted:

> *"O waterfall,*
> *tell me,*
> *tell me what to make of this."*

He tilted his head and listened. I listened too, but heard nothing except the roar of the water.

"The waterfall says you are probably telling the truth. In any case, the waterfall says, it is bad luck to give trouble to travelers or people who ask for help. Therefore I will help you. Come along." He turned and walked up the trail. I hesitated a moment, then followed. It was never a good idea to argue with an oracle, especially one from a society you didn't understand. Soon we were a good distance above the pool. I looked down and saw churning water. Part of a rainbow shone faintly in the mist.

The trail entered a crevice. We walked between black walls of stone. Water trickled down. There were patches of shaggy orange vegetation on the rock. A creature walked between the patches. It was level with my shoulder and moving slowly, Earth-sky-blue with at least a dozen legs. Two antennae stuck out in front of it, waving gently. Two more antennae stuck out behind. They also waved gently. I couldn't see a mouth or eyes.

I assumed that the animal was traveling forward, but I had no way of telling. I thought of picking it up. Maybe there were organs visible on the underside. But I had never liked animals with more than eight legs.

My guide was moving quickly. I followed him, slipping now and then on the wet stone.

We were coming to the end of the passage. The walls were

only a couple of meters tall. On top of them plants grew. I saw leaves and stalks and flowers.

The height of the walls decreased further. I could see over them and over the vegetation. We were coming out onto a plain.

Off to one side was a bluff—a low one, dotted with trees. In every other direction the land was flat and covered by a plant with long, narrow, flexible leaves. The plant was about a meter tall. Its color varied: green and blue-green, yellow-green and a silvery blue-green-grey. I couldn't tell what the differences in color meant. Was there more than one kind of plant growing on the plain? Or did the color represent variations within a species?

"There." The man pointed at the bluff. "The river is there. The trail goes along it. Follow the trail. At nightfall you will come to a village. Ask for the shamaness and say you have a message from the Voice of the Waterfall. Tell her the waterfall says give this person what she asks for. Say there is no harm in this. I know. The waterfall has told me.

"Do not disbelieve me,
O you people.
I know what the river knows.

"I know the secrets
discovered
by the rain."

He waved his pole and danced sideways, then spun and pointed down the trail. "Go!"

I went. When I got to the top of the bluff, I looked back. I could see the trail, winding through the pseudo-grass, but I couldn't see the man. He must have returned to the canyon and the waterfall.

I scrambled down the slope toward the river, which was wide and shallow here, shaded by trees with dark blue leaves.

In the middle of the river was a gravel bar. Half a dozen creatures rested there: large hairless quadrupeds with tails. One lifted its head and stared at me, then croaked a warning. They all got up and lumbered into the water.

Lizards, maybe? The name seemed appropriate, and it gave me a label. Though I would have to remember that these creatures were not real lizards.

I reached the village at sunset. It stood on top of the river bluff, and all I could see at first was a wall made of logs. Smoke rose from behind the wall. Cooking fires. A lot of them. On the wall were standards like the one the oracle had carried: long poles that ended in metal horns. The horns gleamed red in the sunlight. Polished copper, I told myself.

I climbed the trail up to the gate. A woman was standing there, watching the sun as it went down. She was dark like the two men in the canyon and dressed in a bright blue tunic.

"Make me welcome," I said.

The woman turned.

"Who are you?"

"A traveler. The Voice of the Waterfall told me to come here."

"Did he? Come in. You got here just in time."

We entered. She closed the gate and put a bar across it. "There!" She brushed off her hands. "Come with me. I'll take you to the shamaness."

I followed her along a narrow street that wound back and forth between houses. The houses were octagonal, built of logs. The chinks between the logs had been filled with a fuzzy yellow plant that seemed to be alive and growing. The roofs were slanted, going up from the edges to the center, where there was a smoke hole. I couldn't see the holes, but the smoke was obvious, rising from almost every house. The roofs were covered with dirt—an excellent form of insulation—and plants grew in the dirt. They were small and dark. I reached up and picked a leaf. It was round and thick and waxy. I squeezed. Water squirted out. A succulent or something very like. Chances were it would not burn, which was all to the good. Sparks would float out of the smoke hole. If they landed on a dry plant, these people would have a prairie fire going over their heads. What was the plant for? Was it edible? Was it decoration?

The woman stopped in front of an especially large house. "O shamaness, come out!"

The door opened. A woman came out, short and fat, wearing a long robe covered with stains. The robe was off-white, and the stains were easy to see. A poor choice for an obvious slob. She had on at least a dozen necklaces. Some were ordinary strings of beads. Others were elaborate with chains and bells and pendant animals. Everything was copper, and everything was tangled up. I didn't think there was any way she could have taken off just one necklace.

"This very strange person has come, O holy one. She says she has a message from the Voice of the Waterfall."

The shamaness peered at me. "Where is your fur? Have you been sick?"

"No. I come from far away. My people don't have fur."

"Aiya! This is strange indeed. What is your message?"

"The Voice of the Waterfall says he wants you to help me."

"No."

"What?"

"That man could not have said that. He has no wants. He has no opinions. He is the Voice of the Waterfall. When he speaks, it is the waterfall speaking. Therefore, what you said was wrong. It is not that man who wants me to help you. It is the waterfall who wants me to help you."

The other woman made the gesture of agreement.

"What do you need?" the shamaness asked.

"I have a friend who has been injured. She is a day from here—to the east, in the canyon. Will you go for her?"

The shamaness frowned and scratched her chin. Then she made the gesture of assent. "Tomorrow." She turned and went back in the house. The door closed.

"Aiya!" said the other woman. "This is something she never does. She never goes to people. They must go to her. But everyone listens to the Voice of the Waterfall. And that man used to be her son. She used to be fond of him. Come with me."

I followed her to another house. Inside was a single large room. Large pillars held up the roof. They had been carved and painted red, white, black, and brown. The patterns were intricate, made up of curving lines. They seemed to represent animals. Here and there I saw faces and hands with claws. The faces had copper eyes and copper tongues that curled right off the pillar.

In the center of the house was a fire burning in a pit. Three people sat close to it. They were children, about half-grown. They played a game. One threw a bunch of sticks. Another bent and looked at the pattern. "Aiya! What luck you are having!"

The third one looked at us. "What is this?"

"A person. Be courteous. Bring us food to eat."

We sat down. The woman said, "I am Eshtanabai the go-between. It's fortunate that I was at the gate instead of some ordinary woman."

"You are a what?"

The children brought bowls of mush and a jug full of liquid. The liquid was sour. The mush was close to tasteless. We ate and drank. Eshtanabai explained.

"People get angry with one another. They do not talk. They sit in their houses and sulk. I go to each person. I listen to what they say. I say, 'This argument is no good. Is there no way to end it? What do you want? What resolution will satisfy you?' Then I go back and forth, back and forth until everyone agrees on what ought to be done. It's hard work. I get headaches a lot."

"I can imagine."

"Someone must do it. The shamaness is too holy. The Voice of the Waterfall doesn't always make sense. And how could a man—even that man—ever settle a quarrel?"

I had no answer for that question. We finished eating, and I lay down, using my pack as a pillow. One of the children put more wood on the fire. Another child began to play a flute. The tune was soft and melancholy. I closed my eyes and listened. After a while I went to sleep.

I woke in the middle of the night with a terrible crick in my neck. The fire was almost out. Around me in the dark house I heard the sound of breathing. My companions were asleep. I sat up and rubbed my neck, then lay down. This time I didn't use my pack as a pillow. When I woke again it was morning. Sunlight shone through the open door. Eshtanabai was sitting by the fire. The children were gone.

"The shamaness has left the village," she told me. "People have gone with her. They will bring your friend back."

"Good. When?"

"Tomorrow or the next day."

I ate breakfast—more mush—then went outside. The sky was cloudless, and the air was warm. It smelled of midden heaps. I decided to take another look at the plain. I found the village gate and went through it.

A trail led around the village. I followed it. The plain stretched south and east, almost perfectly flat. There were animals in the distance: black dots that moved from time to time. I shaded my eyes, but I couldn't make them out.

On the north side of the village were gardens that looked exactly like the gardens in the village of Nahusai. I stopped by one.

A woman looked up. "You are the stranger."

"Yes."

"You certainly are strange."

I pointed at the animals on the plain. "What are those?"

Her eyes widened. "You don't know?"

I made the gesture that meant "no."

"How can anyone be that ignorant?"

I said nothing. After a moment she said, "They are bowhorns. Most of the herd is in the north. In the fall the men will bring them back. The whole plain will be black then."

"Where are the men now?"

She frowned. "Don't you know anything? They are with the herd. Where else would they be?"

"Thank you." I wandered on.

The next day was overcast. I went down to the river, taking my pack with me. I settled at the foot of a tree and got out my radio.

Eddie was back. "How's your friend?" he asked.

"I don't know. I went to get help, and the help has gone to get Nia. I'll find out how she is sometime today."

"Where are you?"

I described the location of the village and told him about my meeting with the Voice of the Waterfall.

"Now that sounds fascinating." He was silent for a minute or two. Then he said, "I don't know much about oracles. They were big in Greece, weren't they?"

"Yes."

"Maybe I ought to do some reading. What is the village like?"

I described the village. "As far as I can tell all the adults are women. The men are up north, taking care of a herd of animals. They're migratory. The women stay put. How is the ship?"

"Pretty much the same. We got a message from Earth."

"Oh, yeah?" I felt the usual excitement. "Anything interesting?"

"There's a new space colony and the Ukrainians are beginning to settle the wilderness around what used to be Kiev. And someone has come up with a practical faster-than-light radio. They have sent us the plans."

I rocked back on my heels. We wouldn't be isolated any longer. We wouldn't have to wait forty years for the answer to a question. "How long will it take to build the thing?"

Eddie laughed. "We can build the receiver. The engineers are almost sure of that. But in order to send messages we have to be able to generate a very strange new particle, and the machine that does that is *big*."

"Shit."

"My thought exactly. The particle—you might be interested in knowing—is called *fred*. Not in honor of Frederick Engels. The message was very clear about that." Eddie's voice had the tone he used when describing obvious lunacy. "It was found—no, theorized—by two people more or less simultaneously. Everything about this particle happens in sets of two, according to the message. The person in Beijing wanted to call it a *guanyon* in honor of the Chinese goddess of mercy Guan Yin. Apparently the goddess came to her in a dream, standing on a lotus flower and holding the crucial equation written on a fan.

"The person in Santiago wanted to call the particle a *pablon* in honor of the poet Pablo Neruda. I don't know why. Maybe he got an equation in a dream. Neither person was willing to back down. So the particle is being called a *fred.* It always comes as one of a pair. The other particle is named *frieda.*"

"I suppose this is another example of the terrible whimsy of physicists," I said.

"Uh-huh."

"Why did they send the plans if we can't use them?"

"For our information and just in case we ran into a lot of metal and a lot of silica and a modern industrial society. Always be prepared, as somebody said. Frederick Engels maybe."

I scratched my nose. "What is bothering you?"

"Aside from the *fred?* Derek has found a lump of copper. It's a meter across, and as far as he can tell it's pure. It was lying on the edge of a river. Just lying there in plain sight. People are saying maybe we can find the resources to build the new transmitter. You people are finding too much. Why don't you shut up?"

"Come on, Eddie. We can't do that. Secrecy is the enemy of democracy. Is there any other news?"

"Derek's moving north as well as west. He's only a hundred kilometers from you. He'd like to join with you. Do you think your friend would object to traveling with a man?"

"Yes."

"I was afraid of that."

Something moved at the edge of my vision. "I have to go." I turned off the radio and shoved it into my pack, then looked around and saw a bipedal animal something like the one I had seen in the canyon. This was a new variety, however, as tall as I was with a dark blue back. Its belly was cream-white, and it had a crest: a bunch of long feathers that shone bright blue in the sunlight. The animal was feeding off a tree covered with berries, reaching up its long arms and pulling the berries off, handful after handful. It crammed the berries into its mouth, then swallowed and reached for more. I got up. It twisted its long neck and stared at me, then went back to eating. There was something oddly human about its motions. It couldn't be intelligent. Its crested head was tiny. Still and all—I watched till it finished eating and wandered off. Then I walked back to the village.

In the evening the shamaness returned. I saw her enter the village. She was wearing a blue robe and a hat made of feathers. Five women followed her. Two of them carried a litter. Nia was on it. Her eyes were closed. She seemed to be asleep.

"Don't worry," Eshtanabai said. "Our shamaness will cure your friend."

"I hope so."

The shamaness said, "Take the woman to my house. I will go and gather herbs."

Eshtanabai touched my arm. "Come with me. The shamaness will not want visitors, except for the holy spirits. And you wouldn't want to meet them. It isn't safe."

"All right."

I spent the evening in the house of Eshtanabai. I felt restless and uneasy. What was happening to Nia? I bit my fingernails and watched the fire. Eshtanabai played with her children. After a while I went outside. The village was quiet except for the sound of a drum. Was that the shamaness? I didn't know. I looked up. The sky was clear, and the stars shone brightly. A cool wind blew in off the plain. It was a lovely planet: pure and clean and almost empty. We had been working on our own planet for over a century when the ship left and the work had continued. Two centuries so far. There were still scars everywhere: stripped mountains, poisoned marshes, wide stretches where the land was useless, at least to humans—eroded, full of salt or dry, the water gone, pumped up and used in the twentieth century.

What had they been thinking of, those people then? They had left their descendants almost no water and great mountains of uranium. What kind of inheritance was that? How did they think we were going to survive?

We had managed with not much help from them. It was amazing how many people we had been able to save. When

I thought of Earth, I thought of crowds. Only the ocean was really empty and the polar ice caps and the ruined lands.

Looking up at the starry sky I felt a terrible sense of loss.

Not that I objected to my society. It was sane, decent, humane, the best society that Earth had ever known. But it was enormously complex. Nothing was easy. Nothing was straightforward. For the first time history was a conscious process. For the first time people were shaping their lives deliberately, knowing what they did.

We argued every point. We voted. We compromised. We formed factions and coalitions. We thought—always—about justice and fairness, about the consequences of what we did, about the future.

The drum stopped. The breeze shifted. Now I could smell the cooking fires and the outhouses. I decided to go in.

In the morning I went to the house of the shamaness.

Eshtanabai led me. "O holy one," she cried. "The hairless person has come to visit."

The door opened. The shamaness peered out. "Your friend is sick. She burns. I can feel the heat in the places where her fur is thin. And she is weak. But I will cure her. Do not fear."

"Can I come in?"

The shamaness frowned, then made the gesture of assent and opened the door farther.

The fire was out. The only light came in through the smoke hole: a golden beam that slanted down and lit an old basket, faded and bent out of shape. Everything else in the house was hidden by shadows. I saw heaps of stuff, but I couldn't tell what it was.

"Nia?" I looked around.

One of the heaps moved and raised a hand. I went over. It was Nia, lying wrapped in a blanket.

"How are you?"

"I feel terrible. Sit down. Keep me company."

I glanced at the shamaness. She made the gesture of assent. I sat down.

Nia closed her eyes. For a while she said nothing. Then she said, "Is the shamaness good? Do you know?"

"They seem to think well of her."

"Good. Maybe I will live." She opened her eyes. "Enshi came to me last night. It's bad luck to dream about dead people. But he didn't threaten me. He joked and told me what it is like to live in the sky. Not bad, he said, though he goes hungry from time to time. He was always a bad hunter. Even when the animals come to him, as they do in that land, he still misses the shot. What a useless man! But he told good stories, and his temper was wonderful. He never got angry." She closed her eyes. I waited. She opened her eyes. "We did a shameful thing."

I glanced around. The shamaness was at the door, talking to Eshtanabai. She was too far away to hear.

Nia lifted her head and looked at the two women. Then she lay back down. "I won't tell you about it. Not here. I am not crazy. I'm tired. I want to sleep."

I left her and spent the day wandering through the village, watching children as they played in the streets and talking with mothers and grandmothers. They were courteous, friendly people. A coppersmith showed me how she worked the metal. An old woman told me how the world was created out of a seed let fall by the bird who lives in the tree of the sun. In the evening I ate dinner with Eshtanabai.

"Your friend will be fine. The shamaness told me. The shamaness says your friend is a smith. She has promised her a knife."

I made the gesture of affirmation, followed by the one for agreement.

"She is from the Iron People?"

"Yes."

"They live to the west of us, beyond the Amber People. They are fierce, we hear."

"I don't know."

"The Amber People say they quarrel a lot and when they give a gift, they always make sure the gift they get in return is just as good."

I made the gesture that meant "maybe" or "if you say so."

The next day I saw Nia again. A fire burned in the fire pit, and the house of the shamaness was full of aromatic smoke.

My friend was sitting up, her back against a pole. I sat down. The shamaness left, closing the door behind her.

"I asked her to," said Nia. "I had another dream. I saw Hua, the woman who raised me. She died before anyone knew what I had done. But now she knows. She is angry. She spoke sharp words. Aiya! How they cut!

"I told her it was none of her business what I did. And anyway, what I did was nothing bad. She said, 'Everyone will agree with me. It was bad.' I said, 'I will tell the story to Li-sa. She is from far away. She knows how things are done in different places. Let her decide whether or not the thing I did was bad.' Then I woke up." Nia looked at me. I found it hard to read the expression on her face. But I thought she looked tired and unhappy.

I said, "Tell me your story, if you want to."

Nia frowned and scratched her nose. Then she began. Up till then, I had thought she was the strong silent type. She had never said a lot. But now she spoke fluently. She must have practiced the story. I imagined her telling it—to herself, most likely. She must have gone over it again and again, trying to make sense of what had happened.

"The first mistake was this: I helped Enshi meet his mother. I don't know why. He was always good at talking. He could always make the thing he wanted seem reasonable and right.

"I led him into the village—at night, of course, and waited outside the tent. He and his mother talked. She gave him gifts. He had lost the gifts that she had given him before. That was typical of him. When he was done, I went with him to the edge of the village. Now came the next mistake." Nia clenched one hand and struck the ground. "He wanted to come again. He was lonely on the plain. He would die out there in the emptiness, he said, unless he had something to look forward to. The warm fire in his mother's tent, good food, and new clothing. What a talker he was! I agreed to help him." Nia rubbed her face. "What a fool I was!

"His mother began to complain about her neighbors. She said there was too much noise in the village. She was tired of the smell of her neighbors' cooking. There was too much garbage. There were too many bugs. She began to pitch her tent away from all the others. They had planned this together. Now it was easy for him to find her tent, and people were not as likely to see him.

"But they still needed someone to carry messages in and out of the village. They needed someone to keep watch when he came. I did it all summer and through autumn. In the winter he could not come into the village. People would have seen the tracks in the snow. I went out to find him, taking food and a new cloak, a thick one made of fur. In the spring we met and mated. That was in the hills. The young men stay there. He had the worst possible territory. It was all stone, going up and down. There was nothing to eat there. Nonetheless, I went to him." She hit the ground a second time. "Maybe Hua is right. Maybe I am a pervert."

I said nothing. Nia went on. "He had nothing worth giving. He picked things up—feathers out of a bush or stones that glittered in the sunlight. He made up poetry. What kind of gift is that? He was a useless man!" She stopped for a moment. She looked puzzled. "When I was with him, I felt—I do not know what to call the feeling. I felt as if I had found a new relative, a sister or a mother. Someone to sit with in the evening, someone to gossip with. I felt contented. When the time of the lust was over, I stayed on. I liked being there. I stayed another ten days. Then I went home, and people asked me what had happened. I said my bowhorn went lame. I had to walk most of the way back, I told them. Now I was a liar." She frowned. "What happened next? We went north and pitched our tents in the summer country. Old Hua hurt herself. She got a burn working at her forge. The burn did not heal. Her leg began to rot. In the end she died.

"Everyone said she died the way a woman ought to—without complaining or making a lot of noise. The spirits were pleased with her. That is what people said. I found it hard to bear.

"After she was in the ground, the shamaness performed ceremonies of purification and ceremonies to drive away bad luck."

"Why?" I asked.

Nia looked surprised. "Every death is unlucky, and Hua had died unexpectedly. She was old but strong, and she had gotten burned many times before. The burns had always healed."

I made the gesture that meant "I understand" or "I see."

"The bad luck stayed," said Nia. "It did not seem that way at first. The summer was good. There was just enough rain. The rivers were full of fish, and the bushes had so many berries that their branches bent down till they touched the ground. We had plenty to eat.

"At the end of the summer people came to the village out of the west. They brought tin and white fur. One of them got sick. That one died. Then our shamaness died. I got sick and so did Nuha. She was Enshi's mother. She went crazy and cried out, 'Enshi! Enshi!' Then she asked the spirits to forgive her. She said it was my fault. Her son would never have done anything wrong. I had made him behave in a shameful fashion. I had made the spirits angry. She promised everyone if she died, she wouldn't go away. Her ghost would stay in the village and find ways to get even with me.

"She died. I got well, though I thought for a while that I would die, too. When I was able to get up and move about, the old women of the village asked me to leave.

"Aiya! That was difficult! I asked them to let me stay. I pleaded with them. But they said, 'Go.'

"I went to find Enshi, and the two of us went south until we came to the Hills of Iron. They are midway between the land of summer and the winter home. The soil is red there. The streams and rivers are as brown as rust. Every year certain women go there and mine iron. They stay till fall, digging out iron and smelting it into bars. Then they rejoin the village. By the time we got to the hills, the women were packing. We hid in the bushes. They loaded their wagons. At last they were gone.

"We found a shelter at the entrance to a mine. It was built of wood and stone, and the woman who'd built it had left some of her tools behind. We found an axe and a pick and shovel. There was an anvil as well—a big one, too heavy to carry.

"We stayed the winter there. We almost starved. There was a child in me, but it died and came out as blood. Enshi thought his mother was responsible. He begged her to go away, and then he told her, 'Hurt me! Hurt me! I am the one who acted shamefully.'"

Nia stopped talking. I shifted position and rubbed my legs. They were getting numb.

"In the spring we moved farther into the hills. The women came back. We stole from them. Enshi was good at this. Or at least better than I was.

"We found a river full of fish—far back in the hills, away from everyone else. There was a cliff nearby red with iron. I made traps to catch the fish. Enshi learned how to dig out iron. We built a shelter, and I set up a forge. Nuha left us alone." Nia frowned. "I did not feel especially ashamed. On some days it seemed to me that what we did was right. What was wrong with me?"

I made the gesture that meant "no comment."

"That winter we had plenty of food. At the end of the winter I had a child. I gave her the name Hua. Enshi liked her. He held her and talked with her. At times she made him angry, but he didn't yell or strike out. He put her down and went for a walk. He was crazy, without a doubt."

I turned my hand, telling her "maybe yes and maybe no."

"My throat is dry. Will you get me a drink?" She pointed. I went and got a jar of water. She took a big swallow. "Aiya! That is good! What was I saying?"

"You had a child."

"Two. The other was a boy. Anasu. He was born in the third winter that we were in the hills. By then I was used to being alone, except for Enshi and the children. I liked it. I still do. There is too much talk in a village. Too much gossip. Too many arguments. But not in the hills. There it is quiet. Once in a while Enshi got restless and went off by himself. Sometimes I did the same thing. I liked those times the best, I think. I went up till there was nothing above me except the sky. Below me were red cliffs and deep red ravines. There were trees as well, tall ones with leaves the same color as the sky. I was above everything. I sat and listened to the wind. Then I felt contented.

"Afterward I had to go down and help Enshi with the children.

"This went on five winters. Then—in the spring—the crazy man came. He rode up one morning. His bowhorn was so thin that I could count every rib. As for the man, he was ragged and grey. One eye was gone. He looked terrible.

"I was in the forge, beating out a piece of iron for a pick. Enshi was hunting. And the children—I don't remember where they were. Near me, I guess.

"I heard a voice. It was deep and harsh. 'Are you ready, woman?'

"I looked up. He dismounted and came toward me. 'Is it time?' he asked.

" 'No,' I said. 'What are you doing here?'

"He stopped and tilted his head to one side. I remember that and the look in his one eye. He was crazy. This happens to old men. They lose their territories. The younger men drive them away. But they won't give up. They refuse to go to the village. Instead they wander by themselves. They have no place. They forget the rules and customs. They are dangerous.

"I took a tight grip on my hammer.

"He said, 'Soon. Another day or so. I can tell. I used to have five women—six women—in a season. Aiya! The gifts they brought and the smell of their bodies.'

" 'Go away,' I said. 'I don't want you here.'

" 'I can wait,' he said. 'I have waited a long time already. I will stay.'

"Then I saw Enshi behind the man, his bow in his hand. 'No,' he said. 'This woman is mine. Get out.'

"The old man turned. 'You scrawny little thing! Do you think you can confront me? I've met men twice your size. They were the ones to lower their gazes. They were the ones to turn away.'

"Enshi lifted his bow. There was an arrow ready, fitted to the string. He began to draw the bow. 'I will kill you, old man. I will put an arrow through your gut.'

"The old man said, 'This is outrageous. Don't you know how these things are done? No true man ever uses an arrow on another man. A knife is the proper weapon. A club is all right, too. But nothing that kills at a distance. A true confrontation is up close.'

"Enshi spoke in reply. He said, 'I don't care what the rules are. This woman is mine. I will do what I must to keep her.'"

Nia paused for a moment. Her face looked thoughtful. "I lifted up my hammer and said, 'I don't care for the rules, either. If you come close to me, I will kill you, old man. Believe me. I tell the truth.'

"What else is there to say? The old man backed down and went away. A day later the lust began. Enshi and I were together for three days. I think that is right. Maybe four days. One morning I woke. Light came in the door of our shelter. Enshi was close to me. The old man was above him. I saw him drive his knife into Enshi's throat. Anasu cried out. I got up. But it was too late. The old man was completely crazy and strong the way that crazy people sometimes are. He was much stronger than I was, and I am not weak. He pushed me down and stuck his penis into me. I tried to get free. He hit me. The knife he was holding cut my shoulder. I still have the scar. The children were crying. Both of them. The old man made grunting noises. I bit him. He hit me again." Nia frowned. "I dream about that sometimes. There is blood in my mouth. There is blood on the ground. I feel the old man on top of me and inside me. I hear the children cry. I know—in my dream—that Enshi is dead. After a while I wake.

"But then I did not wake. The old man stayed until the lust was over. That was five or six days. We mated again and again." She clenched her hands. "When we were not mating, he kept me tied. He was not stupid, even though he was crazy. He knew I would have taken the children and run. He said I was the crazy one. No ordinary woman would have told him to go away. No ordinary woman would have tried to fight him off.

"The children got hungry. They cried. He untied me then, so I could feed them. But he would not let me bury Enshi. He dragged Enshi out of the shelter and left him to lie in the bare place outside the door. The weather was hot. Enshi swelled up.

He began to stink. Bugs came and birds. When the shelter door was open, I was able to see them feeding. Hua kept saying, 'What is wrong? What has happened to Enshi?'

"I told her to keep quiet. She would make the old man angry.

"What else could I say? Two men had met at the time of mating. One killed the other. This did not happen often, but it wasn't wrong. Why did I think it was wrong? Why did I hate the old man? He had the right to mate with me. He had won, though maybe not entirely fairly.

"It was wrong that Enshi was unburied. It was wrong that the children were there. It was wrong that he tied me up. But it was not wrong that he lay on top of me and stuck his penis in me. Why did I hate him for that? It was not wrong."

Nia stopped talking. I waited. There was a sour taste in my mouth, and I couldn't think of anything to say.

"The lust ended and he left. I buried Enshi. I fed my children and cleaned them and comforted them. Then I saddled our animals.

"I took the children with me. I could do nothing else. Anasu I held. Hua rode on Enshi's bowhorn. I had to tie her into the saddle. We followed the old man's trail. It took two days.

"I found him at the foot of the hills, at the edge of the plain. He had built his fire in the last grove of trees before the plain began. Aiya! I remember how it felt when I saw his smoke twisting up into the sky!

"I tethered the bowhorns. I put the children on the ground and told Hua to watch her brother. I told them not to cry—I would be back soon—and went down the hill. I had a weapon now. A bow. It was the one that had belonged to Enshi. I remember the time of day. Just after sunset. The western sky was orange. The old man's fire shone among the trees. I crept up. I saw him hunched next to the fire." Nia paused. "I shot him in the back. He cried out and fell over. I shot him again.

"What else is there to say? I made sure he was dead. Then I put out his fire and went back to my children. They had kept quiet—hidden in a bush, like a pair of bowhorn fawns. Aiya! How good they had been! I praised them and fed them.

"Later I went north to the village. I left the children with Angai. By this time she was the shamaness. She told me she would raise them the right way. I could not. I went east and ended up where you met me—in the village of Nahusai."

Nia leaned back and closed her eyes. She must have lost weight in the last few days. Her face looked thinner than usual, and the bones were easy to make out, even under the fur. Her jaw was heavy. Her forehead was round and low. She had thick cheekbones, and there was no indentation where her nose met her forehead. It went straight up, wide and flat all the way. She opened her eyes and blinked. "Decide between us. Is Hua right? Am I a pervert?"

I glanced up, seeking inspiration. The smoke hole was dark. Something was up there, blocking the light.

What on earth? I stood.

The thing moved. Sunlight came in. I could see the sky. "I'll be back," I said to Nia. I went out and turned.

Like all the roofs in the village this one was covered with vegetation. The small round leaves shone in the sunlight, and there were orange flowers. Bugs fluttered over the flowers. They had yellow wings. Midway down the roof the shamaness stood. Her robe was kilted up, and I could see her legs. They were bony and hairy with big knees.

"You listened at the smoke hole. You heard what Nia said."

"My eyes are bad, but my ears are the best in the village. Aiya! What a disgusting narration! I ought to make you leave today." She went to the edge of the roof and sat down. "Help me."

I reached up. She dropped into my arms. She was light and she stank. It was a mixture of aromas, I decided as I set her down. Fur, musk, and bad breath. The old lady needed a dentist. I took a step back.

"The Voice of the Waterfall said help you. So I must. That crazy man! Why didn't he grow up the right way and go out to join his brothers? Not him, the lunatic! He had to hear voices and see things in his dreams. I go and talk with him. He dances around and jabbers. Naked, too. He'll catch a bad cold some winter and die. Let me tell you, it's hard to be a mother. Now, go away! The woman in there is weak. She needs to rest."

I opened my mouth.

"I won't tell her what I heard. Go! Get out!"

I turned and walked away. Behind me the shamaness was muttering. I heard the word "perversion" and the word "disgusting." Then she said in a loud voice, "Why do these things happen to me?"

I kept going till I reached the house of Eshtanabai. She was sitting in the doorway, leaning against the door frame, looking sleepy and contented.

I stopped. She looked up. "How is your friend?"

"Better. Tell me, what is the shamaness like?"

"Old and strange. Many people say her mind isn't what it used to be. But she still remembers the ceremonies. She talks about the past. Old women always do. And she worries about her children. Not the daughters. They are in the village. She knows how they are getting on. She worries about the sons. She had five, and they all lived long enough to go through the change. Four are up north, if they haven't died by now. The fifth—the youngest—you know about. He came from her last mating, when she was already getting old. Maybe that's why he became an oracle. Old women have strange children. That is well known. Why do you ask?"

I made the gesture that can mean anything or nothing, the gesture of uncertainty.

"That isn't much of an answer." Eshtanabai got up. "Come in. I have some *bara*."

This was the native alcohol. Or—at least—the native intoxicant in a liquid form.

"We'll get drunk. I have nothing else to do today." She led the way into her house.

I followed. Why not? We sat down near the fire. It was a heap of coals. I saw a tiny red glow at the bottom of the heap. A wisp of smoke drifted up, twisting and coiling in the beam of light which shone through the smoke hole. Eshtanabai filled two bowls and gave one to me. I drank. The liquid was bitter, and it burned in my mouth. I coughed, then swallowed.

"Drink more," she said. She drained her cup, then refilled it. "Listen." She leaned forward. "I think you are worried about the shamaness. She is a good woman. Old and strange, but good. But not everything that comes out of her mouth is holy. Only an oracle is holy all the time, and it's a terrible strain. Most oracles die young. Drink some more. It will do you good. It is hard to sit and wait for someone you love to get better."

I drank the rest of the *bara*.

Eshtanabai poured out more. "The shamaness is often holy. But at times she is a foolish old woman, who talks about her sons. We try to be polite. It isn't easy. Last year we sent a boy out, and she got drunk. She didn't sing the proper songs, the songs that tell the boy, 'Be brave! You are doing what is expected!' She sang about the woman who mated with the wind. That song is not appropriate."

"What is it about?"

"You don't know? It's a very old story. It took place long ago, when we lived like the Amber People. Our houses were tents. We followed the herd. There was a woman who went out at the time of mating. There was a terrible storm that year. The bowhorns stampeded, and the men went after them. As a result this woman did not find a man. Her lust ended. She returned to the village. After a while it became evident that she was pregnant. Late in the winter she had a child. It was a child of the wind. No one could see the baby, and she was hard to get hold of. When she was hungry, she would go to her mother to nurse. Then the mother learned—by touching her—that the baby was a girl and covered with soft fur. But most of the time the baby was restless. She ran in her mother's tent. She ran through the village. One day she ran out onto the plain. She never returned. Her mother knew this would happen. She made a song for the child before she left. It goes like this:

> *"Hola!*
> *my little one.*
> *Hola!*
> *my child of the wind.*
>
> *"Now you whirl*
> *in my tent.*

Now you make
the hangings flutter.

"Soon you will be gone
on the wide plain
forever.

"This is the song the old woman sang when we sent the boy out of the village. Everyone was angry, especially the mother of the boy. A woman has many rituals in her life. A man has one: the ceremony of parting. And the old woman had ruined it. She made it a sad occasion. But what can we do? A good shamaness is hard to find. This one is excellent. She can cure almost any kind of illness. And the spirits send rain for our gardens when she asks them to. Have more to drink."

We drank. Eshtanabai told me about the old shamaness, the one before the one they had now. She had been greedy.

"Aiya! She had a house full of things. The older she got the more she wanted. She asked for more than the ceremonies were worth. We gave it. We had to. No one wants bad luck or the anger of the spirits. But the spirits got angry, anyway. The ceremonies didn't work."

"Why?"

Eshtanabai frowned. "Because we gave too much. Look. I fill your cup. I'm generous. I fill it to the brim. That is a proper giving. You have enough. It makes you happy. I know you will give me something in return. That makes me happy. But if I keep pouring and the *bara* goes over the brim, if it gets your hand wet and spills on your clothing or the floor, that isn't a proper giving. That is an insult and a mess.

"A giving is a binding. But only a fool ties a strong rope to a piece of string. You must tie like to like, otherwise the knot will slip or break."

"Are you sure?"

Eshtanabai blinked. "I know the spirits did not listen to that woman. Her rituals got us nothing. We found a new shamaness—one who takes what is right and gives what is right, even though she is half-crazy and talks about her sons.

Here. Let me show you again." She poured out more of the liquid. "To the brim and no more. What will you give me, O hairless one?"

I went to my pack and got out a necklace and gave it to her. She gave me more *bara*. I gave her a bracelet carved out of a native wood and inlaid with the teeth of a kind of native fish. Derek had made the bracelet. He was a wonderful craftsman. By this time it was dusk. The western sky was orange-pink. One of the moons was up: a brilliant point of light. Too much was happening, I thought, and I wasn't in control. Oh, well. I went to the back of the house and passed out on a heap of furs.

In the morning I went back to the house of the shamaness. Nia was sitting up, eating a bowl of mush. "Why are you having trouble walking?" she asked me.

"I did a stupid thing. Oh, my head!" I sat down.

"You did not come back yesterday."

"The shamaness told me you needed rest." Nia looked blurry. I rubbed my eyes.

"You didn't give me an answer." Nia set down her bowl. There was a blob of mush in the bottom. She picked it up with one finger and put it in her mouth. "Am I right? Or is Hua right?"

"What?"

"Am I a pervert?"

I rubbed the back of my neck. "How do I know? I can tell you this: People have different customs. There are places where men and women live together the way you and Enshi did. There are places where the people would say what the old man did to you was terrible."

"Hu!" said Nia. "Where are these places?"

"A long way from here."

"Maybe someday I will go to a place like that."

I said nothing. My headache was getting worse, and I was having trouble concentrating.

Nia scratched her nose. "But maybe I wouldn't like a place like that."

"Maybe not."

In the evening I went to the river. It was hot and muggy there. The air was full of bugs. I made a call to Eddie and told him the story of Enshi.

"Interesting. They seem to have invented monogamy. Nia and Enshi, I mean."

"And the old man invented rape."

"Uh-huh." He didn't say anything for a minute or two. Rape was a subject that made most men nervous. Finally he said, "We've done another satellite survey. There are no cities. Not one. According to Tony this makes sense. The men can't survive in an urban area. And the men have to be close to the women. Otherwise mating would be difficult, maybe impossible. The whole species is stuck in a pre-urban stage of development. They always will be."

A bug flew up my nose. I snorted and coughed. A second bug flew in my mouth. I spat it out. "Eddie, I can't stay here. There are bugs all over."

"Okay. Harrison says to ask about warfare. He doesn't think it exists on this planet."

"Okay." I ran to the village. The gate was shut. I had to yell and bang on the wood till someone came along and let me in.

The next day I talked to Eshtanabai. She had never heard of organized violence. "How could such a thing happen? Sometimes, when two men meet, they both refuse to back down. Then they fight. And there are crazy women who quarrel with their neighbors. But no one will side with a quarrelsome woman. And no one will ever side with a man."

Hm, I thought. I was on a planet without war or cities or sexual love. Was this good or bad? I didn't know.

Eshtanabai held out a bowl. "Have *bara*. Let's drink and talk about something that makes sense."

After a while I asked, "Why do you have walls around your village?"

"There are animals on the plain. Killers. They follow the herd. And when the herd comes south, they prowl around. They look for anything that can be eaten. Garbage. Children. The wall is to keep them out."

"Aiya!"

"Also, we like walls. We feel more comfortable when we look around and see we are enclosed."

That made sense to me. I had grown up on an island. The wide ocean did not bother me, but I had never been entirely happy with the middle American plain. There was too much of it. I did not feel comfortable standing on a piece of land that went on—apparently—forever.

We talked about other things. I stayed more or less sober. Eshtanabai got obviously fuzzy. Did she have a problem with the intoxicant? If so, why? The strain of being a go-between? Or was there some other problem, psychological or physical, about which I knew nothing?

We slept. I woke to sunshine. Nia came to visit me, limping and leaning on a staff.

"I am ready to go," she said. "This place is making me restless, and the shamaness is giving me some very odd looks."

"You're barely able to walk," I said.

"I know what to do about that. Don't plan on staying here much longer."

She limped away. I went to the house next door. There was an old lady there who knew everything there was to know about kinship. Or so my host had told me.

Late in the afternoon Nia came back. I was sitting outside, next to the old lady. She was explaining the obligations between sisters and the children of sisters.

Nia stopped and leaned on her staff, a rough piece of wood. The bark was still on it, and a twig stuck out near the top. "We go tomorrow. I gave my tools to the coppersmith. She gave me two bowhorns. We can ride."

The old lady frowned. "You are interrupting me. I was about to explain who gives gifts to a boy when he is ready to leave the village. This person without hair is amazing. She knows nothing about anything. But she is willing to listen, and she doesn't interrupt."

Nia made a barking noise. "I will go. But be ready, Li-sa. I want to leave at dawn." She limped away.

The old lady finished her explanation. I gave her a necklace made of wooden beads. The wood came from an island in the western ocean, a cold and rainy place that reminded me of Ecotopia in North America. It—the wood, not Ecotopia—was red and had a fine grain, full of twists and coils. The polished surface glimmered.

"Aiya!" the old lady said. "This will impress everyone." She put the necklace on.

I went back to the house of Eshtanabai. My host was out—working on her garden, I decided. I sat down. In time she returned.

"You are leaving."

I made the gesture of assent.

"Good."

"What?"

"The shamaness is angry. If you stay, there will be a quarrel—a bad one. There is nothing worse than an angry shamaness."

"I suppose you're right." I thought for a moment. "What happened to the old shamaness? The greedy one? She must have been angry when you found someone to replace her."

"She was furious. But she had no power. The spirits had stopped listening to her. She went off onto the plain. Most likely she died. Or found another village." Eshtanabai sounded completely uninterested.

They were a cool people. Was it because they did not love the way we did? Then I remembered Hakht and Nia. Neither one was cool.

"Tonight we will eat well," said Eshtanabai. "Fish from the river and a fat bird. Tomorrow I will give you food for the trip."

"Thank you."

We did eat well. The fish were stuffed with vegetables and roasted. The bird was made into a stew. We drank plenty of *bara*. People came to visit and stare at me. The old lady from next door showed off her necklace. One of Eshtanabai's children played a flute. Another beat on a drum. All at once Eshtanabai jumped up. She grabbed a branch from the fire and whirled it around her head. Then she ran out of the house. The rest of us followed. Out in the street my host was dancing, turning, and waving her torch. The other women shouted, "Hola!" The two children kept playing flute and drum. Eshtanabai sang in her language which I did not understand. She strutted back and forth. The other women made gestures of agreement and affirmation.

What was going on? I looked around. Nia was leaning against the wall of a house. Her arms were folded, and she was frowning.

"What is this?" I asked.

"I can't tell you the words, but I know what they mean. She is bragging. She is saying, 'I am wise. I am prudent. I can settle every quarrel.' She is telling them, 'I am generous. You have eaten my food. I have found a way to get rid of these strange people, who have made everyone uneasy. You see all the good that I do for you.' This is what she is saying."

It was a political speech. I watched with interest. More torches appeared. Everyone was dancing now, except for me and Nia. Children climbed up on top of the houses. They leaped amid the foliage and shouted. Eshtanabai kept up her chant.

After a while Nia said, "The Copper People are always the same. They always make too much noise. I am going to bed." She limped off.

The party broke up an hour or so later. All the food and drink was gone. Eshtanabai had said everything she had to say. We all went to bed. At dawn Nia came and shook me awake. I groaned and rolled over.

"Come on," said Nia.

I stumbled off to the privy. When I got back, Eshtanabai was up. I gathered my belongings. She gave me a bag of food.

"Good-bye, hairless one."

I answered with the gesture of parting, followed by the gesture of gratitude.

Nia said, "Come on."

I followed her out. At the moment the air was cool, but it had the feel of a summer morning in Minnesota or Wisconsin. The day would be hot. Nia led me through the village. She didn't have the staff, and she was having trouble walking. In the end I helped her. We reached the gate. She opened it. We went out. Off to the east the sun was rising, hidden by the village. Its light filled the sky. There were two animals tethered by the gate: quadrupeds—and herbivores, I was almost certain. They had long legs and wide chests. Their tails were deerlike. Their horns were narrow and curved like the horns of antelopes. One jerked its head and snorted. The other stamped a foot.

"These are bowhorns," Nia said. "They are in good enough shape, though one is getting old. I can't say much about the saddles. They ought to last until we get wherever we are going."

She untied one animal and mounted. I hesitated, then untied the other animal. It moved.

"Wait a minute," I said. I put a foot in the stirrup, grabbed onto the saddle, and pulled myself up. The animal moved again, taking a step and tossing its head. Somehow I managed to get into the saddle, but I dropped the bag of food.

"You don't know how to ride," said Nia.

"Not well."

She swung her leg over the saddle and stepped down, as easily and casually as if she were stepping off a curb. As she reached the ground, she winced and groaned. She muttered to herself and reached for the bag. A moment later she was back on top of her animal. "This is going to be a long trip," she told me.

DEREK

We forded the river. On the other side Nia found a trail. We followed it up the bluff and over, onto the plain. In front of us the trail led toward the western horizon.

"Who made it?" I asked.

"Women. The ones who take gifts to the Amber People and bring gifts back." Nia slapped the reins. Her animal started forward. My beast followed, and I shifted position, trying to get comfortable.

The day came through on its promise of heat. Our animals ambled west. Nia was quiet and I spent my time looking. There wasn't much to see. The plain was almost featureless. The sky was clear. I saw no animals except bugs.

At noon we stopped and dismounted. I did stretching exercises, then drank from Nia's water bag. The water was warm and had a funny taste.

"How are you?" Nia asked.

"Sore. But I can keep going."

"That's good." She drank and wiped her mouth with the back of her hand. "I hurt, too. I have not ridden for years. We'll stop early tonight."

Late in the afternoon we stopped by a low mound. I dismounted and stretched and groaned.

"I will take care of the animals," Nia said.

"Are you sure?"

Nia made the gesture of affirmation. "It's evident that you

know nothing about bowhorns."

I made the gesture of agreement and went up on the mound. Above me a single bird moved in a great slow circle. I did my exercises, then meditated. I was so stiff that I could barely get into a half-lotus position.

Nia finished with the animals and wandered off. She came back with her arms full of stuff. It was round and grey and crumbly.

"Dung," she told me. "It's left from the spring, when the herds came through."

She built a fire, using the dung as fuel. We ate dinner: bread and a piece of meat that looked and tasted like leather. When we had finished we sat and watched the fire.

I asked her about her ankle.

"It hurts. So do my other injuries." She paused. "I have felt worse. I will survive."

The word she used meant "last," "keep," "remain usable," "not wear out."

"Good." I glanced at the mound. It seemed unnatural to me. Artificial. What was it doing all by itself in the middle of the plain? "Where did that come from?" I pointed.

"I don't know. It was not built by animals. It's too big. Maybe by women. Or demons. The spirits do not build." She sounded uninterested. Did her people lack a sense of history? Or was she tired?

"Where are we going?" I asked.

Nia frowned. "Is there a place you want to go?"

"Another village. I want to learn more words and customs."

"The people to the west of here all travel, and their villages are in the north right now. But if we keep going we ought to be able to meet the Iron People when they come south." She paused. "It has come to me that I would like to see my children."

"Those people drove you off. Aren't they likely to do that again?"

"They might, if I came to them alone. But you are a stranger. Who could possibly be more strange? And they know—better than the Copper People do—what is owed to strangers."

"What?" I asked.

She looked surprised. "Food. A place to sleep. Help, if help is needed. Stories and gifts. It is never right to drive a stranger off, unless he is violent."

"But it's all right to drive off a member of the village?"

"Yes. What harm can be done by someone who is passing through? If a traveler has unusual ideas, that is to be expected. If she behaves oddly, she'll be gone soon enough. But if a villager is perverted or quarrelsome or crazy . . . Hu! That is a serious problem!"

Wonderful reasoning. I grinned.

"You are showing your teeth," said Nia. "Are you angry?"

"No. My people show their teeth when they are happy."

"Aiya! The Iron People will certainly let us in!"

The next day was like the first one, and the third day like the second. The weather remained hot and clear. The plain continued flat and covered with pseudo-grass, which had not changed either. It remained about a meter tall, green and blue-green and yellow. The dominant form of animal life was bugs. They fluttered and whirred all around us.

What was the story?

A bishop asked a biologist, "What have your studies taught you about the Creator?"

The biologist replied, "He has an inordinate love of bugs."

After four days we came to a new kind of vegetation: a bright green plant that looked like grass or pseudo-grass, except that it was five meters tall. It formed a wall that went north and south as far as we could see.

"There's water here," said Nia. "This stuff grows at the edge of rivers."

We rode north along the barrier. There was no way through. The stalks grew too close together, and the leaves had rough edges.

"They cut," said Nia. "This is what I wanted." She reined her animal and pointed. "A path."

We dismounted. I groaned as usual, but the pain was getting less. Nia went down the path. I followed, leading my animal. It crowded me. It must have smelled water. "Stop that!" I slapped the creature's nose. It snorted.

"Be quiet," said Nia. "You can never tell what is waiting for you at a river."

The vegetation ended. We were on the riverbank. In front of us a narrow trickle wandered over a wide sandy bed. On the far side was more of the monster grass. Downstream was a pool.

"Aiya!" said Nia.

A man stood in the pool. He was naked, and he had no fur. His skin was brown. His long hair was blond. On his back was a tattoo: a complex geometric pattern. It represented the cosmic forces in and around the Grey Whale. It—the whale or rather the pattern of the whale—was the totem of his lodge. Maybe I ought to use his terminology. It was the mandala of his eco-niche.

He had a fishing rod, and he was casting with all his usual skill.

"I have a question for you," said Nia. "Do you know what that is?"

"A person. A friend of mine."

He glanced around and pulled in his line, then waded to shore. His beard and his pubic hair were reddish brown. On his chest and arms were initiation scars. The rod he carried was handmade. It was long—extremely long, and it didn't have any reel.

"How is it?" I asked in English.

"The fishing rod? Not good." He grinned. "But I have fish." He laid the rod down. "You are Nia," he said in the language of gifts. "I am Derek. My tribe is the Angelinos. The house I belong to is the house of . . . " He paused for a moment. "The big fish. The name I got for myself is He-who-fights-in-the-sea. And I had better tell you, I am a man."

"I thought you might be," Nia said. "Though it is hard to be certain about anything when dealing with people who are so different. Are you holy? Like the Voice of the Waterfall? Is that why you are naked?"

"No. I'll be back." He went off along the river, moving quickly, out of sight in a minute.

Nia looked at me. "I didn't really believe there were other people like you. I thought you were something peculiar, like the young our does have now and then. They have five legs or two heads. We kill them, and the shamaness performs ceremonies to avert bad luck."

Derek returned wearing jeans. His hair was pulled back and fastened at the nape of his neck. He had on a necklace made of shells and pieces of bone and a metal pendant. It was the same kind I wore, an AV recorder.

As usual he looked graceful and barbarous. He had a Ph.D. in anthropology, and he was a full professor at the University of San Francisco, on leave at the moment, of course. A rather lengthy leave. He wouldn't be back for another 120 years, at the earliest.

"Now for the fish." He went to the river and pulled out a stringer. There were six fish on it: long, narrow, and silver-grey. He held them up. They twisted and flapped their tails. "You take care of your animals. I'll take care of mine."

"Good," said Nia.

By the time we got back, Derek was cutting the last fish open. A fire burned next to him. The rest of the fish lay on a rock in a neat row, gutted.

"We have two choices," he said. "We can put them on sticks and roast them or wrap them in wet leaves and bake them in the coals."

"Which is faster?"

He grinned. "Roasting. Go cut the sticks."

We turned and walked back to the monster grass.

"He gives a lot of orders," Nia said. "Who does he think he is? A shamaness?"

"He has tenure," I said. "It gives him confidence." I felt a twinge of envy. My own academic history was far less distinguished. The job I had left had been untenured.

"What is that? The word you said?"

"Tenure. It means that what he has, he is able to hold on to."

"He is like the big men among my people," Nia said. "They hold their territories, and no one can make them back down—until they get old."

"I guess that's right."

We got our sticks and went back to the fire. Derek cooked the fish. We ate. Afterward I said, "You aren't supposed to be here."

"I got lonely and from what Eddie told me about Nia, I thought she could tolerate a man."

"That may be," Nia said. "But you are nothing like Enshi, and he was the only man I ever spent time around."

I looked at Nia. She began to lick the inside of her hand, getting the last of the fish oil. "If you mind him, I'll tell him to go."

She glanced up. "No. I want to learn how he catches fish. Now I am going to wash myself." She stood up and undid her belt. Then she pulled off her tunic. Naked, she walked to the river. She knelt and undid her sandals. Her fur shone like copper, and she moved as easily as Derek. No. I was wrong. Her movements were more powerful and less graceful. She stood, kicked off her sandals, and waded into the water.

My companion rubbed his nose, which was peeling a little. "I thought, from what she said before, that nudity wasn't entirely proper. Or does that apply to men only? Or maybe it is appropriate to undress in order to bathe, no matter who is around."

"When in doubt, ask."

"A good idea." He got up. "I imagined her as a tough old lady. A Mother Courage. She's beautiful." He followed her to the edge of the river.

Oh, no, I thought. Derek was notorious. The Don Juan of San Francisco. The Interstellar Lover. He had gone through the ship like a devouring flame. There were even rumors about him and Ivanova, though I found that combination highly unlikely. He wouldn't say if the rumors were true, and I certainly didn't have the nerve to ask her.

I asked him why he was promiscuous, one evening after we had finished making love. Guilt, he told me.

"Among my people, we marry young. I had a wife. She was maybe thirteen, thin like a reed with long brown hair. Her eyes were blue. I left her when I left my people. I will never betray her. I will never settle down with a woman from outside."

Nia was waist deep in the water and splashing her arms. He called to her. I couldn't make out what he said. She answered. They began to talk. She moved closer to the shore. Thank heaven it was the middle of summer. The time for mating was past. Nia couldn't possibly be interested in Derek. Nonetheless, I decided to join them. I heard Nia say, "My people think it's shameful to go without clothes. But the women in the village of Nahusai like to swim. They wash often. They say the only shame is being naked when a man is there. Or even a boy, for they grow up to be men. But I do things my own way." She said this defiantly. "I do not pay attention to the opinions of old women. I do what I think is right."

Derek grinned, then made the gesture of agreement. Nia waded farther out and began to wash her back.

Late in the afternoon he showed her how to use a fishing pole. She caught nothing. We ate dried meat for dinner. Night came. There were shooting stars.

"They come this time of year," said Nia. "We call them the Arrows of Summer."

Derek put more wood on the fire. I went to sleep and dreamt of him. We were in one of the recreation cabins on the ship. The walls were glazed yellowish white. Derek was naked and laughing. His penis was erect. He reached for me. I woke. Off to my right Nia was snoring, and Derek was on the other side of the fire. I could hear his deep, slow breathing. I lay for a while watching the night sky. Then I went back to sleep.

In the morning Derek went fishing. For bait he used a local bug. It looked like a caterpillar: fat and green with a lot of legs. There were hundreds of the creatures along the river. They fed on the monster grass. The fish fed on them. We fed on the fish.

"And thus we understand the great chain of being," Derek said as he finished the last piece of fish.

Nia looked puzzled. He had spoken in English.

"Nature red in tooth and claw," he went on. "That's a line from Tennyson. He also said that we rise on the stepping stones of our dead selves to higher things." He grinned at me. "I used to be fascinated by the history of the West, especially the history of industrial societies. That was when I first left my people. I thought—there is a secret here, in Marx and Tennyson and in the big machines. Later I decided my people were right. It is better to be close to the grey whale and the peyote cactus. But by that time I was used to being comfortable. What do we do now, Lixia?"

"Travel west. There are people on the plain. Nomads. Nia says she can find them for us. I mean to do as much fieldwork as possible. I want my name all over the preliminary report."

He grinned. "Is this ambition in little Lixia?"

"I know what I am. A first-rate collector of facts. But I've never been good at the academic bullshit. The analysis. The playing with theory. If I am ever going to get anywhere, it's going to be on the basis of what I do here in the field."

"Maybe. There's no question about your ability to collect facts. You can learn a language faster than anyone I know."

"Except Gregory."

He made the gesture that acknowledged that I might be right. "But listen to the way you talk. You say 'academic bullshit' and 'playing with theory.' This shows a bias. The refusal to theorize is—in itself—a theoretical position, my love. Unfortunately for you, it is not a popular position. Where would we be without our systems, our hierarchies of information, our analyses? Our points and our morals?"

He got up and stretched. "Those animals of yours don't look any faster than horses. I can keep up." He kicked dirt on the fire. Then he collected his belongings: his pack and fishing line, wound in a coil, a bow and half a dozen arrows.

"You made the bow?"

"Of course." He looked down at his feet. "I can't run like this." He took off his boots and socks. "Here." He gave them to me.

Nia said, "If you are going to travel without shoes, keep to the trail or—if you are off it—watch where you put your feet. There are plants that sting on the plain. Don't step on anything that looks unusual."

"Always good advice," said Derek. He made the gesture of gratitude.

We saddled up. I tied my belongings and Derek's on my animal. Nia and I mounted. We splashed through the river. On the other side we found a trail that wound through the monster grass. Soon we were back on the plain. It stretched to the west and north and south without interruption.

At first Derek tried to walk beside us, but the trail was too narrow. He loped ahead. His hair was untied and flapped in the wind. So did the tail of his shirt. He moved easily, confidently. He looked happy and relaxed.

"This man is strange," said Nia. She glanced at me. I made the gesture of agreement.

"Is this the way your men are?"

"No. He is something special. He makes most of us uneasy."

"Hu!"

The land changed. Now it was rolling. Often, in the distance, I saw clumps of monster grass: tall and brilliant green, like a stand of trees. Late in the afternoon we made camp in a hollow. Derek and Nia went to gather dung. I took care of the animals. They were restless—thirsty, I decided. When Nia came back I said, "Why don't we go into one of those groves? You told me they grow near water."

"There is an animal. The killer-of-the-plain. It lies in wait near water. Bowhorns come to drink. It jumps on them."

"Oh." I thought for a moment. "That's why you were uneasy when we came to the river."

Nia made the gesture of agreement. "I knew there was no way around the river. We had to cross it. But I am afraid of that animal."

After dinner I called the ship. Eddie answered.

"Why is Derek here?"

Eddie laughed. "He made it, eh? Three reasons, Lixia. He is a first-rate field-worker, and he was being wasted off by himself." He paused for a moment. "Nia is our most unusual informant. We wanted a second evaluation of her and her information. That is reason number two. Finally, you don't call in often enough. Derek is there to keep tabs on you and Nia."

"Oh, yeah?"

"Uh-huh. You lack social responsibility. If I were Chinese, I'd be upset with you."

I bit the edge of my thumb. "Is that so?"

"Uh-huh. Speaking of our comrades from East Asia, there are a lot of posters going up along Democracy Wall."

There was a main corridor that went through the living quarters. The Chinese had lined part of it with cork board and named it Democracy Wall. They said it was necessary for the proper expression of the mass will.

What was wrong with computers? the rest of us asked.

Computers isolated people, each one in front of a little screen. The wall brought people together. They could discuss what they read. They could look around and see how their neighbors were reacting. They could tell who was listening.

Computers emphasized linear thinking and logic. The wall, like the Chinese ideogram, used linear *and* nonlinear ways of organizing information: pattern as well as sequence, space as well as time. When one looked at the wall, one used the entire human brain.

Besides, it was traditional. Human beings had always written and drawn on walls.

It was hard to argue with that, and the wall had a certain disheveled charm. There was no telling what people would put up: a clever drawing, a stupid limerick, a papier mâché mask. "Wanted—a partner for chess." And a lot of political arguments. It was a way of getting at the people who would never think of entering any of the political discussion networks.

Eddie went on. "Lu Jiang the plumber has a theory, which she has posted. It goes as follows: if the information we have now is right, all the native societies are stuck at a pre-urban stage. As far as we know, it is impossible to develop an advanced technology outside of cities. Without an advanced technology, there can be no proletariat. Without a proletariat, there can be no socialist revolution. Therefore, she argues, the unfortunate inhabitants of this planet can never achieve a socialist society. She has, of course, been criticized for undervaluing the role of the peasantry in achieving socialism."

"It sounds wonderful."

"It's dangerous, Lixia. People are beginning to say if Jiang is right, then maybe we ought to make contact with the natives of the planet—formal contact, telling them who we are. Maybe we have to offer them our technology. If we don't, we condemn them to an existence without the possibility of progress. They will remain as they are forever."

I rubbed my nose.

He went on. "What I see happening is—an alliance between the altruists and the technologists. The lovers of the people and the lovers of machinery. They will both decide that we have to open up the planet."

"Eddie, you are borrowing trouble."

"Listen to me. My grandfather was a medicine man. He saw things before other people did. And I tell you, right now I have his ability. I can see it like a vision: the mines and the refineries and the furry proletarians, punching the clock every morning."

I decided to stop talking. Eddie was getting angry, and I didn't want any part of one of his rages.

"I'm going to turn this thing off. I want to do my exercises."

"Okay. Tell Derek to call in. No. On second thought don't bother. He always remembers."

I turned off the radio and did my exercises. After that I meditated, fixing my gaze on the eastern horizon. The sky there was a transparent deep blue with a tinge of green. Farther up—where the blue grew lighter and a bit more green—a point of light shone. A planet. I concentrated on my breathing. In. Out. *So. Hum.*

Behind me Derek spoke. "Achieving oneness with the universe?"

I twitched, then looked around. He was standing about a meter away. He had come up soundlessly. He grinned. "Do you want any peyote? I brought some down."

"It seems to me we agreed no narcotics on the surface of the planet. Unless, of course, they were provided by the natives."

"First of all, peyote is a hallucinogen. And second, it is necessary for the practice of my religion."

"The committee agreed with you?"

"Which one? The ship is full of committees."

I opened my mouth. He raised a hand. "You're right. I didn't get permission."

"What is this? Some kind of infantile rebellion?"

"I get tired of rules. I take it you don't want any peyote."

"No."

"How about sex? I've been noticing, you look very good down here. I think it's something to do with the sunlight. Nothing looks right on the ship. But here." He waved a hand at the darkening sky.

I thought for a moment. "Okay."

He sat down next to me, putting an arm around me.

He was, as I had remembered, very good. Not fast. Derek came from a hunting and gathering society. He knew the value of patience and slow, careful work. He knew how to use his hands. He knew what to say and when. Is there any pleasure equal to seeing—or hearing—or feeling—a really good craftsperson at work?

We ended naked in the prickly pseudo-grass. He was on top of me and in me.

Nia said, "What are you doing? Don't you realize it is the middle of summer? No one mates this time of year."

Derek said, "Go away, Nia. We'll explain later."

"Very well. But you people are strange."

Derek lifted his head. "She's gone. Now, where was I?"

I laughed.

Afterward we lay awhile in the vegetation. I felt wonderful. I had been alone too long. How many days? Forty-seven? Forty-eight? I would have to ask Eddie. I had lost count.

Derek got up and started dressing. I followed his example. A meteor fell. We walked to the camp. Nia sat next to the fire, which was dim and had a peculiar aroma. Dung did not burn the same way as wood. She looked up. "Are you through with your mating?"

"Yes."

"You are perverted."

"That may be." Derek sat down.

Nia looked at the fire. "I am unlucky. Everywhere I go, I meet people who do things the wrong way."

Derek grinned. "What do you mean by that? What is the wrong way? Is it what the old women say is wrong? You told us you did not care about their opinions."

"That is true. But everyone knows people feel lust in the spring. Only sick people feel lust at any other time."

"We are not ordinary people, Nia. You must understand that. We are stranger than you can know. But we are not bad. And there is nothing wrong with our health."

"You make me uneasy. I am going to take a walk." She got up and limped away. In a minute she was gone, out of sight in the darkness.

I sat down. He frowned. "How upset is she?"

I made the gesture of uncertainty.

"That's a lot of help."

We waited up for an hour or so. Nia did not return. At last I went to sleep. I woke at dawn. Nia was close to me, lying down, her cloak around her, snoring softly.

We rose at sunrise and continued west. The weather stayed the same: hot and bright. The land continued rolling. To the north of us was a range of low, round hills. Clouds floated above them.

"That is the land of smoke," Nia told us. "It is a holy place. The water there bubbles like the water in a cooking pot. Smoke rises out of cracks in the rock."

"Oh, yes?"

Nia made the gesture of affirmation.

A little past noon Derek stopped. He was on top of a rise. We rode up to him.

"There is someone behind us," he said.

"A man," said Nia. "No woman travels alone." She barked. "No. I do not tell the truth. I have traveled alone. But usually women go together." She glanced back. "I do not see him. You must have good eyes."

"Yes."

Nia shaded her eyes and looked again. "I will believe you. Someone will have to stay awake at night. If the man has decided to come close, he will do it then."

We kept on. By this time there were clouds all across the sky. They were small and fluffy, arranged in rows. The land was dappled with shadows. Here and there I saw outcroppings of dark rock. Basalt? I wondered. According to the planetologists, the rocks here were virtually identical to those on Earth.

The hills to the north were closer than before. Nia kept glancing at them. "I do not like the land of smoke. There are demons there."

"Oh."

In the evening we made camp near the top of a hill, under a huge mass of rock. It was black and rough. Volcanic. Below us was a valley full of bushes. Their leaves were yellowish green. We went down and found dry wood. Nia built a fire. It lit the dark face of the rock and the bodies of my companions: Derek—lean and smooth and brown, Nia—broad and furry.

We ate. Derek stood. "I'll take the first watch." He glanced around. "There ought to be a good view up there." He walked to the rock and began to climb, going up quickly with no hesitation.

Nia watched him. "Can he do everything well?"

"There are times when I think so."

"You do not like him."

"Not much."

"Why not?"

"Because he does everything well. For me nothing is easy. I envy him."

Nia frowned and looked at the fire. "I had a brother like that. Anasu. He did everything that was expected, and he did it better than most. By this time he is a big man. I am sure of it. He wasn't the kind to stay in the hills with the young men, with the men like Enshi. By this time he must have a territory close to the village and many women in the season for mating." Nia scratched her nose. "There was another one. Angai. A friend of mine. She was hard to get along with when she was young. People didn't like her. But she turned out well. She is the shamaness in my village. She has my children." She looked up. I was staring right into her orange eyes. "I do not understand what has happened to me. But I know this. It is wrong to feel envy. Hakht did. It burned in her like fire under the ground. It made her into something disgusting. I will not envy other people." She got up and went to get her cloak. "Now I am going to sleep."

She lay down. I stayed up. The big moon was visible in the west: high up and half-full, a bright lemon-yellow. It lit new clouds. They were large and billowing. A new weather system? I grew drowsy. My mind wandered from subject to subject: envy, then Nia's brother. What was he like? What was it like to have a brother in her culture? I remembered the junior members of my family. Leon. Clarissa. Charlie. Maia. Mark. Fumiko.

Fumiko was the youngest by far. At the time I left she had been finishing college, getting ready for her wander year or years. I had gone early, at the age of twenty. I'd quit school and gone to the Big Island to cut sugarcane. Then I'd worked my way to Asia on one of the new freighters. I cooked and learned to operate the computer that controlled the sails. That was easy. The computer damn near ran itself. But I nearly went crazy, trying to cook in the tiny galley while everything around me moved.

Well, that was long ago and on another planet. I got my poncho and settled down to sleep.

I was awakened by an ululating scream: high-pitched, eerie, inhuman. A moment later I was upright. I didn't remember how I'd gotten into that position. On the other side of the fire was Nia. She was standing, too. Her eyes were wide open, and her knife was in her hand.

"What was that?" I asked.

"I don't know."

I realized I knew and that I had been wrong. The sound wasn't inhuman. It was the battle cry of a California aborigine. I looked around. "Derek?"

Out of the darkness came another sound, a cry of fear in the language of gifts. "Help! Help! A demon!"

I turned and ran downhill. Nia followed. We scrambled through the pseudo-grass. Below us the voice repeated, "Help! Help!"

Derek shouted, "Stop fighting me!"

I saw them, a thrashing mass, barely visible in the moonlight. I stopped. Two bodies rolled back and forth. Derek was on top. I saw his blond hair flipping. The person on the bottom cried, "Help me!"

Nia said, "If you are peaceful, stop struggling. The other person will not harm you. He is not a demon."

"No?" The body on the bottom stopped moving. "Are you sure?"

Derek climbed off the other person and pulled him or her up.

"Aiya! What a thing to happen! Are you absolutely certain that this being is not a demon?"

"Yes," said Nia. "Who are you?"

"I am the Voice of the Waterfall."

"You cannot be! I know about him. He spends his whole life next to the waterfall. When he dies and the people find his body, they throw it into the river. His bones lie among the rocks at the bottom of the waterfall."

"That is true. Can't we talk by the fire? I am afraid to be out here in the dark. And can't this being with the strong hands let go of me?"

"Lixia?" asked Derek.

"It's okay. Let go of him."

We walked up the hill. When we got close to the fire I looked at the oracle. This time he had clothing on: a ragged kilt. I couldn't make out the color. Grey or brown. Around his neck was a necklace: gold beads and big, uneven lumps of turquoise. The turquoise was blue and blue-green. The necklace was magnificent. The man rubbed his arms. "Hu! What a grip that being has!" He looked at Derek. "Another hairless one! What is happening to the world?"

"Why are you here?" asked Derek.

"Can't we sit down? I'm tired. I have walked for days. My feet hurt, and I am so thirsty that I can barely talk."

Nia got her water bag. He drank and then sat down. "Aiya! That is better. Do you have anything to eat?"

Nia gave him a piece of bread. He ate it.

Derek asked, "Why have you been following us?"

"That is a long story. Sit down. All of you. But not too close. I am not used to people."

We sat down. The man took another drink of water. Then he stared at me. "You are the one I met."

"Yes."

"You went to the village. After that my mother came with other women. She—my mother—brought food and a new blanket, a fine, thick, soft one. She told me I wasn't taking care of myself. I would freeze in the winter. I told her, 'Old woman, you are as crazy as I am. Don't worry about me. I belong to the waterfall. The waterfall will take care of me.' She gave me a medicine that is good for a sore throat and for a feeling of thickness in the chest. Then she went on. She came back with that one." He pointed at Nia. "After everyone was gone I had a dream. The Spirit of the Waterfall came to me. It was like a person, except that it was grey like silver, and I couldn't tell if it was male or female. It told me, 'Something important is going on, and it concerns the person without hair. Follow that person. Watch that person. Listen to what that person says.'

"I tried to argue. 'I belong here. The Voice of the Waterfall never leaves this place.' The spirit began to look angry. 'You are *my* voice. Don't talk back to me.' Then I began to shake. The spirit went on. 'I do not belong to any one place, though I like this canyon and this waterfall. As for you, you belong where I tell you to be. Now go! And don't argue. Remember whose voice you are.'

"I woke up. What could I do? Only what the spirit told me. I went to the village. You"—he pointed at me—"were inside. I waited. I ate whatever I could find. When people came near I hid in the bushes. Finally you came out, and I followed you onto the plain.

"What a journey! It took—how many days? Five or six. I wasn't able to keep you in sight. But I knew you would follow the trail. After a day or so one of my sandals broke. I threw both of them away. My feet began to hurt and I was hungry. I dug up the root of the spiny *rukha* plant. It gave me food and water, but I stung my fingers on the spines.

"After four days I came to a river. Hu! What a pleasure! I drank water and gathered bugs. I made a fire and roasted them. How sweet! How delicious! I ate until I was sick, then rested and then crossed the river.

"The next night was terrible." He stopped for a moment and shivered. "I was lying on the plain—alone, with no cloak to cover me. An animal came. I heard the sound of its breath. Oo-ha! Oo-ha! I could smell it. It stank of rotten meat. It prowled around me. It sniffed and made a humming noise. I thought, I know what this is. A killer-of-the-plain, and it is going to eat me. I didn't move. I was too frightened.

"The creature went around me a second time, humming all the while. I felt it. Aiya!" He shivered and blinked. "I felt it take one of my legs between its teeth. It lifted up my leg, then it let go. I let my leg fall as if I were dead already. The spirit must have guided me. The spirit must have told me what to do."

Nia leaned forward. "I have heard of this. They attack if you move. Or if they smell blood. But if a person remains motionless, they will leave her alone."

The oracle frowned. "This is my story. Let me finish it."

"Okay," said Nia.

"What?"

"Go on."

"After that the animal went away. I stayed where I was and thanked the spirit. In the morning I looked at my leg. There was no blood. The animal hadn't broken the skin. Aiya! What luck!"

Derek made the gesture of agreement.

"I got up and went on. What else could I do? I hurried. I was afraid of spending another night alone on the plain. The sun went down. I saw your fire shining in the darkness. I came near and that person"—he pointed at Derek—"jumped on me. I thought, I have met up with a demon. I am going to die, and I only hope the Spirit of the Waterfall is happy with this turn of events.

"But I didn't die and here I am. This is the end of my story."

Derek spoke in English. "Who is this?"

"He's an oracle. I met him after Nia was injured. His mother is the shamaness of the Copper People of the Plain. I think he's a little crazy, though I'm not sure. How does one judge insanity in an alien culture?"

"And how does one tell the difference between craziness and holiness?" Derek changed to the language of gifts. "What next? Do you want to travel with us?"

"Yes. Of course. That is the will of the spirit. I am going to sleep now. You can discuss whether or not you want me as a companion. But I warn you—no matter what you decide, I will follow you." He got up and moved away from the fire to the edge of the darkness. He lay down, his back to the plain, and curled up in a fetal position. After a moment he moved one arm, so it covered his face.

Nia said, "Truly, the world is changing. I meet people who mate in summer, and a holy man now appears, who is willing to leave his holy location and travel with ordinary folk. No." She looked at me and Derek. "I don't mean ordinary folk. I mean, people who aren't holy."

"Well," said Derek in English. "Does he travel with us?"

"Why not?" I looked at Nia and spoke in the language of gifts. "What do you think about him?"

"We can't leave him alone on the plain. He's as helpless as a child or an old woman. Moreover he is holy. If we abandon him, the spirits will be angry. There is no question about it. He must come with us."

Derek nodded and got up. "I'm going back up to watch. Get some sleep, Lixia. I'll wake you later."

He woke me after midnight, and I kept watch. It was cool and still except for the noise the bugs made in the pseudo-grass. Toward morning I woke Nia. She got up, and I went back to sleep.

In the morning we went on. Nia and the oracle rode. I joined Derek on the ground. The trail wound among hills. There was plenty of rock here: cliffs and outcroppings and boulders, all black and rough. The valleys were grassy. Now and then we saw a flock of bipeds: the pseudo-dinosaurs. Most were about a meter tall and bright turquoise-blue.

"It's a beautiful planet," Derek said as he walked next to me.

"Yes."

"What's the line from Donne? 'O my America, my new-found-land!' Of course, he was talking about a woman. A new mistress.

> *"License my roving hands, and let them go,*
> *Before, behind, between, above, below.*
> *O my America! My new-found-land,*
> *My kingdom, safest when with one man manned.*
> *My mine of precious stones, my empirie.*
> *How blest am I in thus discovering thee."*

"Derek, how do you manage to be so literate?"

He glanced over, grinning. "Hard work, my love. And a very high intelligence."

"Oh. Okay."

He laughed. "Anyway, I feel the way Columbus must have. Or stout Cortez, silent on his peak in Darien. What a discovery! What a planet!" He swept out one hand, waving at the hills and the blue-green sky. A pseudo-dinosaur screamed and ran away.

Nia looked back. "What is it?"

"Nothing. Derek likes this country."

"I don't."

"Why not?"

She stopped and glanced around. "I don't remember it. I have taken a wrong turn somewhere. This isn't the trail I wanted."

The oracle made the gesture that meant "don't worry." "The spirit will guide us."

"That may be."

In the afternoon the sky got cloudy. Toward evening rain began to fall: a light drizzle. We made camp in a grove of trees. Derek shot a pseudo-dinosaur. Nia cleaned it. The Voice of the Waterfall and I went looking for wood.

After dinner I called the ship. A computer answered. It had a cool, pleasant female voice with a very slight Russian accent.

"No humans are available at present," it said. "You may report to me."

I did.

The computer thanked me and said the information would be relayed to the appropriate people. "I am a level-six program," it explained. "My intelligence is a construct and—do I mean or?—an illusion. I am therefore not a person, according to the current definition of the term."

"Do you mind?" I asked.

"That is not a meaningful question, at least when addressed to me. I neither think nor feel. I do what I am told to do."

I thought I heard sarcasm in the courteous even voice. But that was hardly likely. Why would anyone write sarcasm into a level-six program?

I turned the radio off, lay down, and listened to the rain pattering on the leaves above me.

The morning was overcast. Nia said, "You ride today, Li-sa. I want to find out how my ankle is doing."

"My feet still hurt," the oracle said. "They are covered with blisters."

Derek laughed. "Don't worry. You can have the other bowhorn."

Rain began to fall, and mist hid the distances. We traveled through greyness, up a long slope. Sometime around noon we reached the top. There was a level area, then a drop-off. We were on the rim of a valley. I reined my animal. The valley floor was visible in spite of the mist. The ground was bare and bright orange.

Derek sniffed. "Rotten eggs or sulfur. I think we can assume geothermal activity." He spoke a mixture of English and the language of gifts. I could understand everything, but our companions looked puzzled.

After a moment Nia said, "I don't know what kind of activity you are talking about. But I don't like the look of this valley. Or the smell for that matter."

Derek glanced to the side. "Don't worry. We aren't going down. The trail goes along the rim."

We followed the trail. The rain stopped. The clouds lifted. I could see the valley clearly. It was shallow and more or less circular. The entire floor was brightly colored: orange, orange-red, and yellow. Here and there plumes of white rose. Steam. The plumes moved, blown by the wind. In the middle of the valley was a lake: round and dark. Derek kept looking at it.

"Something isn't right. The lake is peculiar."

"I can believe that," Nia said. "This land is peculiar." She used the same word Derek had. It meant "unusual," "unexpected," "wrong." After a moment she went on. "I don't remember any of this. I am certain we're on the wrong trail, though I don't know how that is possible. I have a good memory and a good sense of direction. I never get lost."

I twisted in the saddle. She was trudging next to me. Her feet were muddy, and her fur was wet. Her tunic clung to her body. "What shall we do?"

Nia made the gesture of uncertainty.

"Keep going," the oracle said from behind me. "The Spirit of the Waterfall will see to it that we arrive in the right place."

"What a comfort!" Derek said.

We came finally to a place where the valley wall was low. A slope led down toward the orange and yellow floor. At the top the slope was covered with vegetation: little bushes and a lot of pseudo-grass. Farther down the ground was bare. A dark line wound across it: another trail, narrower than ours, less well used, going into the valley.

Derek stopped. I reined my animal.

The oracle rode up beside me. "What is it?" he asked.

"I think we ought to make camp."

"Here?" I asked.

Derek made the gesture of affirmation.

I looked around. On one side of me was the slope. On the other side was an outcropping of rock, black and massive. The trail—the main trail—led past it. There was nothing else. No wood except the little bushes and no evidence of water. "Why?" I asked.

"We aren't going to make it down off the rim before night, and I haven't seen any places that are better than this."

"He's right," said Nia. "That rock has an overhang. It ought to protect us, if it rains, and there is forage for the animals. I admit I would like some fresh water. The water in our bags is getting stale. But when a person travels without her village, she must take what she can get."

"And be grateful for it," said the oracle.

Nia made the gesture of agreement.

I dismounted. The oracle did the same. I stretched up as high as I was able, then bent over. I could barely touch the ground. I brushed it with my fingertips and straightened up, breathing in at the same time. More exercise! This expedition was no excuse for getting lazy.

The oracle said, "He wants to go into the valley."

I looked at Derek. He was staring at the view. The sky was clearing. Sunlight edged the clouds, and the colors of the valley were even more brilliant than before. "Why?" I asked.

He turned. I knew that expression, the lifted eyebrows and the twisted grin. Derek was planning something that was either frivolous or dangerous. And he wanted my approval. The charm had gone on. I had no idea how he did it, but it was as dramatic as a light rod beginning to glow. His smile widened.

"Derek, stop it! Turn it off!"

"What?"

"The masculine beauty, the charm, the sexiness." I had switched to English. Nia began to frown.

"I want to take a look at that lake," Derek said. He was speaking the language of gifts. His voice was low and even. A reasonable voice. The voice of sanity. "I think I can make it there and back before the light is entirely gone."

"I doubt it, and I think you're crazy to try. That is a very active area down there. The ground is probably hot, and it may not be reliable. It may be a crust over something ugly. You could go through. You could end up in the soup, and I am being more literal than metaphoric."

"Speak our language," Nia said. "I am interested in this argument."

"Okay. I'm telling Derek not to go into the valley."

"You won't change his mind," the oracle said.

Derek laughed. "He's right. Give in, Lixia. There is no point in talking. I'm going to go."

I made the gesture that meant "so be it." "Take your boots."

"Why? I move more quickly with bare feet."

"I told you. I think the ground is hot." I bent to the side, raising one arm. With the other arm I reached down toward my ankle, then closed my eyes, concentrating on my breathing. In. Out. *So. Hum.* O jewel of the lotus.

I straightened up and opened my eyes. Derek was on his way: a small dark figure scrambling through the pseudo-grass, a good distance off already. Beyond him and below him was the valley.

Nia unsaddled the bowhorns. We built a fire under the overhang. Dinner was the last of the pseudo-dinosaur.

"Why did he go?" Nia asked.

"I have no idea. He does these things. Not often." I paused. I wanted to say, most of the time he plays by the rules. But I didn't know the native word for "play." I said, "Most of the time, he does what is expected."

Nia finished a piece of meat. She tossed the bone into the fire. "All men are crazy in one way or another."

The oracle made the gesture of agreement.

I stared out at the evening sky. The Great Moon was up. It was more than half-full now, and it looked to be—what?—three quarters the size of Luna when Luna was seen from the Skyline Drive in Duluth on a midsummer night.

Why didn't I know the word for "play"? I looked at Nia. "What is the word for what children do when they throw a ball?"

"It is called 'fooling around.'"

Well, yes. That made sense. That was one meaning of "play." But it had other meanings, too. I thought of *Hamlet* and the triple play, though I wasn't entirely sure what the triple play was. And swordplay. Hamlet and Laertes, for example. And musicians playing their instruments. What I needed was the O.E.D. Eddie had access to the language computers. I reached for the radio, turning it on.

I got a computer again. The same program as before. I recognized the accent and the tone of distant courtesy. There was more static than usual. The cool voice came through a constant faint crackling, like fire.

I asked for a definition of "play."

"Just a moment," the computer said.

I heard the usual noises that computers made when working: a beep, followed by a series of chirps, and then by a bell-like tone. A new voice—another program—told me what "play" meant in English.

This voice was male and had a Chinese accent.

When it finished I thanked it and turned the radio off.

"What is that thing?" asked the oracle.

Nia leaned forward. "Li-sa told me about it. It is a way to talk to people who are beyond the horizon."

"Oh. I thought it might be a musical instrument. It makes a lot of different kinds of noise, and some of them are pleasant."

"What do you do with a musical instrument?" I asked.

The oracle frowned. "What do you mean?"

"What is the word for using it. For making it make a noise."

"Oh. *Nakhtu*."

"That is in his language," said Nia. "In the language of gifts, it is *nahu*."

"Is that like fooling around?" I asked.

"No. Of course not. Children fool around. Grown-up people are sensible. Or—if they are not sensible—they are crazy, which is different from being a fool."

"Oh." I looked at the fire, then at the moon. The aliens had musical instruments. They had ceremonies. They danced. I knew they were capable of competition. Think of Hakht and Nahusai. But did they play as we did? Ritual aggression and competition were absolutely central to the Western cultures. The East Asians had opera and kabuki and all the martial arts. Everyone had soccer. Did these people need to play as much as we did? There was so much tension in human society, so much frustrated aggression. Even now when the old society—the society of greed and deprivation—was gone.

Wait a minute. Not every human society was full of tension. I remembered the California aborigines. They were mellow, consciously and deliberately. Mellowness was central to their religion. It was a sign of enlightenment. The ideal aborigine was mellow and in touch. He or she kept a low profile, close to Mother Earth.

I thought about Derek. He could be mellow, but it was an act. Under the surface he was like a bull walrus. He knew what he wanted, and he would fight to get it. Had he known what he was like as a kid? Was that why he'd left his people? He would have been a failure, frustrated and angry, among people who could sit for hours watching a condor in the sky and be happy.

"That's where it's at," one of them told me, a witch wearing a loincloth and a lot of tattoos. "Mother Earth and Father Sky, the things that live—the plants and animals. All the old mysteries that the prophets spoke about. Black Elk and the Buddha. Jesus and Mother Charity. They all tell us the same thing. No matter how much you struggle and strive, you'll never get out of this world alive. So why struggle? And why strive? Do what you have to. Take what you need. Be thankful and be mellow."

Okay, I told that old memory. I closed my eyes and saw her: lined face and long flat breasts. There was—there had been—a crescent moon on her forehead. Between her breasts was a pendant, a double axe carved out of shell. A wise old lady. Had Derek known her? Not likely. Her tribe was different. They were mountain people, the Bernadinos.

I ate another piece of meat, then went to sleep, waking in the middle of the night. The moon was gone. The sky was full of stars. I sat up. The fire was a heap of coals that still glowed a little. I looked around. Nia was next to me, snoring. Farther off I saw another body. That must be the oracle.

On the far side of the fire was a third person standing upright, tall and pale. "Derek?"

"I just got back." His voice was low. "You were right. The ground is hot. I could feel it through the boots."

"Any trouble?"

"No.—Except, a funny thing. When I was coming back, the moon was setting. Just as it went out of sight I saw a flare. I think the moon is erupting."

I thought for a moment. "That's possible, isn't it? The planetologists said there was evidence that it had been active recently."

"The eruption has to be huge," Derek said. "Really huge, if I can see it."

"You're right." I thought for a moment. Could that be why I hadn't reached Eddie? No one in their right mind would want to miss seeing a major eruption. "More trouble for the planetologists."

"Uh-huh." He laughed. "The poor fools. It serves 'em right. They worked out all their theories on the basis of one system."

"They used what they had, Derek."

He said, "I want to go to sleep. I'll tell you the rest tomorrow."

"Okay." I lay back down. The wind had shifted. It blew out of the valley, bringing the smell of sulfur. I thought about the moon, which had an atmosphere. There was a lot of sulfur in it, as I remembered. It must really stink up there now.

The planetologists had not been happy when they saw the first long-distance holograms. The moon was too big, they told us. All the best theories said that Earth was an anomaly. Small planets didn't have moons. Or if they did, the moons were tiny: pieces of captured space junk.

The ship got closer in. The planetologists discovered the surface of the moon was comparatively smooth.

The system was full of junk. The planet had twelve other moons, all of them clearly captured planetoids. The big moon should have been covered with impact craters. Instead there were wide plains of volcanic origin and some fairly impressive mountains, also of volcanic origin.

The moon was active, and the best theories said that small planets did not have active moons.

Which meant the planetologists had to start working on new theories. I'd heard a couple. One involved tidal pull. The other assumed a really odd composition for the body in question. They were too far outside my area of expertise for me to have an opinion. I simply enjoyed the strangeness of the moon.

I woke at dawn, got up, and went to find a place to pee. Then I did my exercises, ending with the solar salute. I timed it perfectly. When I finished the sun was fully up, round and crimson, right above the eastern wall of the valley.

Nia woke and the oracle. Derek was the last person up. He stretched and groaned, then climbed to his feet. We ate. Nia went to saddle the bowhorns. The oracle followed after her.

Derek yawned. "Coffee. That's what I need."

"What did you find?"

"The lake is mud. Hot mud. Boiling. It's an interesting sight. Bubbles appear on the surface. They get bigger and bigger, then—pssht. They're gone. Exploded." He yawned again. "The smell of sulfur is really offensive. And there are poles along the edge."

"What?"

"Wooden poles. Maybe ten centimeters thick. About three meters high. They're decorated with feathers and pieces of cloth. Some of them have horns on top made of copper. Really badly corroded. The gases from the lake must do that.

"I assume the lake has some kind of religious meaning. Wouldn't you think? I found this on the edge in the mud." He rolled up one sleeve. There was a bracelet on his arm. He pulled it off and handed it to me. It was gold, wide and heavy. I turned it and saw a design, repeated four times: a bowhorn with another animal attacking it, digging in with its claws and biting. What was it? The body was sleek like the body of a panther. The head was long and narrow with huge ears, and the tail ended in a tuft. "Nia?"

She came over.

"What is this?"

She took the bracelet. "Hu! This is good! One of my people made it. No one else can do work of this quality."

"What is the animal? The one on top?"

"A killer-of-the-plain." She tilted the bracelet so the design was more visible. "A killer-of-the-mountains is smaller and has scales as well as fur. I wonder how this got here? Where did you find it?"

"Derek found it in the valley, by the lake."

"Then it is an offering. A gift to the demons of fire. You should not have taken it." She handed the bracelet to Derek.

"Oh, no?" He put the bracelet on.

"I see you are going to keep the thing." Nia made the gesture that meant "so be it." "I think you are making a mistake." She turned and walked away.

Derek grinned, then rolled his sleeve down and fastened it.

"There are times when I think you are crazy," I said.

"No. Only badly alienated. Anyway, I don't believe in demons of fire." He glanced at the valley. "It's a good thing I don't. My own protection is too far away. The Grey Whale can't help me here."

The trail turned south, leaving the rim of the valley. Once again we traveled among hills. The day was overcast, and the sun was a bright white disk. In the diffuse light there were no shadows. I was pretty certain that we were traveling west, but I would not have bet on it. I thought—as well—that we were climbing, but I would not have bet on that, either. The trail wound up and down.

Gradually the slopes of the hills grew gentler. The valleys grew wider and more shallow. The bushes and trees—those few there had been—were gone.

"Nuh," said Nia, sounding satisfied. "We are coming to the plain."

We entered a new valley. A stream ran through the middle of it, and a flock of animals fed along the bank. They were bipeds, a new species, larger and heavier than any I had seen before. Only two were standing on their hind legs. Lookouts maybe. The rest had their front legs on the ground and their heads down, feeding.

Derek said, "They must be more efficient than our dinosaurs. They have competition from mammalian browsers. Or do I mean mammaloid? I don't understand how they manage to survive."

"There are—or were—a lot of odd birds on Earth. Ostriches. Emus. Cassowaries. How about the moa and the great auk? They survived into the age of mammals. In fact, I think they evolved in the age of mammals."

He shook his head. "They evolved from ordinary birds to fill specific ecological niches—on islands, in at least two cases. The moa lived in New Zealand. The great auk nested in Iceland. These creatures are all over. They are obviously competing successfully. And I don't think their ancestors were birds. They look reptilian, if that word has any meaning here."

"They have feathers, and I'm willing to bet they're warm-blooded."

"So were the dinosaurs. Warm-blooded, I mean."

One of the upright animals let out a bellow. The others reared onto their hind legs and moved away up the valley along the stream. They had a funny gait, a lumbering run. As awkward as it seemed, they covered a lot of ground. By the time we reached the bottom of the valley they were gone.

Midway through the afternoon I looked around and realized the hills had ended. We were on a rolling plain, covered with pseudo-grass. It rippled in the wind, changing color as the leaves turned over: green, blue-green, tan, and grey.

Something rose above the horizon in the north. I shaded my eyes and stared. The thing was almost the same color as the sky and so distant that it was barely visible. A cone, wide at the base. The top of the cone—the point—was missing. Instead there was a horizontal line. The rim of a crater.

I turned and waited for Nia, who was riding some distance behind me. The oracle was behind her, also riding. "What is that?" I asked. I pointed.

She glanced, then reined her animal.

"I have not seen it before. But I have heard. That is Hani Akhar. The Great Mountain. The home of the Mistress of the Forge."

The oracle came up beside us. He looked north. "Yes. That is the one. I can feel it even at this distance. It is a very holy place.

Also dangerous. She is not always friendly, that spirit."

"This is definitely the wrong trail," Nia said. "We are way north of where I want to be."

"We will end up in the right place," the oracle said. "The route we take doesn't matter."

Nia scratched her nose. "There is no way to argue with a holy person. They are always certain they know more than we do. And if we say, 'No,' they say, 'The spirits have spoken.'"

I moved on ahead. I didn't like to be on the ground near the bowhorns. They were too big, and Nia's mount was sometimes restless and even nasty. I certainly did not want to follow the animals. It was a hassle to have to keep watching for dung.

That evening we camped by a little marshy lake. Derek and Nia went hunting. They came back at nightfall, empty-handed. We ate stale bread and drank water from the lake. It had a funny flavor.

"Swamp water," said Derek. "I've drunk worse in California."

"In the desert?" I asked.

"Mostly. But also in Berkeley. A couple of the people in my department had really lousy taste in wine. And they were important people. I had to go to their parties."

"What are you talking about?" asked Nia.

"A drink like *bara,*" I said.

"Is it nasty-tasting?"

"Sometimes," Derek said.

He wandered off, taking his radio. I stayed with the two natives by the fire.

The big moon was up and more than half-full. I looked at it, trying to see evidence of a volcanic eruption, but the clouds veiled it and blurred its edges.

I looked at the natives. "Does anything unusual ever happen to the big moon?"

"What do you mean?" asked Nia.

I thought for a moment, trying to figure out how to describe something I had not seen. "Do bright spots ever appear on it? Do things ever appear on the rim, like a wisp of steam rising or like a tongue of flame licking out?"

Nia made the gesture of affirmation. "But that isn't unusual."

"What does it mean?" I asked.

"Nothing that I know of." She frowned, thinking. "There are people in the west who have found a way to look at the sun without harming their eyes. According to them the sun is not flawless and untarnished the way we think it is. They say it is spotted. The spots are black. They crawl around like bugs. When the spots appear—a lot of them—it means the weather is going to get bad."

"I've never heard that story," said the oracle. "But I know what it means when a spot appears on the moon."

I made the gesture of inquiry.

"It means the Mother of Mothers has not been watching her pot."

"What?" I asked.

"The old women say the big moon is a cooking pot. It belongs to the Mother of Mothers. Sometimes she forgets to watch it, and it boils over. Then we see what you have described. The old women say it means the winter will be hungry." He paused. "My mother says the old women are wrong. She has kept a moon string for many years. Every time something happens up there, she ties a knot. And she has other strings that she uses to keep track of the weather. Rain. Snow. A big wind. Drought. She has a string for every kind of weather. There is no connection between what happens on the moon and what happens on the plain. That is her opinion. I think she is right."

"Huh," said Nia. "I have never heard the story about the moon. If it isn't true, I won't repeat it."

"The part about the cooking pot is most likely true," the oracle said. "My mother said nothing about that. Not everything that happens in the world of the spirits has an effect on our world here."

Nia made the gesture of agreement.

Derek came back. I glanced at him. "Did you get through to Eddie?"

"Yes. Why shouldn't I?"

"There was static last night, and I've been talking to computers the past couple of days."

"Eddie didn't mention anything about static." He sat down, folding himself neatly. "Or about computers. But he has been spending time in one of the big holovision rooms. The moon *is* erupting. And the eruption is big. We are missing one heck of a sight."

"What are you talking about?" asked Nia.

"The moon," I said. "It is boiling over."

She looked at the sky. "It's too bad the sky is cloudy."

The next day Nia said she wanted to walk.

"I am feeling restless again. If my ankle begins to bother me, I'll ask you to dismount."

"All right," I said.

The oracle, as always, rode. Now and then we passed little marshes or half-dry lakes. The sky was hazy. Hani Akhar remained just barely visible.

Late in the afternoon we reached the top of a rise. Below us was a lake. It was much larger than the others we had seen, irregular in shape and full of tiny islands. The edges were marshy. Monster grass grew in bunches on the shore.

Nia said, "I know this place, though I haven't been to it before. This is the Lake of Bugs and Stones. We are in the land of the Amber People. They come here in the fall on their way south. They fish and hunt for birds, and they perform ceremonies in honor of the mountain."

The oracle made the gesture of agreement. "Another holy place."

We descended. The sky was clear in the west. The sun was low. The water glittered, and I could barely see. We passed a grove of monster grass. The lake was only a few meters away. Reeds moved in the wind. The water flashed. Something bellowed. It was right in front of me, crashing out of the reeds, rearing up. My God! It was three meters tall! The mouth was open. The forearms reached toward me, claws spread. Another bellow! The animal I rode jerked its head. The reins whipped through my hands. The bowhorn bucked, and I kicked free of the stirrups. A moment later I slammed against the ground. The jolt went through me. I yelled. Then I was standing upright.

"Back off," said Derek. "Slowly. Don't frighten it."

I took a step back. Derek was next to me. I couldn't see Nia or the oracle or my bowhorn. The pseudo-dinosaur bellowed again. But it didn't move. Now, for the first time, I saw it clearly. Three meters tall. Hell! It was more like four. It had a bright pink belly and a crest of yellow feathers. Its arms and shoulders were dark blue-grey.

I took another step. The creature hissed. The open mouth was full of teeth. Blunt teeth. It was an herbivore. But the claws were long and sharp. For digging? Did it fight? The head tilted. A tiny bright eye stared at me.

"Keep moving," Derek said. His voice was low and even. "One step at a time."

I saw Nia on the other side of me, a knife in her hand. A useless weapon against this monster. It made another sound. A moan. What did that mean?

Something was moving behind it, coming up from the lake. Another monster. I blinked, trying to see against the sun. It was smaller than the beast confronting us and went on four feet. Its back was grey.

"The female," Derek said.

It turned its head and bit off a reed. Then it went on, chewing, making a loud crunching sound. Pieces of reed hung from its mouth. Three other animals came after it. These were small, about the size of a St. Bernard. Two were quadrupeds. They waddled after the mother. The third hopped awkwardly.

"Well, what do you know?" said Derek.

We kept moving back, away from the angry male. Where was the oracle? I couldn't see him.

Mother waddled on. The children followed. At last they were out of sight, hidden by a grove of monster grass. The male hissed, then turned and bounded after his family. My shoulder began to hurt. My knees gave out. I sat down.

"Very interesting," said Derek. "They care for their young. That helps explain how they are able to survive in competition with the pseudo-mammals. The mammaloids. We need a whole new vocabulary. O Holy Unity! I thought I was going to piss in my pants."

Nia said, "Hu!" She put her knife away. "I hope the crazy man is all right. His bowhorn took off. The last I saw of it he was still holding on."

"Oh, my God, Derek. Our equipment. The radios."

He laughed. "On the bowhorns. Out there." He waved at the plain. "Are you all right?"

"My shoulder hurts like hell, and I bit my tongue. I don't know when."

He checked me over. "Your shoulder isn't dislocated. Your tongue is still there. I think you'll be okay." He turned and stared at the plain. "I'm going after our equipment. I used to chase horses back in California. Bowhorns aren't any faster. I'll catch up with them." He glanced at me. "You make camp around here somewhere. I'll find you."

"Derek—" I began.

He loped away.

"Derek!" I shouted.

He didn't look back.

"He is very strange," said Nia.

"Yes." I watched till he was out of sight, then I glanced at Nia. "Well, let's go find a place to camp."

INAHOOLI

We followed the trail along the shore until we came to a grove of monster grass. Nia cut branches and wove them into baskets: traps for fish. "This may not work. It is easier to catch fish in a river." She put the traps in the water.

After that we explored the grove. Nia found a patch of plants growing at the eastern edge. Their roots were edible. I gathered firewood. We baked the roots. They were crunchy and almost flavorless.

"They are good in a stew with meat," said Nia. "Alone . . . " She made the gesture that meant "the rest is obvious."

"Better than nothing."

She made the gesture of agreement.

Night came. The wind shifted, blowing off the lake. All at once the grove was full of bugs.

"Biters!" said Nia.

I slapped my neck. "You're right."

We crouched by the fire. The smoke protected us to some extent. I got bit a second time, on the wrist. Nia got bit once, on the palm of her hand, where she had no fur.

"Hu!" She clapped her hands together. "Well, I got the creature. It will not bother another person. How can you bear it, Li-sa? You have no fur. They can bite you anywhere."

Smoke had gotten into my eyes and they were watering. The places where the bugs got me were itching. "I am not fond of situations like this." I scratched one of the bites. "But what can I do about it? I can't grow fur. And anyway, I've been through a lot worse. I used to live in Minnesota."

"Where?" said Nia.

"A land with many lakes and many bugs." I paused and listened. The bugs hummed around my ears. There were a lot of them. They ought to be biting more. Maybe I didn't smell right. Maybe it was only the brave bugs—or the stupid ones—that decided to give me a try.

"Aiya!" Nia hit her forehead. "Another one!"

I waved the smoke out of my face. "They can bite through your fur?"

"Only in a few places, where it is thin. Around the eyes or in the crook of the elbow."

The wind shifted again and blew the bugs away. We lay down. We had nothing to cover us. Nia's cloak was with the rest of our baggage out on the plain. So was my poncho. But the night was mild, and I was exhausted. I curled up and went straight to sleep.

I woke early. The clouds were gone, and the sky above me was brilliant blue-green. Birds made noises in the foliage. Nia snored by the ashes of the fire.

I got up, groaning. My entire body was stiff, and my shoulder felt especially bad. I rubbed it, looking around. There was no wind. The lake was still. Out on the open water beyond the reeds a canoe glided.

"Nia!"

She scrambled to her feet. I pointed. She yelled and waved her arms. The canoe turned in. A moment later it was gone—out of sight among the reeds. We hurried to the shore.

"Who can it be?" I asked.

"I don't know. A woman. One of the Amber People."

The prow pushed through the reeds. A dugout, roughly made. It slid toward us. The woman in the back lifted her paddle from the water, then raised a hand and shaded her eyes. "Am I seeing things? Is one of you hairless?"

"Yes," I said.

The canoe hit shore. The woman climbed out. She was taller than I was and lanky with dark brown fur. Her face was wide and flat. Her eyes were dark orange, almost red. She wore a pale yellow tunic decorated with bands of embroidery. The pattern was intricate and geometric, done in various shades of blue. Her belt was blue, and she had a long knife in a sheath of blue leather. "Were you born like that?" she asked. "Or have you been ill?"

"This is the natural way for me to be." I used the word that meant "usual" or "proper."

She looked me up and down. "Natural, eh? And you?" She turned to Nia. "Who are you? And why do you travel with a freak?"

"I am a woman of the Iron People. Nia the smith."

The new woman frowned. "There is something familiar about that name."

"It's common enough," said Nia.

The woman kept frowning.

Nia went on. "What is your name?"

"Toohala Inahooli. I belong to the Amber People and to the Clan of the Ropemaker. Right now, I have a position of high prestige. I am the guardian of the clan tower."

Nia made the gesture of acknowledgment.

I said, "What is a clan tower?"

She glared at me. "Where do you come from? Don't you know—among the Amber People every clan builds a tower in honor of its First Ancestor? We make each tower as tall as possible. We cover it with decorations and perform ceremonies in front of it in order to impress the other clans and make them feel envious and small."

A new kind of artifact! I thought for a moment. "Can I see the tower?"

"Yes. Of course. What use is a clan tower if people aren't impressed by it? And how can people be impressed unless they come and see? But I warn you—our magic is powerful. If there is anything demonic about you, you will come to harm."

"No. I'm not demonic."

"We can't go," Nia said. "Deragu—" She paused. "I cannot say the name."

"Derek," I said.

"Derag told us to wait."

The woman frowned. "Who is this person? The name sounds male to me."

"The person is a woman," Nia said. "She comes from the same place as Li-sa. They speak a language that is nothing like the languages on the plain. The endings are different."

Inahooli made the gesture that meant she understood what was being said.

Nia went on. "Our bowhorns ran away. She—this person Derag—has gone after them."

Inahooli repeated the gesture of comprehension.

"You stay here," I said. "If Derek comes, tell her where I am. She'll understand."

Nia made the gesture that meant "no."

"Why not?"

Nia scratched the back of her neck. Maybe she had gotten bitten there, though—as I remembered—the fur was pretty thick.

"Listen," Inahooli said. "I will go away. You two can argue. Maybe that one"—she pointed at Nia—"has something bad to say about me." She walked down the shore.

"Okay," I said. "What is the problem? Do you think the woman is dangerous?"

"No. But I think she has heard about me. When my people found out about me and Enshi, it made a big noise. The Amber People could have heard the noise. They trade with us."

"I want to see the tower. Have you heard about things like that?"

"Yes. The Amber People aren't like my folk. We are related to the People of Fur and Tin. We know that. We call them 'kinswoman.' And I think we may be related to the Copper Folk. Their language is not hard to learn. But the Amber People . . . Their language is difficult and their customs are peculiar. They boast a lot. Every clan tries to outdo the others in building towers and dancing. I don't understand it."

"I'm going," I said. "I ought to be back this evening."

Nia made the gesture that meant "so be it." "Don't tell her that we are traveling with men. I don't think she would understand."

"Okay." I waved at Inahooli. She came back. "I'm going with you."

"Good. This will be a remarkable event. No guardian has ever shown our tower to a person without hair."

We pushed the canoe out from shore and climbed in. Inahooli began to paddle. In a minute or so Nia was gone, hidden by the plants that I called reeds. They swayed above us, tall and dull blue-grey. Most of the stalks ended in a cluster of leaves, but here and there I saw a round, dark, shaggy head. The flower of the plant? I didn't know.

We slid out into open water. Ahead of us were islands. They were small, only a few meters across, and made of a soft volcanic stone that had weathered into very odd shapes. One looked like a mushroom. Another—tall and narrow—reminded me of a human woman in a robe. A third island was an arch. A fourth was a miniature cathedral. Late Gothic, I decided. The cathedral had a lot of spires.

We glided among the islands. I looked down. The water was clear. A fish flashed into sight, then turned sideways and vanished. What a planet! All at once I felt horrified at the idea of going home.

Stop it, I told myself. Don't think about Earth. Concentrate on the present. Enjoy what you have now.

I looked ahead. There was another island in sight: long and low, surrounded by reeds. At one end was a construction, twenty meters tall, I estimated, made of rough latticework. Banners hung from it, limp at present. As we drew nearer I saw other kinds of decoration: bunches of feathers and long strings of shells.

"The tower of the Ropemaker," Inahooli said.

We rounded the island. On the far side was a beach. We landed and pulled the canoe up on the gravel. Inahooli led me toward the tower. The island was rocky and mostly bare with scattered patches of vegetation: orange pseudo-mosses and brown pseudo-lichens and a leafy grey plant that came up to the middle of my calf. There were only two objects of any size: the tower and a tent of dark brown fabric.

"That is my home," said Inahooli. "Every spring we come here. The clan rebuilds the tower and performs ceremonies to make it holy. Then we throw dice, and one of us is picked to be the guardian. All summer that woman stays by the tower. She watches it and makes certain that nothing happens to it. In the fall the tribe comes back. The clan invites everyone to a big dance. We eat. We make music. We brag about our ancestors. If everything goes well, the other clans are embarrassed. After that we all go south to the Winter Land. The Groundbird Clan give their dance there. Usually they do badly. For some reason they have never been good at bragging. And anyway, what do they have to brag about? Their ancestor is a miserable groundbird who did only one thing of importance."

"What?"

"She stole fire from the Spirit of the Sky and gave it to the people of the world. That is all well and good. We feel grateful in the middle of winter, when the snow is deep and the wind blows and so on. But our ancestor saved all living things."

"Oh, yes?"

We reached the tent. The tower was only ten meters away. Close to the bottom there was a row of masks hanging on the latticework. They were oval with round eyeholes. Each one was painted a solid color: red, yellow, black, white.

I pointed. "Who do they represent?"

"The black one is the Ropemaker. Yellow is the Trickster. Red is the Mistress of the Forge. And white is the Old Woman in the North."

"Tell me about them."

She looked me up and down. It was a calculating look, the look of a storyteller who has gotten an opening. "All right. But I can't use the masks. They have to stay where they are until the big dance. Sit down. I will make the story plain and as short as possible."

I sat down in front of the tent. Inahooli sat down facing me. Overhead a bird whistled, soaring over the lake.

"This is the story of the ivory comb," she told me in a loud voice.

"In the far north there is an old woman. Her tent is in the sky. The walls of the tent are made of light, hanging in folds from the tent poles, which are made from the bones of the original world-monster. How they got in the sky is another story, which I don't have time to tell. The old woman has a comb, which is made from one of the monster's teeth. It is ivory, as white as snow. She uses it to comb her fur. When she does this, she pulls creatures out. They fall to the floor and vanish, going through the floor into the world. All the animals in the world come into existence this way.

"When the old woman combs the left side of her body, the animals that come out are good and useful: the bowhorns we herd, the birds we hunt and eat. When she combs the right side of her body, the animals that come out are harmful: lizards with venomous bites and bugs that sting. The people of the world sing to the old woman, praising her and asking her for help. This is one of the songs:

"Grandmother, be generous.
Comb the left side of your body.
Then we will be prosperous.
Then we will be happy.
Our children will be fat
In our tents by the fire.

"Grandmother, be compassionate.
Don't comb the right side of your body.
Leave the lizards where they are.
Don't send us
the bugs that bite and sting.

"In the far south there is a young man. He is tall and handsome. His eyes are as yellow as fire. No one is certain who his mother is. Some people say it is the great spirit, the Mother of Mothers. Other people say it is a demon of fire.

"The young man is called the Trickster. He is the one who comes to men in the winter, when they guard the herd. Each man sits alone under a tent that is made by stretching a cloak over the branches of a bush or tree. Snow comes down on him. The fire in front of him is low. The man sits and shivers, holding his arms close to his body. Then the Trickster comes. His voice is like the wind. He says, 'Why are you doing this? Why do you suffer for the ungrateful women of the village? Forget your mother. Forget your sisters. Forget the sons and daughters you may have. Go off into the hills and live like an animal without obligations, pleasing yourself alone.'

"Most men ignore the voice. But some listen. They go crazy and leave the herd, wandering into the hills. No one sees them after that.

"The Trickster is the same one who goes to meet women in the spring, when it is mating time. He looks like the best kind of man, large and strong and self-confident. He establishes his territory close to the village. No other man dares to confront him. When the women come out full of lust, they meet him. Some of them meet him, anyway. Each woman who mates with him thinks, What an excellent father! My child will be hardy and resourceful. Good-looking, too.

"But the mating produces no children. Or if children are born, they are sickly and bad-tempered. They cause nothing but trouble.

"This is usually so. But the Trickster is never reliable, even in the evil he does. Once in a while a woman mates with him, and the child who comes out is like her father, large and strong and self-confident: a true heroine.

"One of these was my ancestor, the Ropemaker. But first I must tell how the Trickster stole the ivory comb.

"He was in the far north, cold and hungry. There was nothing around except the wide plain covered with snow. After a while he came to the tent of the old woman. It shone above him, white and yellow and green. He took off his snowshoes and stuck them in a bank of snow. Then he climbed up into the sky. He entered the tent. The old woman was there, sitting in the middle of the floor. Her fur was grey with age. She was combing it with the ivory comb.

"The Trickster sat down. He watched greedily. The old woman was pulling the comb through the fur on her left forearm. Out came animals. They were little and dark. The old woman shook her comb. The animals tumbled down. When they reached the floor, they vanished. They were going into the world, into the deep burrows of the builders-of-mounds.

"'Grandmother,' the Trickster said. 'Give me some of your animals. I am hungry, and they look delicious.'

"The old woman stared at him. 'I know who you are. The Trickster, the One Who Tells Lies.' She gave the comb a shake, then she caught one of the animals in midair. It sat up on her hand. Its tiny nose twitched. Its whiskers quivered. It looked at the Trickster with bright dark eyes. 'These animals are part of me. I give them to people who treat them with respect. But you—O Evil One—you misuse everything you get hold of. There is no respect in you. I will give you nothing.' She turned her hand over. The animal fell to the floor. It was gone.

"The Trickster ground his teeth. 'Grandmother, have pity.'

"'No,' the old woman said. 'You can starve for all I care. And let it be a lesson to you.' She turned around so her back was to the Trickster.

"He leaped up. 'You will regret this, your old biddy!' He ran from the tent. He climbed down out of the sky and sat next to his snowshoes in a heap of snow. There he waited till the old woman went to sleep. The sound of her snoring filled the plain. The Trickster climbed back up. He crept into the tent. The walls shone as brightly as ever, and the tent was full of a pale flickering light. He saw the old woman stretched out on her back. Next to her was the ivory comb. He picked it up.

"'But where am I going to hide?' he asked himself. 'When the spirits hear that this is gone, they will search the whole world. What place is safe?'

"Then he had an idea. He made himself small—and the comb as well—and crawled into the old woman's vagina. She groaned and scratched herself, but she did not wake.

"'This is not the most pleasant place that I have ever been,' the Trickster said. 'I'd like more light and a bit less moisture. But no one will think of looking here.'

"The old woman woke and reached for her comb. It wasn't there. She let out a scream. All over the world the spirits leaped up. 'What is it?' they cried. 'What is going on?'

"Then the search began. Up and down, back and forth, in and out. The spirits searched everywhere. But they didn't find the comb.

"'What will I do?' the old woman said. 'The comb is irreplaceable. There is none like it, and without it I cannot comb my fur.'

"The spirits had no answer.

"Spring came. Vegetation appeared. The hills and the plain turned blue. The people of the world noticed that something was wrong. In every village they went to the shamaness.

"'What is going on?' they asked. 'Fish thrash in the river as they do every year. But no one has seen any fingerlings. The birds build nests as usual. The nests are empty. As for the little animals, the builders-of-mounds, they puff up the sacks in their necks. They scream and moan and carry on. But they produce no young.'

"The shamanesses ate narcotic plants. They danced and had visions. They said, 'The Trickster has stolen the ivory comb. Without it no more animals will come into existence. We will all starve because of that malevolent person.'

"All the people cried out. They beat their chests and thighs. They prayed to the spirits. But what could the spirits do?

"Now the story turns to the Ropemaker. She was a woman of the Amber People. She was large with glossy fur. Her eyes were as yellow as fire. Her arms were strong, and her fingers were nimble. Most people believed she was a child of the Trickster. She had the look.

"Her craft was making rope out of leather. She was very skillful at this. Her ropes were narrow and flexible. They did not stretch. They were hard to break, and they lasted for years.

"In any case, the time for mating came. The women of the Amber People felt the spring lust grow in them. But this year they were unwilling to go out onto the plain. 'What is the point of leaving the village?' they said. 'Why should we bother to go and find a man? The children we conceive will die of starvation.'

"But the lust grew stronger. Each woman packed the gifts she had made during the winter. Each woman saddled a bowhorn and rode out onto the plain. The Ropemaker was among them. In her saddlebag was a fine long rope. It was her mating gift.

"Now the story turns back to the Trickster. By this time he was getting restless. There was nothing to do in the old woman's vagina. He knew it was spring. He wanted to go out into the world and play a mean trick on someone. He waited till the old woman was asleep and crept out. He left the comb behind. Off he went toward the south. After a while he came to the land of the Amber People. He found a territory close to the village. There was a man there already: a big man with many scars. The Trickster went up to him and said, 'You'd better leave.'

"'Are you crazy?' the big man said. 'I got here first. And anyway, I'm bigger than you.'

"The Trickster stretched himself till he was taller than the big man. He glared down. His yellow eyes shone like fire.

"'Well,' said the big man. 'If you put it that way.' He mounted his bowhorn and rode off.

"The Trickster shouted insults at his back. The big man did not turn.

"After that the Trickster settled down and waited. A day passed and then another. On the third day a woman rode into sight. It was the Ropemaker. The Trickster felt satisfied. This was an impressive woman. This was a person worth misleading.

"As for the Ropemaker, she liked what she saw: a big wide man. He was standing on the plain with his feet apart and his shoulders back. His fur was thick and glossy. He wore a fine tunic, covered with embroidery. On his arms were silver bracelets. They were wide and bright.

"When she got close, she noticed that he had a peculiar aroma. 'Well, no one is perfect,' she told herself.

"When she reached the man, she dismounted. They lay on the ground and mated. Afterward she said, 'I have some bad news.'

"'Oh, yes?' said the Trickster.

"'The Old Woman of the North has lost her comb. Because of this, she cannot comb her fur, and no more animals will come into the world.'

"'So what?'

"'If we have a child, it will die of starvation.'

"'So what? It's no concern of mine. As long as I am able to mate, I'm satisfied. Who cares what comes of the thing we do together?'

"'I care. And anyway, if this situation continues, we'll all die. For how can we live without the bowhorns and the birds in the air and the fish in the rivers?'

"'If you want to die, then go ahead and do it. I'm not worried. I intend to go on living, no matter what happens to the rest of the world.' The Trickster rolled over and went to sleep.

"The Ropemaker looked at him. His fur shone like copper, and there was a glow around his body. This was no ordinary man, she realized. It was a spirit. A nasty spirit. The Trickster.

"She got her rope and tied him up. Then she waited. He woke and tried to stretch. He could not. 'What is this?' he cried.

"'You are caught,' said the Ropemaker. 'And I will not let you go until you give me the ivory comb.'

"The Trickster ground his teeth. He thrashed and rolled. One heel struck the land and made a hole. Water rushed up and made a lake. The lake is still there. It is wide and shallow and full of stones and reeds. It is called the Trickster's Lake or the Lake of Bugs and Stones.

"The rope did not break. The Trickster continued to struggle. He rolled away from the Ropemaker. He beat on the earth with his bound hands. He made another hole, deeper than the first.

Hot mud rushed up. It seethed around the Trickster. He was boiling like a bird in a pot. His magic was powerful. He took no harm. The rope, however, could not survive the heat and moisture. It began to stretch. The Trickster pulled free. He jumped up. He shouted:

"'I am the Trickster,
oh, you foolish woman!
I cannot be held.
I know no obligation.

"'I am the Trickster,
oh, you foolish woman!
No one can hold me.
No one can make me stop.'

"After that he ran off across the plain. He went north, back to his hiding place. The Ropemaker watched him go. She bit her lip and clenched her hands. 'He is a great spirit, and he may be a relative of mine. But I won't let him get away with this.'

"She mounted her bowhorn and rode north. For a long time she traveled, and she had many adventures. But I don't have the time to tell you about them.

"At last she came to the place where the old woman lived. It was midsummer. The plain was yellow. The rivers were low. The Ropemaker dismounted. She tethered her animal. Then she climbed into the sky.

"'Grandmother,' she called. 'Will you let me in? I have come a long way in order to see you.'

"'Come in,' the old woman said. 'But I can't help you. I have lost my comb. I have nothing to give.'

"The Ropemaker entered the tent. The old woman was there, sitting in the middle of the floor. She was naked and scratching her belly with both hands. 'I am going crazy,' she said. 'My fur is full of animals, and I can't get them out. I can feel them crawling in the folds of my belly. I can feel them in my armpits. I can feel them on my back. Granddaughter, I beg you. Be kind to me! Scratch me between the shoulder blades.'

"The Ropemaker scratched her back. The old woman kept on complaining. 'I can even feel them in my vagina, though I have no fur there. They stir from time to time and tickle me. Oh! This is terrible!'

"The Ropemaker frowned. She remembered the way the Trickster had smelled. All at once she knew his hiding place. 'But how will I get him out?' she asked herself. 'And how will I catch him and hold him, once he is out?'

"She decided to go to sleep. She lay down and closed her eyes. The old woman sat next to her, scratching. Soon the Ropemaker began to dream. Three spirits came to her. One was a woman of middle age with a big belly and noticeable breasts. She wore a long robe, covered with embroidery.

"The next spirit was a man. His fur was blue-green, and he had wings instead of arms. He wore a kilt the same color as his fur. His belt buckle was round and made of gold. It glittered brilliantly.

"The third spirit was a young woman. She was large and muscular. She carried a hammer, and she wore a leather apron. Her eyes were orange-red.

"The Ropemaker knew them. The first was the Mother of Mothers. The second was the Spirit of the Sky. And the third was the Mistress of the Forge, who lives in Hani Akhar, the great volcano.

"'O holy ones,' the Ropemaker said. 'Help me out! I know where the Trickster is. But I need a way to get him out of his hiding place. And once he is out, he will try to run away. I need a way to catch him.'

"The Spirit of the Sky spoke first. 'I will keep watch. If he tries to run away, I will see where he goes. He won't be able to find a new hiding place.'

"The Mistress of the Forge spoke next. 'I will make a rope out of iron, forged with magic so it will never break. It will be self-fastening and able to move. The Trickster won't escape from it.'

"The Mother of Mothers spoke last. 'I know how to get the Trickster out of his hiding place.' She leaned forward and whispered into the Ropemaker's ear.

"In the morning the Ropemaker woke. There was a rope lying next to her in a coil. It was dull grey in color, and it had a peculiar texture like the scales of a lizard. The Ropemaker took a close look at it. It was made of many tiny links of iron fastened together.

"'Good morning, grandmother,' she said to the Old Woman of the North. 'I've had an idea. You said that your vagina tickled, even though it has no fur.'

"The old woman made the gesture of agreement.

"'I don't think there's an animal in there. I think you need sex.'

"'You're crazy!' the old woman cried. 'It's the wrong time of year. And anyway, I'm too old to feel lust.'

"'Remember,' the Ropemaker said. 'A woman doesn't grow old easily. The feeling of lust doesn't vanish all at once. Often a woman becomes irritable and uncertain. Her behavior changes from day to day. She feels lust at the wrong time. At the right time, in the spring, she feels nothing at all. She cannot understand what is going on—any more than a young girl can when she becomes a woman. I think this is what has happened to you.'

"'No!' cried the old woman.

"'In any case, try sex. I will go and find a young man for you. If I'm right, and you are feeling lust—a bit late, I will admit—then the young man will respond to you. And maybe you will feel better afterward.'

"The Ropemaker got up and left the tent. She took the iron rope with her.

"The Trickster heard all this. He became uneasy. 'If that crazy woman can find a man willing to mate with this old biddy—well, my position will not be comfortable. I am likely to take a terrible beating. I'd better get out of here.'

"He waited till it was night, and the old woman was snoring. Then he crept out. The comb was in his hand. He stole to the door. Out he stepped. The Ropemaker was waiting there. The Great Moon was up. It lit the sky and the plain. It lit the man as he came through the doorway.

"'This is it, you nasty spirit!' the woman cried. She threw the iron rope.

"It twisted in midair. It wrapped itself around him. He stumbled and fell. The comb flew out of his hand. The Ropemaker caught it. As for the Trickster, he fell out of the sky and landed on the plain. He rolled back and forth. He yelled. He struggled. But the rope would not break. After a while he gave up. He lay still, breathing heavily.

"Three spirits appeared around him. He looked up at them. 'I can tell that you are responsible for this.'

"'Yes,' said the Mother of Mothers. 'This is the end of all your malevolent tricks. We are going to take you far from here and drop you in the ocean. You'll cause no further trouble.'

"'Don't be sure,' the Trickster said.

"They picked him up and carried him through the air. In the middle of the ocean they let go of him. He splashed into the water. Down and down he sank. At last he hit the bottom. Aiya! It was dark and cold! Deep-sea fish nibbled on his toes. He twisted and tried to yell. Instead he swallowed water. But he could not drown. His life was everlasting. He stayed there for more years than we can count. He gave his nature to the ocean. It became changeable and unreliable, impossible to trust. In the end he broke free. But that is another story.

"As for the Ropemaker, she went back into the tent. She woke the old woman and gave her the comb.

"'Oh! This is wonderful!' the old woman cried. She began to comb her fur. Animals came out, hundreds of them. They tumbled out of the sky and filled the world. All the people rejoiced."

Inahooli stopped talking. I unfolded my legs and stood. By this time it was noon. Sunlight poured down. The air was still and hot. I was sweating.

"Well," said Inahooli. "Are you impressed? Do you think my ancestor is great?"

"Yes." I turned and looked at the tower. A trickster god like Anansi the Spider and Coyote and B'rer Rabbit. There were other odd similarities. The Old Woman in the North reminded me of a character out of Inuit mythology. Was there such a thing as a universal archetype? Would we find the same characters on planet after planet? I imagined a collective unconscious that extended across—or maybe under—the galaxy. What an idea! But I was moving too fast. I didn't have the data. I stretched. "I have to go."

"No! Don't leave. I have other stories."

I made the gesture of polite refusal, followed by the gesture of extreme regret. "Nia is waiting."

She stood up, frowning. "There is something about that name . . . " Her eyes widened. "I remember! Nia the smith. The woman who loved a man." She used the word that meant familial affection, the love between sisters or between a mother and her daughters. "They told us about her, the Iron Folk. They said the man died. But she was still out on the plain. A big woman with the look of bad luck. They warned us about her. They said, 'If she comes to your village, let her stay only as long as is decent. Then tell her to move on. If you let her move in, she'll sour the milk in your pots. She'll make your fires go out.'"

"Nia does no harm," I said. I kept my voice low and even. A confident voice. The voice of sanity.

Inahooli was silent, still frowning, obviously thinking. "She hasn't given up her old behavior. When she mentioned your friend she wasn't using an ending from your language. You said the name differently. I heard. I didn't understand. She gave the name an ending from her own language or from the language of gifts. In either case it is a male ending. Your friend is a man."

I opened my mouth. What could I say? I didn't like to lie, and I didn't think Inahooli would believe any lie I told. "I'd better go."

She stared at me, her eyes narrow. "What are you? Why do you travel with a woman like that? And with a man?"

"I told you, I am ordinary. Among my own people, anyway."

She made the gesture of disagreement, moving her hand emphatically. "I have met the Iron People and the Copper People and the People of Fur and Tin. No one is really different. Not about things that are important. I think you are a demon."

How does one reason with a religious fanatic? I thought for a moment. "Remember what you said before I came here. The tower is magical. If I am a demon, why hasn't it harmed me?"

She turned, staring at the latticework. At the top a couple of banners moved languidly. A couple of feathers fluttered. A wind must be rising, though I couldn't feel it.

Inahooli made the gesture of agreement. "I did say that."

"And I am fine."

There was a pause. Then Inahooli spoke. Her voice was slow at first. She was obviously thinking out loud. "You are right. The tower should have harmed you. It hasn't." She turned back toward me. "You have overcome our magic. The tower is something."

I didn't know the word, but I could guess the meaning. The tower was polluted, desanctified. It had lost its power.

"I brought you here," said Inahooli. "I am the guardian. This will destroy my reputation." She pulled out her knife.

"Listen to me," I said.

She grabbed my arm and raised the knife. I twisted and kicked, hitting her in the crotch. It was a good solid kick. She staggered back. I ran.

I made it to the canoe, but she was close behind me. There wasn't time to get the damn thing into the water. I grabbed a paddle and turned to face her. "Can't we talk?"

"No!" She lunged at me. I brought the paddle down on her shoulder. She yelled and dropped the knife.

"Listen to me! I mean no harm!"

She grabbed up the knife with her other hand. "How can we use the tower? The masks are ruined. The magic is gone."

She ducked to the left. My left. I turned and raised the paddle. The knife flashed. I swung. Inahooli jumped back.

"I got you, demon!" she cried.

"What?"

"Don't you see the blood on the ground?"

I glanced down and saw only the rocky beach. No blood. Something moved at the edge of my vision. Inahooli. She was coming at me, her knife raised again. I jerked the paddle up and out. It hit her in the gut. She grunted and bent double. I brought the paddle down on the back of her head.

She fell. I picked up the knife and threw it out into the reeds, then looked back at her. She lay facedown, motionless.

I knelt and felt her neck, then ran my hand over the back of her head. Her pulse was strong and regular. Her head felt rock solid. Good! But I wasn't going to stick around and nurse her. She was too likely to make another attempt to kill me. I pushed the canoe into the water, jumped in, and paddled away from the island. The things I did in order to get a myth!

After I was well out past the reeds, I noticed something was wrong with my left arm. I pulled in the paddle and took a look. My shirt was slit from the elbow to the wrist. Blood dripped onto the dark wood of the canoe and onto my jeans. "Goddammit." I took off the shirt and twisted my arm, trying to see the cut. There was a twinge of pain in my shoulder. Funny. I had forgotten how stiff the shoulder was. The cut was long and shallow. A scratch. Nothing to worry about. It was bleeding well, which ought to reduce the risk of infection. Not that infection was likely, unless from something that I had brought with me. I wrapped my shirt around the arm and tied the sleeves together. Then I went back to paddling.

A wind blew, light and fitful. Waves splashed against the canoe. My arm began to ache. My shoulder also. I concentrated on my breathing: in and out, keeping time with the motion of my arms as I lifted the paddle and brought it forward, drove it into the water and pulled it back.

Ahead of me was the shore. Where could I land? I shaded my eyes. There was a figure on the bank above the reeds. No. Two figures. They waved at me. I turned the canoe and paddled toward them. In a moment they were out of sight. The reeds leaned over me, their shaggy heads swaying, and I had no room to move. I stuck the paddle down, hit bottom, and pushed. The canoe went forward through the vegetation into an area of clear water. Nia and Derek waded out and pulled me to shore.

"Where is Inahooli?" Nia asked.

I stood. The canoe shifted under me. Derek grabbed my arm.

"No!"

He let go. "What is this?" He held out his hand. The palm was red.

"Blood." I stepped onto dry land, sat down, and fainted.

When I came to, I was on my back, looking up at foliage, the long narrow leaves of monster grass. They shone, edged with sunlight.

Derek said, "Can you understand me?"

"Yes. Of course." I turned my head. He sat cross-legged on the ground. His upper body was naked, and I could see the bracelet on his arm. The wide band of gold. It kept going in and out of focus.

"What happened?"

"The woman. Inahooli."

"Nia told me about her. What did she do?"

"She thought I was a demon. I was bad luck for her"—I paused, trying to think of the right word—"artifact. The one she was guarding. She came after me with a knife. I hit her. Derek, she's alive. What if she comes after me?"

He smiled briefly. "I'll worry about that. You rest."

"Okay." I closed my eyes, then opened them. "The bowhorns."

"I found one. The Voice of the Waterfall managed to stay on. I don't know how. He let it run till it was exhausted. He had no choice, he told me. In the end it had to stop. He calmed it and let it rest. Then he turned back. I met him at sundown. We camped on the plain. And in the morning . . . " He made a gesture I didn't recognize.

"What was that?"

"What?"

"The gesture. The wave."

He grinned. "It's a human gesture, Lixia. It means—approximately—'skip it' or 'why bother' or 'you can imagine the rest.'"

"Oh," I said.

"We got here at midmorning, after you left."

"Oh." I closed my eyes, then remembered something else. "The radios."

Derek laughed. "They're on the other bowhorn. The one I didn't find."

"Shit."

"Uh-huh. I thought I ought to make sure the Voice of the Waterfall got back to the lake. Nia will go out tomorrow on the animal we have. She's a better rider than I am, and this is her planet. With any luck she'll find the radios. And I will make sure what's her name—the woman who cut you up."

"Inahooli."

"I'll make sure she doesn't cause any more trouble."

"What does that mean?"

He grinned. "Nothing dramatic. I'll stay here and keep my eyes open. Now, go to sleep."

Derek left. I worried. What if Nia couldn't find the other animal? We'd be alone for the first time. Really alone on an alien planet. It might be days before the people on the ship realized that something was wrong. Then what would they do? How would they find us? I tried to think of signals. A huge fire. That would be best. But could we make one that was big enough? And would they know it was made by us?

I dozed and had bad dreams. Inahooli was after me. I ran down a long corridor between ceramic walls. Then the corridor was gone. I was on a plain. I turned and saw a wall of flame advancing toward me. A grass fire! I ran. But it was so difficult. The grass was tall and thick. I kept tripping. The fire was gaining.

I fell, rolled over, and opened my eyes. Smoke drifted above me. I sat up, terrified.

Oh, yes. The campfire. It burned three meters away. My companions sat around it. Beyond them was the lake and the low sun. It was late afternoon. My arm hurt, my head ached, and my throat was dry. "Is there anything to drink?"

They looked at me.

"Are you all right?" said Nia.

"I'm thirsty."

Nia brought me a green sphere with a hole punched in the top: something like a gourd or maybe a coconut. Where had she found it? I took it and drank. The liquid inside was cool and had a sharp flavor. Like what? A citrus fruit? Not quite. I drank again.

"Can you talk now?" asked Derek. "What was the woman guarding? And why did she decide you were a demon?"

I looked at Nia, who was squatting next to me. "You were right. Your people have talked about you. Inahooli remembered. Nia the smith. The woman who loved a man."

Nia frowned. "There are times I think my people talk too much. Don't they have anything better to do?"

"And she figured out that Derek was a man."

"Because I used the male ending on his name."

"Yes."

She stood up and clenched her hand into a fist, then hit her thigh. "I am just like my relatives. My tongue goes up and down like a banner in the wind, and I do not think." She opened her hand and made the gesture that meant "so be it."

"One of us ought to stay up tonight and keep watch. That woman is probably a little crazy. She has been alone too long, and she has been too close to something that is holy. She may come after Li-sa."

Derek made the gesture of agreement.

"I hit her pretty hard," I said. "For all I know, she is still"—I paused and tried to think of the right word in the language of gifts—"asleep. Or maybe dead."

Derek looked out at the water. "Maybe. I don't intend to go and check. The island is holy. She's made it very clear that she doesn't want us on it. And as a rule, I don't interfere with other people's karma. She chose to invite you to the island, and she chose to try and kill you. If those choices end in her death—well." He paused, then used the same gesture that Nia had used a minute or so before. "That is the way it is," the gesture said.

The oracle leaned forward. "I don't know what you did in the past, Nia, and I don't know why your people tell stories about you. But this situation is not your fault."

"Why not?"

The oracle pointed at Derek. "He went into the valley of demons. He took the bracelet. Now, the demons are angry.

They are causing all this trouble—the *shuwahara* and the angry woman."

Shuwahara? Was that the name of the animal that had frightened our bowhorns?

The oracle stood up. He held out his hand. "Give me the bracelet."

Derek frowned.

"Do it," I said in English. "We're in enough trouble already."

Derek pulled off the bracelet. The oracle took it and slid it onto his arm.

"What are you going to do with it?" I asked.

"The spirit will tell me." The oracle pulled off his tunic. He was naked except for the bracelet and his necklace. His dark fur shone. The jewelry glistened. Taken all in all, he was impressive. He tossed the tunic on the ground. "I am going off by myself. I will dance and sing until I am in a frenzy. Then—maybe—the spirit will come to me." He walked away toward the lake.

"Do you think I'll get it back?" asked Derek.

"No."

"Goddammit." He laughed and shrugged. "Oh, well."

Nia fixed dinner: fresh fish, gutted and stuffed with herbs, then wrapped in leaves and roasted in the coals. It was delicious, but I was too tired to be hungry. I ate half a fish and lay down. The sun had set. Clouds were moving in. They were high and hazy, golden in the last light of day. My companions talked quietly. The birds made little evening noises. I closed my eyes.

When I woke, the sun was up again. Who had guarded the camp? Had Derek remembered? I climbed to my feet, groaning. A body—dark and furry—sprawled by the fire. The oracle. Asleep. There was no sign of Nia or Derek or the bowhorn. I walked through the grove. The animal was definitely gone. Nia must have left as soon as there was any light. I looked out on the plain, shading my eyes against the sun. Nothing. I went back through the grove. The oracle had rolled over on his back. His arm was over his face. He was snoring.

Down to the lake. Birds flapped in the reeds. On the shore were two canoes. I stopped, terrified. I was in no condition to fight Inahooli. Had she done something to Derek? I needed a weapon. A paddle had worked before. I went to the canoes.

Inahooli was in one of them, on her back. She was naked. Her feet were tied with a strip of yellow cloth, and she was gagged with another piece of yellow fabric. Her hands were behind her. I couldn't see how they were tied. She glared at me.

I laughed, relieved. I hadn't killed her. "You must have met Derek."

She grunted.

"I don't think I'll take out the gag. I'd like to know where he is. But I don't suppose you'd tell me, even if you knew."

Inahooli growled and twisted. Was there any chance that she could get free? Of course not. Derek had tied her. I wondered if he would ever make a serious mistake.

"I have to go. I'll be back later."

Inahooli growled a second time.

I found Derek farther along the shore, on a beach of black gravel. There was a break in the reeds. A channel—two or three meters wide—led out into the lake. A bird floated in the channel. It was perfectly ordinary-looking.

"It has teeth," said Derek.

His long hair was wet, and there were patches of dampness on his shirt. He tucked the shirt into his jeans, then grinned at me.

"A morning swim?" I asked.

"Uh-huh." He fastened one of his sleeves. I saw a glint just before he sealed the fabric. He had something metallic on his arm.

"I found Inahooli. What happened?"

"Nia went to sleep, and I went off to watch the oracle. I figured, never pass up a ritual. He did exactly what he said he would do. Danced and sang and waved a branch around, all under a moon that was three-quarters full and clearly erupting. You can see the plume above the rim. It starts in sunlight and then curves over the part of the moon that is still in shadow. A heck of a sight.

"I couldn't understand what he was saying. He wasn't using the language of gifts. But I got it all on my recorder."

"What did he do with the bracelet?"

"Tossed it into the lake. That was the end of the ceremony. He went back to camp. I wandered around and kept my eyes open. I figured he would be tired after all that jumping around. You were injured, and Nia had to get up early. That left me to keep watch, and I wanted to keep looking at the moon." He closed the front of his shirt.

"The woman came two hours later. No. More like three. The moon was still up. She came in the second canoe. I guess that's obvious. I didn't see her land—or hear her. She is a very quiet lady. But she woke up a bird, coming in through the reeds, and it whistled.

"I waited in the shadows. The fire—our fire—was burning. She moved toward it. I knew she would. When she came into the grove, I jumped her." He grinned. "She's strong as well as quiet. But I had the advantage of surprise. After she was unconscious, I dragged her back to the canoe and tied her up. I didn't have any rope. I cut up her tunic and used it. I'm hungry. Let's go back to camp."

We walked along the shore. Derek continued. "Nia left at dawn. I didn't tell her about what's her name. It was something else to worry about, and she looked moody enough. Nia, I mean. I guess she isn't a morning person."

"What are we going to do with Inahooli?"

"Hold her until Nia gets back, then let her go, but only when we're ready to leave. She won't follow us. She has her tower to guard."

"I wonder if we're driving her crazy."

"What?" He stopped and stared at me.

"She struck me as a vulnerable person, though it's hard to judge a person from another culture. Maybe they're all like that: boastful and defensive. In any case, her self-esteem is all tied up with the tower and her position as the guardian. Now she's failed. I'm pretty sure that she thinks the tower is ruined, and I don't think she'll be able to handle failure. I don't think she has the—what?—elasticity of spirit."

Derek made the gesture of doubt. "I think you underestimate that woman. Her technology is primitive—what you call primitive, anyway. But I don't think she's simple. I know Nia isn't. And the oracle is so damn complex, I don't know where I am with him. Most likely this lady—I've forgotten her name again."

"Inahooli."

"Most likely she'd do what I'd do in her place."

"What?" I started walking again.

Derek kept pace. "I'd lie. I'd pretend nothing had happened. When my people came, I'd say, 'Everything is fine.'"

I frowned. Derek glanced at me, then continued, "Every society has standards for proper conduct, and in every society people fail to meet those standards. Reality and human frailty get in the way. Well, you can't abandon the standards, and you can't have everyone in the society going around crying 'Mea culpa.' So you invent hypocrisy. It's present in every society I've ever studied. I'm sure they have it here on this planet."

"Maybe."

We turned away from the shore, walking toward the grove.

"Think of my people," Derek said. "To them two qualities are important. Mellowness and honesty. Well, what do you do when honesty will create an unpleasant situation?"

He paused. I said nothing. "First of all, you try to evade the problem. You eat a little peyote. You concentrate on the cosmic patterns. That's what's important, after all—all that energy, pouring down from the stars and rising up from the ground.

> *"The world is charged with the grandeur of God.*
> *It will flame out, like shining from shook foil;*
> *It gathers to a greatness, like the ooze of oil*
> *Crushed . . .*

"And so on. If you can't escape from the problem, if you are pulled back to the here and now, then you lie. Which is dishonest and hypocritical, but natural and human, and it keeps everything mellow."

We reached the camp. The oracle was up, rebuilding the fire. He glanced at us. "Nia has gone?"

"Yes," said Derek. "And that woman came. Inahooli. She's down by the water. I tied her up."

"Our luck is changing. Nia will find the bowhorn, and everything will come out the way it is supposed to. My spirit has promised me."

Derek made the gesture that meant he had heard what had been said, but was reserving judgment.

Late in the morning we went down to the canoe, all three of us. Inahooli was in the same position as before. Her head was turned, and her eyes closed against the glare of the sun.

I looked at her a moment. "This isn't going to work," I said in English. "Nia could be gone for days. We can't keep the woman like this."

She opened her eyes, frowning and squinting.

"It's uncomfortable. It's humiliating. And it's undemocratic. What right do we have to deprive her of freedom?"

"We have the right to protect ourselves," Derek said.

"Well, maybe. In any case, this isn't practical. How is she going to eat? Or go to the bathroom? We can't let her lie in her own excrement like a character in a novel about the old society."

The oracle bent over Inahooli. He loosened her gag.

"Demon," she said.

"No. I am a holy man. An oracle. I serve the Spirit of the Waterfall, who is large and powerful and able to handle any kind of evil."

An interesting word, that one. I translated it as "evil," an abstract noun. In his language it was an adjective coupled with a noun that meant "thing." The adjective meant "bad," as in a bad taste. It also meant "unlucky" or "peculiar."

"You are a demon," the woman said. "You travel with demons."

"They are not demons. They are people without hair."

"One of them is male. And you are a man."

The oracle made the gesture of agreement.

"Everyone knows that men are solitary by nature and have bad tempers and are unwilling to share anything with other men. But you travel with that one." She nodded toward Derek.

"You must be a demon or a monster."

"You are thinking badly," the oracle said.

Again the same word, the one that meant "bad" or "evil" or "strange." This time the form was adverbial.

The oracle straightened up. "You have been alone too long. It isn't natural for a woman to sit by herself on an island."

"I am the guardian. And that one—the woman—has done harm to my tower."

"How?" asked the Voice of the Waterfall.

"She came to the island. She sat in the shadow of the tower."

"No I didn't. It was noon. There wasn't any shade. Right below the tower, maybe, but not where I was."

"You were on the island. Bad people—people who are unlucky—cannot go to a holy place. Not until they have taken part in a ceremony of purification. But there is no way to purify a demon."

"You said if I was a demon, the tower would harm me. I wasn't harmed. How can I be a demon?"

The woman closed her eyes for a moment, frowning. Then she looked at me. "I explained this before. You are a demon. I can see that now. You have to be a demon. Who else would travel with men? And with a woman like Nia? The magic in the tower should have destroyed you. Or—at the very least—given you a terrible pain. But you are fine. Therefore, it must be the tower that has come to harm. And I am the guardian! How will I ever explain?"

Derek said, "This kind of thinking goes around in a circle. If Lixia is a demon, the tower will hurt her. The tower does not hurt her, and this means she is a demon."

I made the gesture of disagreement. "You haven't understood the argument."

"Help me sit up," the woman said. "I can't talk like this."

The oracle took hold of her shoulders. He pulled her into a sitting position. She grunted and twisted, moving the upper portion of her body from side to side. "My arms are numb. I can't feel anything. And how can I talk without using my hands?"

The oracle looked at me.

"Free her. But only her hands."

"I need a knife," he said.

Derek gave him one.

The oracle cut.

"Are they free?" the woman said. "I can't move them."

"They are free."

She leaned forward. Her arms fell apart, and her hands knocked against the sides of the canoe. "I feel nothing! I cannot make them work!"

"Your arms are sleeping," Derek said. He pulled her arms forward, till her hands were resting on her thighs. Then he began to rub one of the arms.

"Aiya! It hurts! It tingles!"

Derek kept rubbing. "Lixia?"

"Yes?"

"Explain the argument. The one I didn't understand. And you—" He looked at Inahooli. "Remember, your feet are tied. Don't try anything humorous."

Inahooli frowned. "This is no time for a joke. And anyway, I am not good at joking. Everyone tells me that."

"The problem is Nia," I said. "I am a demon because I travel with her. And with you and the oracle."

The woman raised her arm. She clenched her hand, then opened it and made the gesture of agreement. Then she began to rub her other arm. Derek stood up and stepped back.

"If I am a demon, then it follows that the tower is my enemy. If the magic of the tower does not harm me, then it follows that my magic must have harmed the tower. —An elegant line of reasoning," I added in English. "I don't see any flaw."

"This is stupid," the oracle said. "You talk and talk, and you don't settle anything. You are all thinking badly and more than that"—he raised one hand for emphasis—"you are fooling around with words. You are like children with bright stones. You toss the words. You line them in rows. Aiya! How pretty! But what does it mean?" He paced around the canoe, then turned and stared at us. "Listen to me, all of you! Among my people there is a woman who is called the go-between.

When there is an argument, she goes to the women who are involved. She asks questions. Each woman tells her side of the argument. Then the go-between goes off by herself. She thinks over everything she has heard. She picks through the stories, and she throws away anything that seems malicious or foolish. When people argue, they begin to brood. The memory of the argument stays in their minds. It becomes like food that has been stored all winter: half-rotten and full of bugs. And it is hard to tell what is good from the garbage.

"But the go-between learns to turn ideas over. She knows how to find the soft spots and the little holes where bugs have burrowed in. She throws away all the bad ideas. Whatever is left is the real reason for the argument. Once she knows that, she can begin to settle the argument."

He paused for a moment. Inahooli opened her mouth. He held up his hand, flat with the palm forward. The gesture meant "stop" or "wait." It was identical with the human gesture.

"Sometimes the go-between can find no good reason for the argument. Then she looks further. Is there a malicious neighbor who has been telling lies or carrying stories? Have the women in the argument done anything that is unlucky or likely to cause anger either in the land of the spirits or in the rest of the village? The go-between keeps looking until she finds a good reason for the argument. Now—" He touched his chest, then straightened his arm, moving it out to the side. I didn't recognize the gesture. It had a formal look, like the gestures used by professional speakers. Maybe it was a gesture reserved for special occasions: feasts and religious ceremonies. "I have been thinking about the reason for this argument. Everything you people have said is stupid. And we have no neighbors here to carry stories and tell lies. Therefore, the cause of this argument is magical."

Inahooli frowned. "You are talking too much. I am getting confused. Everything was simple and clear before you people arrived."

The oracle looked at Derek. "I thought maybe this is happening because of the bracelet. But I gave it back, and I performed a ceremony of propitiation."

I grabbed Derek's arm and pulled on his shirtsleeve. He jerked away from me. Too late. The cuff was open, and the thing on his wrist was visible. It was the bracelet, of course. Sunlight hit it. The metal glittered.

"He watched you last night," I told the oracle. "He saw where you threw the bracelet. This morning he went swimming. Derek never gives up. That's why he has tenure."

"What?" the oracle asked.

"It's difficult to explain."

Derek took off the bracelet. "Okay. You win, Lixia." He tossed the bracelet to the oracle. "Get rid of it. Lixia can watch me to make sure I don't watch you."

"What is this about?" Inahooli asked.

The Voice of the Waterfall answered. "This one"—he waved to Derek—"took the bracelet, and he had no right to. It was a gift to a spirit or demon, whoever inhabits the lake of boiling mud that is to the east of here."

"It belongs to the Trickster." The woman stared at Derek. "You are very unlucky. He does not forget. And it is very hard to get away from him."

"You see?" said the oracle. "There is always a good reason for everything. This"—he held up the bracelet—"is the reason for our argument."

"Do you believe this?" Derek asked the woman.

She frowned. "No. The Trickster is angry with you. But I am the one who is having the bad luck. That doesn't seem right." She closed her eyes and pressed her lips together. We all waited. After a minute she opened her eyes. "The Groundbird Clan!"

"What?" said Derek.

"Their ceremony follows ours, and we always overshadow them. Our tower is always taller and better-looking. Our dancers and storytellers have more skill. I know they are envious, and the new shamaness was born in their clan—though now, of course, she belongs to the Clan of the First Magician. But a woman does not forget what she learned as a child in the tent of her mother. Yes!" She made the gesture of affirmation. "She has performed some kind of magic rite and made this happen." She looked at the oracle. "You were right about the malicious neighbors. I should have thought of this before. There is nothing wrong with the tower. She drove me crazy with magic and made me think the tower is ruined."

"What about the bracelet?" the oracle said.

"That will certainly cause bad luck, but not to me. No, this is due to the Groundbird Clan." She fell quiet, obviously brooding.

"You said, the groundbird stole fire from the sky."

She looked at me, then made the gesture of agreement.

"Did you see the moon last night? It is on fire. Could that have anything to do with what is happening here? Could it be an omen? A sign of magic?"

"No." She paused. "Yes. Maybe. I have never been good with omens. Someone else has to explain them. I never understand what they mean. I have to get back to the tower. If the shamaness is trying to drive me crazy, then I must try to be ordinary. I have to go back to my usual behavior. I have to do what I'm supposed to do." She reached down and pulled at the fabric that held her feet. "Help me! I can't stay here. Who knows what is happening to the tower?"

The oracle cut her free. She pushed herself up on her knees, then tried to get up on one foot. She couldn't. "My ankles don't work."

"To hell with it," said Derek. He grabbed the woman under the arms and pulled her up. "Hold on to me." He lifted her out of the canoe. "Can you stand?"

"No."

He kept one arm around her. "Lean on me. Try to walk."

She stumbled forward.

"Okay. Keep going."

They walked back and forth. I watched and tried to figure out what had happened. What had we been talking about? What had been resolved?

After a while she was able to walk on her own. She made the gesture that indicated completion and then the gesture that meant gratitude. "I will go now. The tower must be guarded. And if you are willing to take my advice, get rid of the bracelet. Give it back to the Trickster, or else he will cause you a lot of trouble." She pushed one of the canoes out into the water, jumped in, and began to paddle. In a minute or two she was gone, out of sight among the reeds.

"I am going to hide the bracelet," the oracle said. "Lixia, you watch that man. He cannot be trusted." The oracle walked away.

I looked at Derek.

He grinned and shrugged. "I seem to be getting a bad reputation."

"Uh-huh. And you deserve it. I've always heard that you were first-rate in the field. Well, if this is a sample . . . "

He began to frown, drawing down his thick blond eyebrows.

"You interfered with a ceremony. You stole something that's magical or—at least—owned by a magical being. Are you out of your mind? How could you risk your relationship with the oracle? He's an excellent informant. Do you think people like that grow on trees?"

"He never would have known except for you. You decided it was time for a big revelation."

I thought for a moment. "That's true enough."

"I ought to be angry with you, Lixia. I've lost a valuable artifact, and I'm going to have to spend a lot of time convincing the oracle that I am not—most of the time—a thief. Well—" He made the gesture that meant "so be it." "I'll talk him around. And I don't believe in holding a grudge. So what do you say we forget this?"

I laughed. The man was superb. After everything he'd done, he was willing to forgive me. "Okay. Do you want to shake on it?" I held out my hand. We shook.

"I'm getting hungry," Derek said. "What do you say we check the fish traps?"

I made the gesture of agreement. We waded out. The traps were empty, though something had paid a visit to them. The bait was gone.

"Dammit," I said.

We waded back to shore, bringing the traps with us.

The oracle came down the beach. His hands were empty. He had gotten rid of the bracelet. "No fish?"

"Not a thing."

"Aiya!" He paused and scratched his nose. "We should have asked the crazy woman if she had anything to spare. Well, I have seen plants that are edible. We will gather them."

Derek shook his head, then made the gesture that meant "no." "You two go. It's time I began to think about hunting. I'll look for wood. Maybe I can make a new bow or a spear."

I went with the oracle. We dug roots and gathered berries. He told me stories about the various kinds of vegetation: how the bloodroot got its color and why the sunleaf turned always toward the sun and why no man would eat any part of the *hubaia* vine, though women relished it.

Late in the afternoon we went back to camp. Derek was there. He had a long piece of wood. "A spear," he said.

We roasted the bloodroots. They were pale orange when we put them in the fire. By the time we raked them out, they had turned dark red. They had a sweet flavor and a mealy texture. Imagine a potato with the taste of a ripe sweet pepper. Not bad, I thought. But they needed butter.

Derek stripped the bark off his piece of wood and scraped the wood with a knife, cutting away irregularities I couldn't even see. Then he sat and twisted the bark into cord.

"This man is skillful," the oracle said. "Even though he has no hair, he knows the things a man has to know."

Derek glanced up and grinned, then went back to twisting.

"Though I don't understand," the oracle said, "why he likes to show his teeth. He does it over and over."

"It is an expression of pleasure or happiness," I said.

"Oh," said the oracle.

Night came. The wind was off the lake. It carried bugs to us: a new variety, tiny and numerous.

I cursed and waved my hands.

"Ignore them," Derek said.

I moved closer to the fire. Smoke swirled around me, and the bugs left me alone. But now—of course—my eyes were watering. I looked at the oracle. "Don't they bother you?"

"Yes," he said. "But there is nothing to be done. A lake like this always has bugs. And these ones do not bite. That is the best we can hope for." He opened his mouth in a really wide yawn and I saw his canines. They were long and sharp. No wonder these people did not express happiness by grinning. Those teeth looked menacing. "Are we going to keep watch?"

"Derek?" I asked.

"Yes. I'm not certain we did the right thing by letting that woman go. She gives me a humorous feeling. I don't like her aura."

"We couldn't keep her tied up for days," I said. "Anyway, she has a real problem to deal with now. Her enemies in the Groundbird Clan." I grinned.

The oracle lay down. I watched Derek. He split the piece of wood at one end and wedged the knife in, the blade pointing out. Then he wound the cord around the split wood and the knife. "Crude but effective. I hope." He kept winding and knotting. I put more branches on the fire. Then I lay down.

I woke. Something was biting my hand. A mosquito. I slapped and got the little varmint. At the same moment I remembered that it could not possibly be a mosquito. I looked at the fire. It was a heap of coals, glowing dimly, not giving off much smoke at all. Off to the west above the lake the Great Moon shone. It was getting close to full. I squinted and thought I saw a line above the upper edge. It was curved like a handle, going up and over the terminator, then back down—from sunlight into shadow. Derek had better eyes than I did. To me it was just barely visible.

"Goddammit!" Another biter got me on the neck. I looked around for wood. There wasn't any. I couldn't rebuild the fire.

I lay down and put my arm over my face, trying to protect it. The bugs hummed around me. They didn't bite often, but the sound and the expectation kept me awake. I gave up finally. It was time for a walk. Maybe I would find a late-night store that sold bug repellent or one of those hats with a veil made of mosquito netting.

I started toward the reeds. The wind was still blowing. Leaves rustled, and the grove was full of moving shadows. Here and there a beam of moonlight penetrated the foliage, and I could make out a branch or a stem of monster grass.

But for the most part I saw very little, except for the moon ahead of me and the lake aglitter with yellow light. A lovely evening, except for the bugs.

When I was a short distance from camp—thirty meters at the most—hands grabbed my neck. I tried to yell and couldn't. The hands pressed in, choking. I grabbed at them. I couldn't break the grip. "Unh," said the person in back of me. It was a deep, low, satisfied sound. The person turned, dragging me around, and slammed my body against something that was hard.

The person let go. A moment later I was on the ground, belly down with my face pressed against something that felt lumpy. A root? The base of a tree?

The person rolled me onto my back. I kept still. Maybe he or she would think I was already dead. He or she leaned close. I heard heavy breathing, then smelled the person's breath.

Mouthwash, I thought.

More heavy breathing. I had a sense the person was going to touch me.

Someone shouted nearby.

The person straightened up. A moment later he or she was gone.

My throat hurt. So did my shoulder and my arm. I inhaled slowly and carefully. So far, so good. My lungs still seemed to work. I exhaled, then raised myself up on one elbow. I could move. My neck was not broken.

I turned my head and felt a twinge of pain. The camp. Where was it? I saw a dim red glow. The fire. I got up on my knees. As I did so a figure jumped in front of the glow, visible for a moment. Then it was gone.

What?

There was something next to me. I touched it. Monster grass. A big smooth stem. That must have been what I'd hit when my attacker swung me around. I'd been picked up and slammed against a tree, the way a human would knock a shoe against a post to get off dry mud.

Aiya! I climbed to my feet, bracing myself against the stem of the monster grass. For a moment I felt dizzy. I closed my eyes and tried to breathe evenly, but not deeply.

"Monster!" It was a scream. Inahooli. That lunatic.

I opened my eyes. Next to the fire two figures struggled. They were on the ground, rolling over and over. I couldn't make out who they were.

I began to walk. It was possible, though I still felt dizzy. The campfire—and the two figures—went in and out of focus.

A voice cried, "Help me!"

It was the oracle. He was in the fight. But where was Derek? I reached the edge of the camp and looked around. There he was. Three meters away. He lay on his back, half in moonlight and half in shadow. His hair was loose and had fallen forward. Long, pale, and tangled, it covered most of his face. I bent and brushed it to one side. His eyes were closed. There was blood around his nose and mouth.

"Help!" the oracle cried again.

I saw Derek's spear near him on the ground. The blade shone faintly in the moonlight. He must have dropped it when Inahooli got him. I picked it up and walked around the fire, moving carefully. There was something wrong with my sense of balance.

Inahooli was on top. It had to be her. She wore a new tunic, pale with a lot of embroidery. The oracle had nothing like that. She straddled him. Her hands were on his face. I thought I saw her thumbs go into his eyes. The oracle screamed. I raised the spear and drove it into her back.

She cried out. There was fury in the sound. No pain. She twisted, trying to see who had done this thing. I let go of the spear. The oracle pushed up. She tumbled off him. A moment later he was on his feet. She was on the ground, on her side, groaning, beginning to feel the pain.

"Are you all right?" the oracle asked.

"No. Find out how Derek is." I went down on my knees next to the woman. The knife blade had gone into her lower back under the ribs. What had it hit? I had no idea. There wasn't much blood. Should I try to pull the spear out? Or would that increase the bleeding? My eyes went out of focus. I lifted my head and breathed fresh air. Inahooli was moving, trying to find a comfortable position. "Be still," I said.

"Demon."

I took her wrist and tried to find a pulse. She pulled her arm away. "Leave me alone." She grimaced. "Aiya! The pain!" She closed her eyes and pressed her lips together.

I took hold of her wrist again. This time she didn't pull away. I found the pulse. But how was I going to measure it? Not in beats per minute. I didn't have a way to measure time. And I didn't know what was normal for her people. Fifty beats a minute? Seventy? Or a hundred? I would have to compare her pulse rate with that of another native. "Oracle?"

"Give us a minute," Derek said in English.

I looked around. He was standing, holding on to the oracle with one hand. With the other hand he rubbed his forehead. "Ouch!"

"A concussion?" I said.

"Maybe. I can remember what happened. I think I can. That argues against a concussion. Maybe you had better check the size of my pupils."

"Okay."

The oracle said, "Speak a language I can understand."

Derek made the gesture of assent. "I was checking the grove, going in a circle, making sure everything was okay.

"When I got back to camp, you were gone, Lixia. I called your name and got no answer. That worried me—a little, not enough. I thought Inahooli was a fool. I didn't think she'd be able to get past me. I went looking for you.

"I found Inahooli." He sounded puzzled, as if he could not understand how any of this could have happened to Derek Seawarrior, Ph.D. "I didn't see her coming. She appeared out of nowhere and grabbed the spear from me. She just grabbed and pulled and it was gone. She used it as a club. Right across the face." He felt his nose. "I don't think it's broken."

"Is that where the blood came from?"

"What blood?" He wiped below his nose, then looked at his hand. "Oh. That blood. I think so. The thing I don't understand is—why didn't she stab me?"

"She was going to," the oracle said. "After you fell. But you yelled before she hit you. I woke up and saw what was happening. I got to her before she drove the spear in. I jumped on her back and bit her shoulder. That made her drop the spear."

Inahooli groaned. I was still holding her wrist. Her pulse seemed slower than before. "Oracle, come here. I want to find out how quickly your heart is beating."

"Why?"

I thought for a moment. How was I going to explain? "When one of my people is sick, her heart beats differently."

"Than what?"

"Than it does when she is well. And a wise person—a person skilled in healing—can listen to the heart or feel the way it beats and tell how sick the woman is."

"I know that," the oracle said. "Remember, my mother is a shamaness. She taught me a few things when I lived in her house. But I haven't been injured. Why do you want to know how my heart is doing?"

"To compare." I waved at Inahooli with my free hand. "I don't know what her heartbeat ought to be. I don't know what is right for your people."

The oracle glanced at Derek. "Can you stand by yourself?"

"I think so." Derek let go of him.

The oracle walked over to Inahooli. He crouched down and took her wrist from me. "We don't belong to the same people, Inahooli and I. But all hearts beat in the same fashion." He paused, tilting his head and frowning. "It is going a little too fast, but remember she has been fighting." He laid the wrist down. "We will pull out the spear and bind up the wound. Even though I am a man and she is crazy, I cannot walk away and leave her in this condition."

Inahooli opened her eyes. "You are all demons."

"Don't talk," the oracle said. He took hold of her tunic where the spear had cut it and pulled gently. The fabric tore. In a moment or two he had the tunic off. He gave it to me. "Tear it in pieces."

I did what he asked. It wasn't easy. I kept running into embroidery. Fortunately I had sharp incisors. I bit through the threads, then went back to tearing. When I was done the oracle said, "We need more cloth."

What did we have? My shirt and Derek's. I looked at my comrade. He was still upright, but he hadn't moved any closer to us. He seemed—in the dim light—to be swaying. He looked worse than I felt. I unfastened my shirt and pulled it off.

The oracle looked at me. "What is that across your chest?"

How does one explain a brassiere to an alien? I tugged at the shirt. There was a weak seam. It tore. "I'll tell you later," I said.

Derek walked over to us. He stumbled once.

"How are you?" I asked.

"Okay. Dizzy and confused. I didn't really expect her to come back. I was only being careful. Why'd she do it?"

I finished tearing, then I made the gesture of uncertainty.

The oracle had his hand on the spear. He began to pull. Inahooli gasped. "It will be over soon," he told her. He glanced at me. "Have the cloth ready." He pulled again. The spear came out. I saw the blade, covered with dark blood. He laid the weapon down, then leaned forward and peered at the wound. "It is bleeding, but slowly. It is a flow, not a rush. That is a good sign. Give me the cloth."

I handed him a piece of tunic. He made it into a pad and tied it in place over the wound, using the rest of the cloth, the beautifully embroidered pieces of native fabric and my denim shirt.

A bug got me on my bare shoulder. I slapped it.

"Wood," said Derek. "There's a tree—I guess you would call it a tree—down and dry not far from here. Come on."

We went into the dark grove. Derek found his piece of monster grass: a huge fallen stem. It lay in moonlight. There was a growth on it, something analogous to fungus. It looked like coral, delicate and intricate. Pale branches divided and redivided. Either they were translucent or they glowed with their own light. I couldn't tell which. But the thing had a dim radiance. I stared at it. Another bug bit me, this time on the arm. "Let's hurry," I said.

We gathered wood and carried it back to camp. Derek rebuilt the fire. When it was burning brightly, I checked his eyes. The pupils were of equal size. No concussion.

I went over to the oracle. "How is she?"

"Her heartbeat has slowed down. But I do not like the way she breathes. My mother's sister made a noise like that when she had the coughing sickness. She did not live."

I listened. The oracle was right. Inahooli sounded congested, as if she had a bad cold or pneumonia.

"She told me she was cold," the oracle said. "I put Nia's cloak over her. Aiya! It is good that Nia left it!"

Derek spoke in English, "If she doesn't make it, remember it was self-defense."

"I should have hit her over the head or kicked her. Distracted her and given the oracle a chance to get away. Do you have any idea what this is going to do to my karma?"

"I told you before," the oracle said. "Speak a language I can understand."

"This will bring bad luck," I said. "To do this—to harm another person—is to act like an animal, without reason or compassion. People—true people—don't harm each other."

"Do you really believe that?" Derek asked. "And if so, what about the man in the canyon? He's dead, and—from what I heard—you helped."

"I didn't intend to kill him, and I did not deliver the fatal blow. Nia did. I don't know what was going through her mind. In any case, that's her problem, not mine. I try not to impose my system of ethics on the people I study. Here—" I paused. "I drove the blade in. So it's my problem and my karma. And I'm not entirely sure what I was intending. Maybe I wanted to kill Inahooli. —I never expected to become a Buddha, but I thought I'd do better than this."

"What is a Buddha?" the oracle asked.

"A person who understands what is going on. Or maybe a person who doesn't understand what is going on and doesn't care."

"That makes no sense."

Inahooli groaned and moved restlessly. Her eyes opened, but she didn't look at us. She was staring up at nothing.

Derek leaned forward. "Inahooli? Can you hear what I'm saying?"

She looked at me. "I thought when autumn came I would be an important woman."

"Why did you come back?"

She moved her head slightly. Her eyes met his. "Do you think I believed you? Those crazy stories? I knew that you were demons."

I said, "You mean you were pretending? The story about the shamaness was a lie?"

"A trick." She pulled her lips back, so her teeth were exposed. It was not a smile. "You are very stupid demons." She paused for a moment and breathed in and out. Her eyes narrowed. "The pain is terrible." She looked at the oracle. "Will I live through this?"

"I don't know."

She blinked. "Aiya! The luck that I've been having!"

"What do you expect when you creep up on people in the darkness and try to do them harm? What spirit will approve of behavior like that?"

"I was angry."

The oracle frowned. "That is no excuse. When I get angry, I throw rocks or jump up and down and scream or—if I am very angry—I make up a nasty song and sing it as loudly as I can. That is the right way to be angry. It is not right to throw people around. Only crazy men do that."

"I tried to yell and jump up and down. It did no good. There was too much anger." Inahooli frowned. "It was like the lake of boiling mud—in me, in my gut, churning and exploding."

Derek said in English, "Bicarbonate of soda."

"Be quiet," I said.

"I could not endure the anger. I had to do something big." She closed her eyes a moment, then opened them. "I am not going to talk anymore. It hurts. It is too much trouble." She closed her eyes again.

I shivered. Derek put more wood on the fire. Flames leaped up. "It's burning too quickly. I don't think it will last till morning." He looked at me. "You're cold, aren't you?"

I made the gesture of agreement. "And the bugs are getting to me. They must have decided I smell like food."

He unfastened his shirt and took it off. "Here."

"What are you going to do?"

"Stay in motion." He looked at the lake. "The moon is still up. I think I have time. You stay here, Lixia." He walked into the darkness.

I opened my mouth to call after him, then decided what the heck. I put the shirt on.

The oracle said, "Where is he going?"

I made the gesture that meant "who knows?"

"He certainly moves quickly when he decides he ought to do something."

"Yes."

Inahooli groaned and bit her lip. The oracle took hold of her wrist. "The beat is getting weaker. I think she will die."

She opened her eyes. Her pupils had expanded, and I could barely see her irises. There was a little orange in the corners, but the middle of each eye was dark. "No."

"Yes," said the oracle. "I do not lie."

She closed her eyes and concentrated on breathing. It was becoming more difficult for her. Strange! To watch a person struggle to do something as easy and as ordinary as drawing a breath.

I got up and put more wood on the fire. Then I came back and sat down. I listened. Each inhalation was a gasp. When she exhaled I heard a whistle. The air was coming out through some kind of obstruction. A liquid. Blood. I must have gotten a lung when I drove the spear into her.

The breathing went on for another hour or two. I got up once and put more wood on the fire, then stood leaning over the flames. Hot air rose around me. My goose bumps disappeared and feeling returned to my hands. Odd! That I was so cold. It was, after all, the middle of summer. But the night was cool, and there was a wind blowing. The bugs were gone. The wind must have blown them away.

I went back to Inahooli. I sat down and listened. Her breath went in and out. The sound was harsh and desperate. Toward dawn it became erratic. There were pauses, as if she were drifting in and out of sleep—the breath stopping for a moment as she came awake. But she wasn't ever really awake. I rubbed my hands. They were numb with cold. The oracle sat quietly.

At dawn the breathing stopped. The oracle felt her wrist and then her neck. "No beat." He stood up. "Aiya! I am stiff." He stretched and yawned, then rubbed his arms. "My feet are numb." He hopped from one foot to the other.

I got up and stretched. My neck and shoulder hurt, and there were minor things wrong all over my body: aches, twinges, areas of stiffness.

I looked at Inahooli. I could make out her position, even under the cloak. She lay on her side, her knees drawn up and her arms folded against her chest. Her head was bent forward. Her chin was tucked in. I couldn't see her face.

I was a killer. The real thing this time, not merely an accomplice. I looked east. Red light shone between two stems of monster grass. The sun was coming up.

The oracle stopped hopping. "This is a good time for a song. One came to me while I watched her." He pointed at Inahooli, then sang, using the language of gifts. I was able to get most of the song. Later he explained the verses I had not understood.

"Aiya! Hai-aiya!
What a situation!
Even you, Inahooli,
don't deserve
to end like this.

"Where are your sisters?
They ought to mourn you,
rocking and moaning
at the entrance to your house.

"Where are your cousins?
They ought to mourn you,
bringing gifts
to bury in your grave.

"Aiya! Hai-aiya!
What a situation!
Even you, Inahooli,
don't deserve
to end like this."

He paused for a moment, frowning and scratching the back of his neck. "There is one more verse," he said. "I just heard it in my mind. Give me a moment to arrange the words." He bit his thumbnail, then sang:

"This is a man's death,
to die without presents.
This is a man's death,
to die on the plain."

The sun finished rising. Derek came up from the lake. He was carrying a pair of saddlebags.

"Where have you been?" I asked.

"On the island, the one you visited." He set down the bags and opened one. "I'll trade you. My shirt for this." He pulled out a tunic. It was cream-white with blue and red embroidery.

I undid the fasteners on Derek's shirt. "Do you have something for Inahooli? I'd like to get Nia's cloak back. It doesn't seem right for it to be on her."

He glanced at the body. "Dead?"

"Yes."

He opened the other bag and pulled out a cloak. It was rust-brown with a yellow border. The oracle pulled Nia's cloak off Inahooli. I had a brief glimpse of the body, naked except for the dark fur and the bandage made of denim. Then it was gone from sight.

Derek said, "There was food on the island. Dried meat and fruit. I filled a bag."

"This has to be wrong, Derek. We're stealing from the dead."

He went down on his knees and put his hands on his thighs. For a moment or two he remained in that position, his arms braced, his head a little bent, looking at the body under the rust-brown cloak. "Listen to me, Inahooli. We take these things because we need them. We are cold. We are hungry. Two of us have traveled farther than you can imagine, and we may never make it home. Believe me, we aren't doing this out of malice or anger or any bad emotion, but out of need." He paused. "I promise you we will use what we take with respect. We won't be ungrateful, and we certainly won't use this as an excuse to go on a journey of strength.

"This happened the way it happened according to the turning of the wheel. Accept it, Inahooli. Don't be angry with us." He stood up and walked back to me.

"Journey of strength?" I said.

"Power trip," he said in English. "I couldn't think of a better way to translate it." He went back to the language of gifts. "I'd like my shirt back."

I gave it to him. He handed me the tunic in return. I pulled it over my head. The fabric was soft and warm, like fine wool. It had a furry aroma, the smell of the aliens.

"I'll get the food," Derek said. "After we eat, we can bury her."

We dug a grave in the sand by the lake, using the oars as shovels. Derek and the oracle got Inahooli and carried her to the grave. Hard work. They gasped and grunted and almost dropped her once. I carried the cloak, which was easy. They laid her in the grave. I laid the cloak over her.

"Wait for me," the oracle said. He walked into the grove.

I rubbed my shoulder, then looked at Derek. He had washed his face, but he still looked pretty awful. His nose was red and swollen, and one eye was almost closed. There was a bruise on his forehead above the eye.

"Why did you make that speech to Inahooli? To reassure the oracle?"

He nodded. "And me. One must never take without explaining and never kill without making an apology."

"How civilized are you, anyway?"

He grinned. "Not very."

The oracle came back. He carried food: a strip of dried meat and a handful of fresh berries. He laid these in the grave next to

Inahooli. Then he unfastened his necklace of gold and turquoise and laid it next to the food. "Maybe she will be less angry if we give her presents. Though I doubt it. She is the kind that holds on to anger. What a bad way to be!"

We piled sand over Inahooli, then found rocks and put them on top of the sand. When we were done the oracle said, "We ought to perform ceremonies of aversion and purification. But I am not a shamaness. I don't know the ceremonies the holy women learn. I don't even know the ceremonies that men learn to help them after they leave the village. All I know is what the waterfall has told me." He sang:

"O holy one!
O being of power!
Why don't you help me?
What should I do next?

"O holy one!
O being of power!
Why don't you help me?
Tell me what to do!"

He tilted his head and listened. The wind blew. Reeds rustled. Water lapped the shore. "All I can hear is, 'Take a swim.' Maybe we can wash off what has happened in the last few days."

Derek made the gesture of agreement. The two of them undressed and waded in. They washed in the deep water by the reeds, then swam. I was worried about the cut on my arm. I didn't want to get it wet. And I didn't think my shoulder was up to swimming. I took off my boots and rolled up my jeans and waded in the shallows, looking for shells and polished stones. The stones were uninteresting: black stuff like pumice, worn round or oval. The shells were lovely: tiny spirals, pale lavender or pink. I gathered a dozen, then waded to the beach. I laid the shells on the grave. A ridiculous gesture. What use was the gift? I did not believe in an afterlife, so it wasn't an attempt to buy off Inahooli's anger. And it wasn't enough to buy off my feeling of responsibility.

"Killer," I said out loud.

That mood was dangerous. I refused to give in to it. Why should I? Guilt was not part of my heritage. The senior members of my family had disapproved of it. One must recognize mistakes and acknowledge them and work to break the patterns of behavior that led to them. But guilt was unproductive.

"Life is a process," Theresa had said. She was one of my co-mothers, a medical technician who specialized in psychology. Half the year she worked on a deep-sea mining ship, the *Pacific Aurora,* out of Pearl Harbor. The other half of the year, she helped to raise the junior members of the family. "We make and remake ourselves, responding to changes both external and internal. But guilt is static, as are related ideas and emotions: sin, for example, regret, and maybe shame. Though I am not certain about the effect of shame. But the others anchor you in the past. They hold you, so you can't move freely in the present.

"Imagine guilt as an iron band fastened around something that is growing: the trunk of a tree, the neck of a child. Sooner or later, one of two things must happen. If the band does not break, the growing thing will be deformed.

"Commit yourself to change, Lixia, to living in the present, to making and remaking who you are. Do the best you can. Understand what you do. And do not feel guilty."

Good advice, I told the memory of Theresa. I picked up my boots and walked to our camp.

INZARA

The oracle went off to gather roots and berries. Derek went for wood, and I sorted through Inahooli's belongings. Two tunics—three, if I counted the one I had on, a leather cloak, a pair of sandals, and a knife. All the tunics had embroidery: geometric patterns. The cloak had a fastener, similar to a fibula, made of bronze and covered with silver. The silver was wearing thin.

"Lixia!" Derek shouted.

I threw down the cloak and ran through the grove. He was at the eastern edge.

"There!" He pointed.

Out on the plain was a rider. He or she was astride a bowhorn. I could make out the animal's long curving horns. A second animal—another bowhorn—followed the first.

"Nia?" I asked.

"I think so."

The rider came closer. I recognized the wide shoulders and the way she rode: easily, comfortably, slouching a little in the saddle. "We have to call Eddie at once," I said.

Derek glanced at me. "Shall I do the talking? I'm a better politician than you are, and we have some explaining to do. The unfortunate death of a native religious leader."

"Okay."

She reached us and dismounted. "Well, I found it." She waved at the bowhorn. "And the gear. I'm hungry. Is there any food?"

"Yes," I said.

"I'll take care of the animals," Derek said. He held out his hand. Nia gave him the reins.

"Where did you get that tunic? And what happened to his face?" She pointed to Derek.

"Inahooli came back."

"Aiya!"

"She came after us at night. We had to kill her. I had to kill her."

"You?" Nia stared at me, her eyes wide open.

"Yes."

Nia was silent for a while. At last she said, "Any unexpected death is bad. A death like this—that happens in a fight—is worse than other kinds. The ghost of the dead person is certain to be angry. There is likely to be bad luck. When we get to a place where there is a shamaness, we will ask for ceremonies to placate Inahooli or drive her away. We'd better do something about the man in the canyon as well. Though it doesn't matter in the same way when a man dies suddenly." She frowned. "Did you bury Inahooli?"

"Yes."

"With gifts?"

"Yes. The oracle gave his necklace."

"Good. Maybe there will be no bad luck." Nia did not sound confident. "The woman was crazy and dangerous. She brought this on herself. The spirits will not blame us, and ghosts do not usually travel any great distance. Once we are gone from here, we ought to be safe." Nia made the gesture that meant "I wish, I hope."

We returned to camp. I got out food: dried meat and dried fruit. Nia ate. "Hu! I have been starving on the plain." She leaned back and sighed. "The food is from the woman?"

I made the gesture of agreement. "Derek explained to her."

She looked at the piece of fruit in her hand. After a moment she popped it in her mouth. "I thought about it while I looked for the bowhorn. I thought—at first—that I was responsible for what was happening. But that can't be." She finished chewing and swallowed, then she scratched her nose. "Most of the time, bad luck comes from something that is unexpected or peculiar. Well, I have done strange things and had my share of bad luck. But in this case it was Inahooli who was behaving oddly. We came to her land. We were strangers. But she did not welcome us. Instead she tried to kill us. Now, everyone knows that women do not quarrel with strangers. That is male behavior."

"Women never quarrel with strangers?" I asked.

"Once in a while. Hakht did. She is a bad person." Nia said this firmly with conviction. "And Inahooli did. She was crazy. And I killed the old man who killed Enshi. But ordinary women, women with self-respect, never quarrel except with people they know. Kinfolk and close neighbors. That is the right way to have an argument." Nia ate more fruit. "There is no way to be certain who a stranger is or what will happen if you give her trouble."

It made sense. The people on this planet did not have war—nor, as far as I could tell, any kind of organized theft. When they saw a stranger—a strange woman, at least—they did not have to wonder: Is this person a thief? A killer? Someone who will do us harm? They could instead anticipate with pleasure the gifts and the stories the stranger would bring.

Aggression and exchange were, or seemed to be, entirely separate. How different from Earth. The old Earth, anyway, where it had been legitimate to say, "Property is theft."

Derek walked into camp, carrying our two packs.

"What happened?" Nia asked. "How did Inahooli die?"

He set the packs down and told her. It was a fine report, brief and vivid with a lot of gesturing. "My luck was bad yesterday," he said at the end. "But hers was a lot worse. If things had gone a little more slowly, if she'd had a bit more time, Inahooli would have killed all three of us. Maybe the Trickster had decided that I had suffered enough."

"Who is the Trickster?" Nia asked. "And why does he want to make Derek suffer?"

"Remember the bracelet he found?" I said.

"Yes."

"It belonged to a spirit called the Trickster. Inahooli told Derek the Trickster was certain to be angry and give him a lot of grief."

"Ah!" said Nia.

"I know that spirit," said Derek. "Among my people he is called Coyote."

"I'm not entirely sure of that, Derek. Coyote is a sneak, but he isn't a bad person. I got the impression from Inahooli that the Trickster is bad. Selfish and malevolent. He's like Loki."

"Once again, I don't know what you are talking about," Nia said.

"Don't worry about it. Lixia has a habit of wandering away from whatever people are talking about. She thinks too much, and her thinking goes off in every possible direction."

I gave him the finger.

"Is that a gesture your people use?" asked Nia.

"Yes. It is a gesture of disrespect."

"Ah! Let me see it again."

I repeated the gesture. Nia imitated me. "I thought you people had no gestures. It is good to know you are not utterly strange." She looked at Derek. "Is your story over?"

He made the gesture of affirmation.

"Hu! I wish this had not happened. It has." She made the gesture that meant "so be it." "We'll go on tomorrow. I want to get away from here, before her ghost manages to pull free of her body."

"All right," said Derek.

The oracle came back with berries. We ate dinner. Derek called the ship.

"What happened?" asked Eddie. "Where in hell have you been?"

"We encountered some of the local fauna. Four meters tall with claws. Our animals bolted, and we lost them. Our radios were on the animals." Derek looked up. I was watching him. So were Nia and the oracle. "Have you managed to learn the native language, Eddie?"

"No. Why?"

"I have two natives here, and I think they're wondering what I'm saying."

"You let them know about the radios?"

"Yes."

"We were going to try to keep the natives ignorant of our technology," Eddie said. He spoke slowly and clearly, his voice even. "It was part of our policy of noninterference."

"Eddie, it wasn't possible. We couldn't keep creeping off into the darkness. 'Pardon me, I'm going to take this box and go off and pee. I'll be back in half an hour. Oh, by the way, I talk to myself while urinating, so if you hear voices in the night, don't worry.'"

Eddie said, "This is getting to be more and more of a mess." He paused. "Do you have anything to report?"

"Yes," said Derek. "A native attacked us. She's dead."

"What?"

Derek told the story. After he finished Eddie said, "I want to see what your recorders got. Transmit information."

Derek pulled off his medallion and put it into the radio. He looked at me. "I keep forgetting about the medallions."

"Don't worry, Derek. You can talk your way out of almost anything." I took off my medallion and tossed it to him. "Send that up, too."

A couple of minutes later Eddie came back on. "We'll get back to you after we've looked at your information. I warn you, I'm not happy about this. I am going to ask Lysenko if there is any place near you where he can land."

Lysenko was the senior rocket plane pilot: a man with an unfortunate name. Biologists laughed at him.

"Are you going to pull us out?" asked Derek.

"I want that option. Ask Nia and the oracle if they know of any place. A dry lake bed is best. A lake with water might be possible, if it's deep enough."

"Okay."

"And try to stay out of trouble for a while."

Derek turned the radio off. He got up and stretched. I could see the tension in his body. "One trouble with Eddie—he was born to sit at a desk. He can organize, supervise, analyze, and criticize, but he doesn't know what it's like in the field."

"What did your box say?" Nia asked. "Why is Derek angry?"

I stood up. "You explain, Derek. I'm tired of talking about Inahooli." I walked to the edge of the plain. Before me was the plain, dark and featureless. Above me the sky was full of stars. I listened to night noises: rustles in the branches and a low buzzing in the pseudo-grass. I thought about my career. There was a chance it was ruined. Who would trust me in the field after this? Especially if Eddie and the others on the soc. sci. committee decided I had been really out of line. They could attach a reprimand to my record or insist that I undergo group criticism.

Now that was an unpleasant idea. I had seen a group in action once. I'd made friends with a man on the long trip out of the solar system, before we went to sleep. A master chef from China. He had the moody personality that one associates with artists and an extraordinary face: pale and smooth, like a mask carved out of white jade. His hair was black, long and thick and lustrous. When he cooked, it was tucked up in a cap. But when he sat and talked with friends, it fell around his face and touched his shoulders. I was maybe a little in love with him. I was certainly in love with his Mu Shu Iguana.

He woke at the edge of this system and realized—finally—what he had done. Left his family, his home, his society, his planet. When he returned, everything would be changed.

He got depressed—which was hardly surprising. Most of us got depressed at one point or another. But De was a real expert at depression. He brooded the same way as he cooked: with skill and passion.

He started drinking, which led to trouble on the job.

Most of his colleagues were Chinese, and they insisted on group criticism. I went to lend moral support—to De, not to his critics. We met in a small room with celadon walls. De sat in front, facing twenty people. Most were kitchen workers, a few were people he knew outside work, and a few were comparative strangers. The meeting was open to everyone, and everyone could speak. The voice of the masses had to be heard.

One by one the kitchen workers spoke. De had missed a lot of work, forcing others to cover for him. He had refused advice and constructive criticism. His attitude was negative. He had argued with decisions made democratically by the kitchen workers. He had lied about his drinking.

Someone from his dormitory got up. De had come in at all hours and made a lot of noise, waking other people. Once he had thrown up in the hall, right outside the speaker's cabin.

Another person—a blonde with a Scandinavian accent—got up and spoke about the evils of drink. A couple of other people got up and argued with her. The problem wasn't alcohol, it was the lack of a decent recreational program. It was the Western cult of individuality. It was the miserable performance of the psychology team.

De sat and listened. His face was paler than usual. There were dark patches under his eyes. He looked exhausted and unhappy. At last, when everyone was done, he stood up. He apologized to his colleagues, to the people on the ship, and to the entire human race. He promised to mend his ways, to come to work promptly, and to go into therapy. Finally, he thanked everyone in the room for their concern and good advice. As far as I could tell, he was being sincere. My family had been in the West too long. I would never really understand the Chinese.

The senior nutritionist stood up and praised De for his new constructive and cooperative attitude. The meeting ended. I went to find a drink.

Never, I thought. I would never go through group criticism. I wasn't sure what I'd do if the committee insisted on it. I couldn't quit nor could they fire me. Not this far from Earth. Most likely, if it came to a crisis, they'd relieve me of my duties and refer me to the committee in charge of nonmechanical maintenance. I'd wash walls or replace cracked tiles until it was time to leave the system.

Once again I was thinking too far ahead. Stop it! I told myself and went back to camp. Derek sat by the fire, his knees up, his arms around them.

"Well?"

He glanced at me and grinned. "The oracle offered to talk to Eddie and explain it isn't wrong to kill in self-defense. He seems to think Eddie is some kind of idiot. And Nia said there is a river that goes between the country of the Amber People and her country, the land of the Iron People. At one point the river spreads out into a long narrow lake. The lake is deep and there are no islands. It might be a safe place to land."

"How far?"

"She isn't entirely certain. Nine or ten days, she thinks."

"Do we go there?" I asked.

He made the gesture of affirmation. "It will make Eddie happy, and it's on the way to Nia's people."

Sunlight woke me, slanting into the grove. A grey line of smoke curled up through it, moving languidly. The oracle crouched by the fire. He was skinning a fish.

"You reset the traps," I said.

"Yes, and we have been lucky. This is a greenfish. It is delicious, especially when baked. Go and perform your morning ceremony."

I obeyed him, doing yoga by the lake. I was still very stiff. But as far as I could tell, no major damage had been done. Talk about lucky!

When I got back to camp, Nia was pulling on one of Inahooli's tunics. It was dull blue, embroidered in orange: a pattern of triangles. She put on her own belt and her knife with the bone handle and the sheath of dark leather. After that she tugged at the hem of the tunic and smoothed it across her chest. "Hu! This is better! There is something to be said for new clothes with bright colors and no bad aroma."

We ate and broke camp, following the trail around the lake, then back onto the plain. To the west and south were clouds. They were high up, fluffy and thin, arranged in flocks or clusters. In the north the sky was clear. I could make out Hani Akhar.

I thought about the *China Clipper:* corridors and little rooms and far too many people. There would be no sky and no wind and no birds, except in the aviary. Maybe I should make a run for it, toss away my radio and AV recorder, and vanish into the wilderness. That was one way to avoid group criticism—unless, of course, they caught me.

I looked around at the plain. It was—or seemed to be—almost empty. A few orange bugs fluttered above the pseudo-grass. A few birds soared in the sky. Way off in the distance I saw a herd of animals. They were black dots moving through the yellow and green vegetation. I had no idea what they were.

This land was too vast and too alien. I couldn't turn my back on my civilization and live utterly alone without hope or help from my people.

That night we camped on top of a low hill. There was nothing in sight except for pseudo-grass. We ate Inahooli's food. Eddie did not call.

"Should we call him?" I asked.

Derek made the gesture that meant "no." "We don't have to go hunting for aggravation. It will find us, more than we want or need."

I made the gesture of agreement.

In the middle of the night rain began to fall. Thunder grumbled, and there were flashes of lightning. We huddled under our cloaks and ponchos and got wet.

By morning the rain had stopped, but the air remained humid, and the vegetation on the plain was beaded with water. It bent over the narrow path. Derek and I pushed through it, getting wet a second time. The natives, riding in back of us, looked as if they were more comfortable, but not by much.

"A person is coming," Nia said.

I looked ahead. The trail was a dark line winding through the vegetation. A bowhorn moved along it. A person rode the animal.

"A man," said Nia. "He travels alone."

"No," said Derek. "There is someone else—off on the plain." He pointed north.

I peered and saw a dot moving down a slope. "Why aren't they together?"

"I don't know," Nia said. "Maybe they are both men."

The trail went into a hollow, and I lost sight of the riders, though only for a few minutes. We came out onto a low rise.

A bowhorn stood in the middle of the trail: a large animal, dun-colored with a white spot on its chest. Its horns were as black and shiny as obsidian.

Derek and I stopped. The two natives rode up on either side of us and reined their animals. I looked at the bowhorn's rider.

A male, almost certainly. He was wide and tall with dark, shaggy fur. His tunic was like the one I had on: cream-colored with geometric embroidery. On his arms were thick gold bracelets, and he wore a necklace of gold and amber.

He looked us over calmly, then spoke in the language of gifts. "I see that you have met my sister." His voice was deep and soft.

"Inahooli," Derek said.

The man made the gesture of assent. "I am Toohala Inzara of the Clan of the Ropemaker and the People of Amber." He waved to the north. "My brother Tzoon is off in that direction. I haven't seen my brother Ara for a couple of days. But he is out there somewhere, probably to the south. How is our sister?"

"As well as can be expected," Derek said. "She has been alone for a long time."

The man made the gesture of agreement. "She has always been edgy and hard to get along with. I was hoping her temperament would improve, now that she has—at long last—achieved something of importance. But it hasn't?"

"No," said Derek.

"Aiya! Such a difficult person! If you don't mind, I'll be going. I don't like being with so many people. And two of you—I have to say it—are very odd-looking. That makes me even more uneasy." He looked us over again. "It's too bad Ara didn't see you. He is the curious one." He turned his animal off the trail and rode around us.

Derek started walking, more quickly than before. The rest of us followed. After a while Derek said, "He's going to visit Inahooli. Is that possible?"

"No one among my people would do a thing like that," said Nia. "Though I went to find my brother years ago."

The oracle said, "I visit with my mother from time to time. But I am holy and a little crazy as well. An ordinary man would not go looking for his relatives."

"This man must not be ordinary," Derek said. "He will reach the lake tomorrow in the afternoon and find the grave. What will he do then?"

Nia made the gesture of uncertainty. "I do not know."

"He was huge," I said. "Are most of your men that big?"

"No," said Nia.

"Thank God," said Derek. "I was beginning to think of meeting three brothers the size of gorillas and trying to explain to them what happened to their sister."

"As big as what?" asked Nia.

"Gorillas. They are relatives of ours, but much bigger than we are." Derek was still walking quickly. "He'll be a couple of days behind us when he starts."

"What are you talking about?" I asked.

"Inzara. If he decides to come after us. Maybe three days, if we're lucky and he spends time at the lake. Nia? How fast can a bowhorn travel?"

"The Amber People follow the herds. They understand animals and they understand patience. He will know better than to push his bowhorn too hard. Most likely, he will keep to a pace that is twice ours."

"I used to hate problems like this. Bob has twice as many pieces of fruit as Alice, who is half again as tall as Krishna. How many days until Inzara catches up with us?"

"What is he talking about now?" asked the oracle.

"Nothing important." I thought for a while. "It'll take him two days, Derek. We ought to start worrying in the evening of the day after tomorrow. No, the day after that."

"Okay. We are going to move as quickly as we can. Maybe the river is closer than we think."

"Are you frightened?" I asked.

"Yes, of course," he said in English. "If we kill any more natives, we are going to end up on the ship—cleaning out sewer lines, most likely. Or maybe cleaning cages in the laboratories. Anyway, we'll be finished down here forever." He glanced at me. "I bend rules a lot, and I operate close to the edge. But I have no intention of getting myself in serious trouble."

"Why do you bend rules?"

He laughed. "To prove I can."

We traveled till sunset, then made camp. The clouds parted and the Great Moon shone down on us. It was a little past full. Derek peered up at it. "The eruption must have ended."

"Uh-huh." I got out my one remaining human shirt and looked it over. A little dirty and with one tear. I decided to put it on.

"It's too late," said Derek. "That man has already seen Inahooli's shirt."

"Nonetheless—" I changed into my shirt and folded Inahooli's, putting it away.

My radio rang. I turned it on.

"First the good news," said Eddie. "The committee has decided to approve—with regret—your action in relation to Inahooli. You had no choice. Maybe if you hadn't been half-unconscious, you could have figured out another way to stop her. But it was her fault that you were in no condition to think. Her karma was working itself out. There should not be any increase in your karmic burden, at least in the opinion of the committee." I could hear a certain aloofness in his voice. Eddie had nothing against the various Asian religions—in their place, which was not a committee in charge of establishing policy for a scientific team. "Nothing bad is going on your record."

I felt my body relax. I let my breath out in a sigh, then rubbed the back of my neck. "Okay. What is the bad news?"

"There are three pieces. Derek got a reprimand for that silliness about the bracelet."

I looked over at Derek. He shrugged.

"However, that is not going to slow down anyone with his list of publications. The second piece of bad news is—the committee has decided to recommend a ship-wide discussion of our policy re the natives."

"Nonintervention?" I asked.

"Uh-huh." Eddie sounded grim. "They want to reopen the question. I really would like you up here, or at least I would like the option. And that brings me to the third piece of bad news. Lysenko has gone over all the information we have about your part of the continent. The nearest place he is willing to land a plane is to the west of you. It's a river that widens into a lake. He says it's not good, but it's possible."

"How far?" I asked.

"Our best estimate is eight days. I am going to try to stall the first meeting of the all-ship committee."

"That isn't the worst of it, Eddie."

"Oh, no? What is?"

"We met a native today. Inahooli's brother. He is going to visit his sister."

"Does he know you met her?"

"I had on a tunic that belonged to Inahooli. So did Nia. He recognized the clothes. That didn't bother him. The natives are always exchanging gifts. But when he finds the grave . . ."

"Oh, damn."

"And he has two brothers. They are traveling together or—at least—in the same direction. We may have three large angry natives after us."

Eddie was silent for a minute or two. "What do you plan to do?"

Derek said, "Run like hell and hope they don't follow."

"I guess that's the best idea. The committee is right about one thing. There have been too many incidents. I can't figure out why." Eddie sounded plaintive.

"You aren't thinking," Derek said. "Consider the people who've been having all the trouble. Me. Harrison. Gregory. All men. We all ran into the same problem: the social role of adult males. I don't know how Santha managed to avoid trouble. Do his people allow men into their village?"

"Now, that is an interesting story," Eddie said. "But it is pretty long, and diagrams help a lot. I'll tell you about Santha when you get back up here."

"Okay," said Derek.

"I'm not sure your explanation works. What about Lixia? Why has she had so much trouble?"

"Remember her traveling companions. Two men and a woman who has a widespread reputation for perversion."

There was a silence. "You're right, aren't you? This is my mistake. I should have pulled Lixia out after the fiasco in that first village and reassigned her, maybe to the other continent."

Derek made the gesture of uncertainty, then said, "I don't know. I am not crazy about second-guessing history. And I don't like words like 'should.'"

"Well, do the best you can. Lysenko will be waiting when you reach the lake."

Derek turned off the radio. "Do you notice how much Eddie uses the first person singular? The way he talks, he is the one who makes all the decisions and takes all the responsibility with no help from the rest of the committee.

"I, me, my, mine—
Each one a danger sign.

"That's what the witches used to tell us. Listen for those words they said. If a person uses them too often or with too much emphasis, then he or she is sinking down into the well of self. And that is a dangerous situation. You may be face-to-face with a greed head or a power freak."

I made the gesture of acknowledgment. I didn't want to discuss the social theories of the California aborigines—not in English in front of Nia and the oracle. It was rude. I looked at Nia. "Our friend, the one whose voice is in the box, is worried about the amount of trouble we've encountered."

"It is never easy to travel," the oracle said. "I know that. One of my sisters is a great traveler. She has been as far north as the men go and met the Iron People in their summer range. She has been south as well and seen the ocean and gotten gifts from the people who live there: the Fishbone People and the People of Dark Green Dye. My mother has told me about her adventures. Hola! What a tale!" He bit one of his fingernails. "What does your friend expect?"

"A good question. I'm not entirely sure."

For the next three days we traveled as quickly as possible. Nothing much happened. The sky was mostly clear, and the land rolled gently. We saw animals in the distance: flocks of grazing bipeds and once a solitary animal that Nia said was a killer-of-the-plain.

"A male. See how big he is and how he shambles?"

"Nia, that thing is a black spot to me. I thought it might be a person."

"What eyes you have! It is certainly a killer and a male. A female would be traveling with her children. The children would be hungry, and she would be dangerous. But a male is not much of a problem."

"You say that!" the oracle put in. "I know better."

"You were alone and had no fire."

"We'll make one tonight," said the oracle.

This was in the middle of the third day. By then we were all getting uneasy, looking behind us and around us.

We stopped early atop a rise that was higher than the other little hills. Derek peered east. "Nothing," he said. "I can't see them. But nonetheless, we are going to keep watch. And I don't think I want to risk a fire."

"We have to," Nia said. "There are worse things here than men. I do not want to lie in the darkness and wait for a killer-of-the-plain."

"All right," Derek said.

We built the fire and huddled around it. Derek took the first watch. I sat and worried. Finally, when I couldn't stand the worry anymore, I called Eddie.

"Any sign of the three brothers?" he asked.

"No. And I don't want to think about them. How are things on the ship?"

"Not good. Meiling went over to the opposition."

"What?"

"She has filed a report against nonintervention. The natives are not fools, according to her. They have eyes to see and minds to think with. They know that she is something utterly different, something utterly outside their experience *and* the experience of their ancestors. Hairless people are not mentioned in the stories about creation.

"Knowledge—by itself—is an intervention. Our presence

changes the way the natives see the world. According to her, there is no way to study these people without causing change."

"The Heisenberg Uncertainty Principle," I said.

"So I am told. I'm not an expert on the history of science. And I don't think it's possible to apply the laws of physics to the behavior of people. That is like Social Darwinism. A stupid and dangerous theory.

"Meiling says the policy of nonintervention does only one thing. It makes life hard for the workers in the field. They can't trade information with the natives, and they can't offer help. Simple medical care, for example."

"I did," I said. "When Nia got hurt."

"I know. But that was only one person, and you and Nia were alone. It wasn't as if you had set yourself up as the village doctor. Meiling wants to. She has medical training and worked in Tibet. We told her no. She is still angry."

I thought of Meiling: thin and intense, a person who had trouble with detachment. Nonaction was not for her. She had no interest in the ideas of Lao Zi or the Buddha. She came from the second great tradition in China, that of Mao Zi and Men Zi and Master Kong. The tradition of social responsibility.

"She has a point," Eddie said. "I know that nonintervention makes everything more difficult. And maybe it is a farce. Maybe there is no way we can avoid changing this planet. But the policy makes us go slowly. If we abandon it or even begin to modify it, then it's only a matter of time—and not much time—before the planet looks the way America did in the nineteenth century. The natives will be knee deep in explorers and prospectors and Marxist missionaries."

"Eddie, you worry even more than I do."

"I'm not going to say wait and see. I'm going to do everything I can to make sure my predictions don't come true."

"Good night, Eddie."

I meditated for a while, looking at the fire. Then I dozed, sitting in the half-lotus position. Finally Derek shook me.

"It's your turn. I haven't seen anyone."

I kept watch until the middle of the night. Nothing much

happened. Meteors fell, and a night bug came out of the darkness. It glided above the fire on huge pale wings. A moment later it was gone.

I woke Nia. She got up, groaning softly.

"I saw a bug this wide." I held my hands forty centimeters apart. "Is that possible?"

She frowned. "Is that why you woke me?"

"No. It's your turn to keep watch. Could the bug have been that big?"

"Yes." Nia stretched and yawned. "Go to sleep, Li-sa. I don't feel like talking."

I did as I was told.

The morning was bright. Above us and to the east the sky was clear. The west was full of clouds. They were a kind of cirrus.

"New weather," Nia said.

We saddled the animals and went on. I rode, as did the oracle.

The clouds spread east, covering the sky. By midmorning the sun shone through a white haze. Derek kept looking back. "Maybe they've decided to forget the whole thing," he said at last. He didn't speak with much conviction.

At noon we came to a valley. We stopped on the bluff above it. The bluff was low. The valley was shallow and not especially wide. A river ran through the middle of it, brown and slow. Monster grass grew on the banks. A new variety. The leaves were distinctly blue. The slopes of the valley were covered with the usual yellow vegetation. Here and there I saw patches of red: a plant I did not recognize.

The trail descended into the valley. We followed it over the yellow slopes. I saw animals: a herd or flock of quadrupeds. They were tiny, no more than a meter high, and shy. As soon as we came near they bounded away in great leaps like so many gazelles. They were brown with white stripes down their backs, and they looked furry.

"What are they?" asked Derek.

"Silverbacks," Nia said. "In the winter they turn entirely white, and their fur is warm and thick. Some people keep them. The People of Fur and Tin, for example. But we—the Iron People—think they are more trouble than they are worth. They do not keep their horns, but drop them every fall and grow new ones in the spring. While the horns are coming in the animals are irritable and hard to manage. They rub their horns against anything they can find: tent poles and the wheels of wagons and even the tripods we use to hang up cooking pots."

The trail went along the river. Bipeds with long necks grazed on the leaves of the monster grass. They were almost the same color as the grass. In the shadows, among the blue leaves, they were hard to make out. Often I did not see one until it moved, reaching up a long thin arm to grab some food or twisting its neck and cocking its tiny head in order to stare at us. And I had no idea how many there were. Two? Three? A dozen?

"We don't have to worry about killers-of-the-plain," Nia said. "There are too many animals around. They aren't smart—these creatures—but they wouldn't stay if they saw one of their kind being eaten."

We continued along the river all afternoon. Gradually it widened, growing increasingly shallow. There were sandbars and patches of reed. The trail ended. We came to a halt.

Nia stared at the river. "This is the ford." She shaded her eyes. "There is a man on the other side in the shadows. He is standing watching us."

Derek shaded his eyes. "You're right. Goddammit!"

Behind us a voice spoke. "That is my brother Tzoon."

I looked around. A man stood five meters away from us, next to a stem of monster grass. Inzara. I recognized the tunic.

"And that is Ara." He waved and a man stepped onto the trail we had just come down. He was as big as Inzara. His tunic was blue and covered with embroidery. He wore a belt made of linked copper and a knife in a blue leather sheath. His boots were blue leather. Around one wrist he wore a dozen or so bracelets of copper wire. He moved his hand slightly, gesturing to his brother. I heard the bracelets chime.

"What do you want?" asked Derek.

"You killed Inahooli," Inzara said. "We dug her up. There was a deep wound in her back."

Derek said nothing.

After a moment Nia said, "Yes. We did. What about it?"

"We want an explanation."

Ara said, "The ceremony to honor the Ropemaker is ruined. We are men. We don't care about these things as much as the women do. But it is no good thing to see the clan of our mother embarrassed."

"Inahooli will be known as the guardian who failed," Inzara said. "Her ghost will be furious. She was never easy to get along with. Now, who knows what she will do? There will have to be ceremonies of aversion and ceremonies of purification." Inzara paused.

Ara continued, "And ceremonies to drive away the anger of Inahooli and of our ancestor the Ropemaker. This is a bad situation. We want to know how it came about."

"All right," Nia said. "We will tell you. Does the other one—the one across the river—want to hear?"

"Yes." Inzara waved and shouted.

The third brother appeared a few minutes later, riding out of the grove into sunlight. He led two bowhorns with empty saddles. They forded the river, splashing through the shallows. When they reached our side, the man reined his animal. "Well?" His voice was as deep as Inzara's but much harsher.

"Tie up the animals," Inzara said.

Nia looked at me and the oracle. "Get down, both of you."

We dismounted. Nia took our reins and led our animals into the nearest grove. The third brother rode after her.

They came back together, but walking some distance apart. Both of them looked wary. Nia was a big woman. The man dwarfed her. He was as huge as his brothers. He wore a kilt of dark green fabric and a yellow belt. The buckle was silver. His boots were green leather. On his broad chest he wore a necklace. It was tangled in his shaggy hair and more than half-hidden. I made out beads of silver, long and narrow, alternating with round amber beads as yellow as butter.

Inzara waved at him. "This, as I told you before, is my brother Tzoon."

The man looked at us, then grunted. "Unh!"

"Who are you?" asked Ara. He had remained to the north of us on the trail. Inzara was a little to the south, close to the bank of the river. The third brother was to the east, at the edge of the grove. We were surrounded. Trapped.

Nia scratched her nose. "Will you answer a question for me? Then I will tell you who we are."

Inzara made the gesture of assent.

"Why do you travel together?"

"We are not ordinary men," said Inzara. "We were born together, all three of us in one birth."

"Aiya!" said the oracle.

Nia said, "Hu!"

"No one in our village had ever seen a thing like that. Two children at once, yes. That has happened, though not often. Usually the children are small and weak. They die. But three— That was unheard of. And we were all large and healthy. People said our mother must have met the Trickster on the plain. We had to be unlucky. No woman could nurse three children. One of us, at least, would have to die."

Ara continued the story: "Our mother said we were all fine babies. She couldn't decide which one of us should be carried out on the plain and left for scavengers to find. She wanted to keep us all. Our mother never liked any kind of waste."

The third brother—Tzoon—made the gesture of agreement.

Ara went on. "Our mother took gifts to the shamaness: a fine long rope and a piece of cloth covered with embroidery."

"And a pot made by the Iron People," Inzara said. "She was never one to keep things hidden in her tent. She knew the importance of giving."

Ara made the gesture of agreement. "She asked the shamaness to perform the ceremony of interpretation. This took three days. Our mother nursed us as best she could. On the second day of the ceremony, when the shamaness was in a deep trance, our aunt Iatzi lost her baby."

"It had always been sick," Inzara added.

Once again Ara made the gesture of agreement. "It was her first child. Now her tent was empty and she had plenty of milk. She offered to help our mother.

"Our mother said that proved we were not unlucky. In fact we were luckier than most, since what we needed came to us."

Inzara said, "When the shamaness woke, she told the villagers she had gone up into the sky and met the Ropemaker, the Mother of Mothers, and the Master of the Herds. They told her, 'These children belong to us, and we will provide for them as we see fit. If we intend them to live, they will live. If we decide it is time for them to die—together or each one separately, you will see the result. Do not interfere and do not presume to understand our intentions.' That was the end of her vision.

"What else is there to say? When we were children, we liked to be together. We almost never argued. There were people in the village who said we had only one spirit among the three of us. Maybe they were right. We don't know. There are differences among us. Tzoon is silent. Ara is curious. I am unusually even-tempered. But it is true we are as close as sisters, and each one of us knows what the others are thinking. We went through the change at the same time exactly."

"Even then," Ara said. "We didn't quarrel, though Tzoon became more silent than before."

I looked at the third brother. He frowned.

"In the Summer Land and when the herd is moving, we stay close together. We like to look around and see a brother off in the distance. And we like to meet now and then to share food and talk. Inzara and I talk. Tzoon listens."

The third brother said, "In the spring we stay apart."

Inzara made the gesture of agreement. "We do not know what would happen then. What if a woman came out of the village full of lust, and two of us saw her? Would we fight? That would be terrible!"

"We make sure our territories are widely separated, though all equally close to the village," Ara said. "This has become difficult in recent years. We are all big men, and the territories we have now are almost in the village."

Inzara said, "We let other men—men we could face down—

creep in between us. We lose some women that way. But our mother always said, 'Nothing is gained by greed.'"

"Now," said Tzoon. "Tell us who you are."

Nia pointed at each one of us and gave our names. She gave her name last.

"You are the woman who loved a man," Inzara said.

Nia made the gesture of agreement.

"And now you travel with another man." He pointed at the oracle. "And with two people who have almost no hair."

"Yes."

"What sex are those people?"

"One is a woman. The other is a man."

"Aiya!" said Inzara.

Tzoon made the gesture that meant "no matter." "This is no concern of ours. If they want to risk bad luck—well, let them. They do not belong to our village."

Ara made the gesture of agreement. "Our concern is Inahooli. How did she die?"

Nia rubbed the back of her neck. "This is not easy to explain."

Tzoon frowned.

She glanced at him, then at his brothers. "First of all, we met with a *suwahara*. A male with a family to protect. He frightened our bowhorns, and they ran away. We were stuck on the shore of the Lake of Bugs and Stones. This is important for you to know. We had no way to escape Inahooli after she went crazy."

"Ah," said Inzara.

"The first time she came, Li-sa and I were alone. She wanted to show off her tower, and Li-sa was curious. She is a peculiar person, always asking questions, like a little girl, poking at things and prying them open and asking and asking. Aiya!"

Ara frowned. "Anything can be taken too far. But there is nothing wrong with curiosity."

"Anyway," Nia said. "Li-sa went to see the tower. Then Inahooli decided she was a demon and pulled out a knife. She tried to kill Li-sa. But Li-sa got away."

"Why did she think that one was a demon?" Ara waved at me.

Nia paused, frowning. She bit her thumbnail. "Inahooli remembered who I am. And she thought a person without hair who travels with a pervert must be a demon."

"That makes sense," said Tzoon.

Inzara made the gesture of disagreement. "The tower is protected. The shamaness performed ceremonies in the spring after it was built. There is magic all through it, woven into every piece of rope and around every piece of wood."

"Does the magic protect it against everything?" I asked.

"No. Of course not. A high wind can blow it down, and hail can tear the banners. Animals can chew on it or perch on it and cause damage. But the tower ought to be safe from demons. If that one"—he pointed at me—"was able to get near the tower, she isn't a demon. Though she might be something else unlucky. A person in need of purification, for example."

"No," said Nia. "Inahooli was definite. Li-sa was a demon. Inahooli decided the tower was ruined. Li-sa had taken away all of its power. She came to our camp at night, planning to get back at us in some way. That one"—she pointed at Derek—"saw her coming. He fought with Inahooli and won. He tied her up, and we tried to talk with her. They—the others—tried to talk with her. I was on the plain, looking for our bowhorns."

"I will tell this part," the oracle said. "We talked and talked, trying to convince her that we had done nothing to her tower. I understand these things. I am an oracle and the holiest person among the Copper People of the Plain."

"Aiya!" said Inzara.

"Oracles don't travel," said Ara. "Why are you here?"

"My spirit told me to go with these people. They are important in some way or other."

Ara looked at me and at Derek. He made the gesture of doubt and then the gesture of agreement. Together, they meant "if you say so."

The oracle continued: "In the end Inahooli decided that the cause of all her trouble was your shamaness. She had put a spell on Inahooli and made her believe the tower was ruined."

Tzoon grunted. "I never liked the shamaness. I remember

what she was like as a girl. Always talking. Always being clever."

Inzara frowned. "Why would the shamaness do a thing like that?"

"Inahooli said she used to belong to the Groundbird Clan, and they are rivals of your clan."

I added, "She told us—the big moon was involved."

Inzara looked at me, frowning. "The moon? How?"

"It was boiling over then."

"We know," said Ara. "We saw it, but that has nothing to do with the making or unmaking of towers. That means we are going to be short of food in the winter."

"The old women say," Tzoon added.

Inzara made the gesture of disagreement. "Inahooli was not telling the truth. The moon had nothing to do with what was happening, and our shamaness is the daughter of the old shamaness. A true daughter, born out of the old woman's body. She has always belonged to the Clan of the First Magician."

Ara said, "The mother of the old shamaness was born in the Clan of the Groundbird. She was adopted by the shamaness of that time, who had only sons. Some people said that she—the mother of the old shamaness—favored the Groundbird Clan more than she should have. But that was three generations ago."

"Well, then," the oracle said. "Inahooli was lying. We believed her and let her go. She came back at night and attacked us. In my opinion she was crazy. She fought without caring what happened. She almost won. But one of us managed to stab her before she killed all of us. That is what she was trying to do."

"That is the whole story," Nia said.

There was a silence. The three brothers were frowning.

"Well?" said Tzoon at last. "Are they telling the truth?"

Inzara made the gesture of affirmation. "It sounds like Inahooli. Deep inside her, she always believed things would go wrong for her. She looked for bad luck. When that one arrived"—he waved at Nia—"she must have thought, this is it. The thing I have been waiting for. The thing that will make me fail."

"What are you talking about?" I asked.

"I'm thirsty," Inzara replied. "Let's drink from the river and then sit down. I will tell you about Inahooli."

"All right," said Nia.

The three brothers drank, kneeling one by one at the edge of the river. As one drank, the other two kept watch, glancing at us and the grove of monster grass and the far side of the river. Tzoon was the last to drink. He rose and wiped his mouth. "Unh!"

Inzara moved away from the bank. He sat down with his back against a stem of monster grass, stretched out his legs, and rubbed one thigh. "It was a hard ride from the lake. We had to rebury Inahooli and do it the right way, with singing and with gifts of parting. All that took time."

Ara sat down at the edge of the grove, not far from Inzara. He folded his legs into a half-lotus position. "We could not do the entire ceremony. A shamaness is necessary for that. But we performed the parts we could remember from when we were children in the village."

"Tell the story," the third brother said. He remained standing on the bank of the river. How tall was he, anyway? Over two meters. In the sunlight his fur was dark brown instead of black. There were reddish highlights in the fur. His eyes were partially closed. The pupils had contracted to lines. The irises were pale yellow.

Inzara pointed at the ground, and the four of us sat down. We were facing Inzara and Ara. Tzoon was behind us. There was no way to watch him and his brothers at the same time. If anything went wrong, if the brothers became angry, he would be on us before we could rise and turn.

"Inahooli was the first born," Inzara said. "The oldest daughter. She should have been the most important child. But we came next, and we were magical."

"Ah," said Nia.

Inzara made the gesture of affirmation. "Everyone watched us. Everyone talked about us. We were the important ones."

Ara said, "I used to wonder why she looked unhappy. But I couldn't ask her. It was never easy talking to her. She was quieter than he is." Ara waved at Tzoon. "And she had a bad temper. Either she said nothing or she yelled and jumped up and down."

"I never noticed that she was unhappy," Inzara said. "But I have to say I never paid much attention to her. I was happy with my brothers and our mother and Iatzi."

Behind us Tzoon grunted. In agreement, I decided.

Inzara went on. "I met Inahooli again—for the first time since we left the village—the spring before last. I had a territory close to the village in between two men who were getting old. They no longer had the strength for confrontation, not with me or Ara or Tzoon. But we let them in, so we would be safe from one another.

"The first woman who came into my territory was Inahooli. She looked good. She was an impressive woman. And I was glad to see her. She was my sister, after all. We had shared the same tent and the same fire. I thought, this is good luck. I will be able to ask about our mother and about Iatzi.

"But the moment she saw who I was, she became furious. 'Can't I ever get away from you?' she yelled at me. I was surprised.

"We mated—"

"Why?" I asked.

"What do you mean?"

"Why did you mate, if she was angry with you?"

"Because that is what a man and woman do when they meet in the time of mating." He spoke slowly and clearly, as if he were talking to a child. "Unless, of course, they are mother and son."

An incest taboo, I thought. Why? Maybe to protect young boys from their mothers. Was that possible? Or maybe to allow the men one relationship that was not sexual.

"Go on," said Ara. "Tell the rest."

"After we mated, I asked her why she was angry. She said I was a child of the Trickster, born to cause trouble. She had waited and waited for the change. She had given us—all three of us—fine gifts and told us good-bye. At last, she told herself, she was out of the shadow and into the light. We were gone.

She was free of us. But we wouldn't leave her alone. Every spring, Inahooli said, the woman asked, 'Who has mated with Inzara and Ara and Tzoon? Are they all right? Did they make it through the winter? Are they as lucky as they have always been?'"

"Unh!"

I looked around at Tzoon. His eyes were almost entirely closed, and he looked as satisfied as a cat in a patch of sunlight. Nothing wrong with that, I told myself. Everyone enjoyed appreciation.

Inzara continued: "Her luck was always bad, she told me. Her children were ordinary. She had no special skill. No one respected her. She had no friends.

"I told her it wasn't my fault. Then she hit me. I thought, she will make me angry. I got out a mating gift. 'Get out of here,' I told her. 'If you still feel the lust, go east. Old Hoopatoo is there. He isn't much good at confronting, but he ought to be able to mate.'

"She gave me a gift, then rode away. I did not see her again until I dug into her grave." Inzara paused a moment. "The next spring I asked the women—the ones who came to me—how Inahooli was doing. She had gotten pregnant, they said. Her child had been born too early. It died. That was bad news. But there was good news. The clan had chosen her to be the guardian of the tower. She was a difficult woman, they told me, but impressive. Strong and forceful, and her family was respected by everyone. A good choice for the guardian, all the women said.

"I thought, Now she will have prestige. She will stop being envious." He looked at us. "I do not like being on bad terms with anyone—except other men, of course. And even then I don't want a serious quarrel. Everything will be fine, as far as I'm concerned, as long as they back down."

Ara made the gesture of agreement. Behind me Tzoon grunted.

Inzara went on. "No man ever sees the ceremonies in front of a clan tower—not unless he is very old and has gone through the second change and chosen to return to the village. But now and then, men go to look at a tower—usually after the ceremonies are over and the tower has been abandoned. Most of the time, the tower had been damaged in one way or another, and the holy masks are gone. They are always destroyed after the big dance. I thought, I want to see this tower—our sister's tower—when it is new. I talked to my brothers. They decided to come with me. We rode south ahead of the herd."

"We lost nothing," said Ara. "In the summer, in the north, it doesn't really matter what kind of territory a man has. Some areas are more comfortable than others. This summer, for example, I had a stretch of river full of fish and an outcropping of rock where berry vines grew. A good territory! I enjoyed it, especially the berries. They were as big as the end of my thumb and juicy. But it wasn't really difficult to ride away and leave everything to that fat fool Oopai. I knew he would sneak in the moment I was gone."

"No matter," said Tzoon. "When the herd reaches the Winter Land, we will be there. Then Oopai can remember his berries. We will be the ones who are close to the village."

Ara made the gesture of agreement.

"In any case," said Inzara. "We rode to the Lake of Bugs and Stones. We found our sister and we came after you."

Ara repeated the gesture of agreement. For a moment or two there was silence. What was next? What were they going to do? I glanced at the two brothers in front of me. Their faces—dark and furry—told me nothing. I twisted around and looked at Tzoon. He frowned and scratched his forehead—a wide, low expanse, covered with fur. The ridges above his eyes were prominent. His eyes were deep-set, his nose was flat, and his cheekbones were broad. An almost perfect Neanderthal. I had seen people like him in dioramas in museums. No. I was wrong. His jaw wasn't as heavy as the jaws of those museum people; and his forehead—though it was low—did not recede. From the look of it, he had a lot of forebrain. Whatever that might mean in his species.

He grunted and made the gesture that meant "so be it." After that he walked past us, away from the river.

Ara got up and stretched. A moment later Inzara stood.

We got up, all four of us.

"What now?" asked Derek.

"We got the explanation we wanted," Inzara said. "We don't mind being around each other, but you make us uneasy. We will go. East of here, we saw tracks. A flock of *shuwahara*. Tzoon is a fine archer, and Ara isn't bad. We will kill an animal—a young one, fat and tender—and roast it."

"Good," said Tzoon.

Ara said, "We will eat and then ride south and wait in the land of winter for the herd to arrive."

They got their animals and led them onto the trail, mounted and settled themselves in their saddles. Like Nia they slouched, looking relaxed and comfortable. They gathered their reins, turned their animals, and rode away. At first they were close together. But after a short while Tzoon turned off the trail, riding into the grove. I lost sight of him. A minute or two later Ara turned his animal into the grove and—like his brother—was gone from view. Inzara rode on alone. The trail curved. He rode around the curve and was gone.

Derek exhaled. "Thank the Holy Unity or the wheel of fate or whatever is responsible. I hate to admit it, but that trio frightened me."

"Why?" asked the oracle. "They weren't crazy. Only crazy men fight when there is nothing to be won—no territory and no women."

Nia made the gesture of agreement. "They are big men. Those ones rarely go crazy. They know their own strength. They have the best of everything, and they know they are able to hold on to what they have. It is the young men in the hills who go crazy from frustration. Or the old men who have lost their territories."

"I forgot," a voice said.

I jumped. So did everyone else. We turned, all of us.

A bowhorn came out of the grove. The rider wore blue. Ara. The curious brother. He reined his animal and looked down at us.

"Yes?" said Derek. "What is it?"

"You two. The ones without hair. What are you?"

"People," I said. "We come from a long distance away. In our land all the people are more or less like us."

"With no hair?"

"Only on the head. And there are a few patches in other places."

"Where?"

"Under the arms and between our legs," I said.

"Aiya! You must get cold in the winter."

"We wear more clothes than you do," I said. "In the summer we take off almost everything, and we are probably more comfortable than you are."

Nia made the gesture of disagreement. "In the summer you have no protection against the bugs that sting or bite."

I thought for a moment. "We have ointments with aromas the bugs don't like. We smear them on us, and the bugs stay away."

"It sounds messy," Ara told me. "Fur would have been better. And handsomer, too. Whatever spirit made you wasn't thinking about what she was doing."

"That often happens," the oracle said. "The spirits are very powerful, but they aren't always smart."

Ara made the gesture of agreement. "You are right about that. Look at the Trickster. He thinks he is so clever. He runs around setting traps and telling lies. And what happens? He falls into his own traps half the time, and his lies get so complicated that he can't keep track of them. That isn't clever. It's stupid-smart." He paused. "What is the name of your people?"

"Humans," I said.

He repeated the word. "What does it mean?"

"People."

Ara frowned. "But what kind of people? What do you carry when you travel? What is your gift?"

Derek said, "At times we call ourselves Homo sapiens, which means the People of Wisdom."

"Aiya! That is a gift indeed! Do you have any with you? Tell me something wise."

Derek was silent for a moment. Then he looked pleased. He had come up with something. "If I tell you something wise, then you will have a gift from me. But I won't have anything from you. So I will have given you something for nothing, which is hardly wise."

"Ah," said Ara. He scratched his forehead. "You prove yourself wise by telling me nothing. Is that what you are trying to say?"

Derek made the gesture of agreement.

Ara made the gesture that meant "no." "Your answer is not wise. It is stupid-smart. You think the way the Trickster does. He worries about being cheated. He wastes his time looking for tricks and lies when there are none. 'Those branches by the trail hide a trap,' he says. 'A deep hole or a noose tied to a sapling. I'm no fool. I will go through the field.' And he leaves the safe way, trodden by people, and goes off to tangle himself in briers or to fall in a bog. If that is the best you can offer, I do not think your people are the People of Wisdom."

I looked at Derek. His face was red. He opened his mouth, then closed it. He wasn't going to argue with Ara. I could understand that. Ara was very large and not especially polite. Inzara was the one who liked to get along with people. Ara didn't seem to care.

"Most of the time," I said. "We call ourselves after the land we live in. Derek is an Angelino, because his people live near a place called Los Angeles. I am Hawaiian. I come from an island called Hawaii."

That wasn't exactly true. I was from the island of Kauai. But I didn't know the word for a collection of islands. Herd? Flock? Heap? Arrangement? Gathering? Lacking the word I could not say I was from the Hawaiian Islands.

Ara frowned again. "You have a lot of names for yourselves. Can't you decide what you are?"

"No," I said.

"Ah. Well, if I meet any more hairless people, I will ask them for a name. Maybe they will come up with a better answer than you have." He turned his animal and rode off along the trail.

"I liked my answer," Derek said. "I guess these people don't appreciate wit." He used the English word for "wit." Was there a native word? I didn't know.

Nia got the bowhorns. We mounted double, Nia behind the oracle, Derek behind me. In that way we crossed the river. At the deepest point the water came to the bellies of our animals. I had to pull my feet up in order to keep them dry. Derek didn't bother. As usual he was barefooted. The water felt good, he said.

On the far side Nia and Derek dismounted. We found the trail. It went south and west along the river. We followed it.

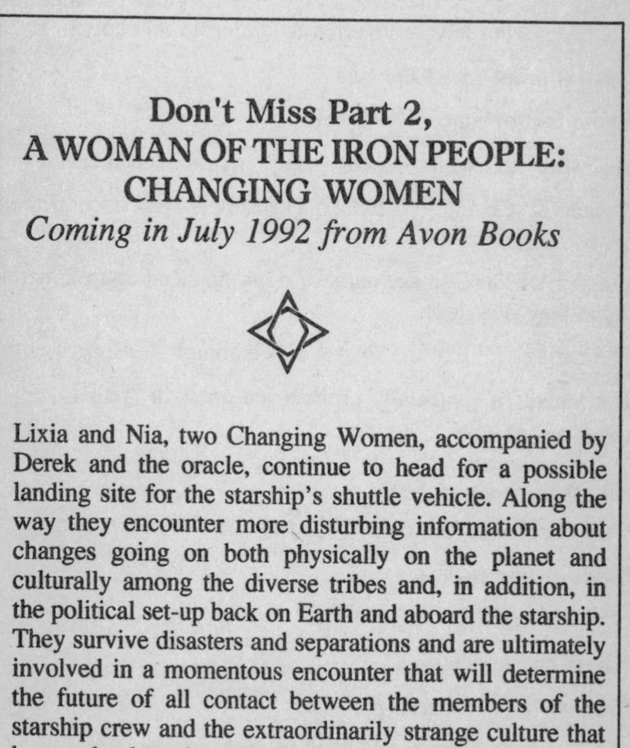

APPENDIX A:
A Note on Pronunciation

I was raised on the Wade-Giles system of transliterating Chinese, but have converted to Pinyin in this novel.

Lixia is pronounced *Lee-sha.*

Yunqi is pronounced *Yoon-chee.*

The word "zi" which means "sage" is pronounced *zee.*

Zhuang Zi (Chuang-tzu in the old system) is pronounced *Juang-zee.*

The rest of the Chinese names are pronounced approximately the way they look.

The native "i," like the Pinyin "i," is long.

The native "a" is usually pronounced *ah* as in "father."

Nia is *Nee-ah.*

"In" is pronounced *inn.*

"Ar" is pronounced as in "car" and "far."

Inzara is *Innzarah.*

"Ai" is pronounced as in "hay."

"U" is pronounced *oo.*

Nahusai is pronounced *Nahoosay.*

"E" is usually the vowel sound in "air" or "care."

Gersu is *Gairsoo.*

"O" is the sound in "Oh" and "Oklahoma."

Yohai is *Yohay.*

The sound spelled "kh" in the language of the Copper People is pronounced like the "ch" in "Bach."

The natives all speak the language of gifts, but their pronunciation varies.

Nia can say "g" but not "k." This is why her version of Derek's name is "Deragu." There is no "sh" in her language. Lixia becomes "Li-sa." The oracle can say "k" and "sh," but not "p." The native animal which Nia calls an "osupa" is an "osuba" to him.

All the native languages are accented. Usually the accent falls on the first syllable.

There are three native gestures that could be translated as "yes."

One is the gesture of affirmation which means "yes, that is so."

Another is the gesture of agreement which means "yes, I agree with you."

The third is the gesture of assent which means "yes, that should, can, or will be done."

APPENDIX B: Starship Design by Albert W. Kuhfeld, Ph.D.

For a reaction drive to push a ship near light-speed, the reaction mass itself must travel at relativistic velocities in a jet so hot no material substance can withstand it. Only a force field can handle the job.

Magnetic fields are the best-trained force fields we know: They're used in laboratories everywhere to control the paths of charged particles. Nuclear fusion is nature's way of making hot ions. A magnetic-mirror fusion reactor, with a leaky mirror to the aft, would create a rocketlike nuclear exhaust.

The reaction $Li^7 + h^1 = 2\ He^4$ releases 17.3 MeV, with no neutral particles to carry off energy in random and uncontrollable directions. It's one of the more enthusiastic reactions of starbirth—any technology with fusion power should be able to handle it.[1]

Lithium hydride has a specific gravity of 0.78 and a melting point of 689 Celsius. Living quarters built inside a large chunk of this solid fuel are protected by sheer mass against most of the interstellar dust and gases. Hydrogen atoms make good shielding against neutrons, while magnetic fields steer away interstellar ions.

17.3 MeV_e, evenly divided between the two product nuclei, works out to about 22% of the speed of light. The (non-relativistic) equation for ship velocity is $m\ dV + v_e\ dm = 0$

[1]Harwit, Martin, *Astrophysical Concepts* (New York: John Wiley & Sons, 1973) pp 335–43.

which integrates out to $V = v_e \ln(m_o/m)$.

To reach 10% of light-speed, the ship would have to burn 37% of its mass; for 20% c, 61% of the mass. If you then slow back to zero, you will burn 61% and 85% of the mass respectively. 15% of light-speed would be a reasonable compromise. At 100% efficiency, accelerating to 15% of light-speed and then decelerating to rest, the ship would arrive with 25% of its starting mass, having used 75% as fuel and reaction mass. (Errors introduced by ignoring relativity are minor compared to those caused by assuming complete efficiency. Time dilation effects are only about 1%.) It takes less than two months at one gravity to reach 15% of light-speed. Even at a fraction of a g, the majority of the trip could be spent coasting.

(The rocket exhaust is powerful alpha radiation. This is an ideal vehicle for leaving your enemies behind, but be careful where you point the thing if you hope for a welcome upon your return.)

A ship traveling the 18.2 light-years to Sigma Draconis at 0.15c would take 122 years one-way. It has to refuel (hope for a planet with a water ocean to supply lithium and hydrogen!) before returning. The round trip could barely be made in 250 years; with study time, more would be probable.

Most of the ship is fuel, a giant lithium-hydride cigar—white when pure, but who knows what impurities will creep in (or be found useful)? The long axis points in the direction of travel, to minimize cross-section and put as much mass as possible between the crew and anything they collide with. (At 0.15 c, cosmic gases become low-energy cosmic rays: grains of dust make large craters where they hit.)

Well ahead of the cigar is a repairable "umbrella" shield—very little mass, but enough to vaporize cosmic dust, spreading it out so it'll cause less damage to the main body of the ship. The living quarters are inside the "cigar," protected from the hazards of travel. Spiral tunnels wind forward and aft to the end caps; since radiation travels in straight lines, a spiral tunnel blocks it effectively.

A fusion rocket is behind the cigar, built of magnetic fields controlled and confined by superconducting magnets. There are many magnetic mirrors in series, so a particle leaking through one mirror finds itself confined in the next chamber. The fields move the ionized gases along in a manner similar to peristalsis with regions of high and low magnetic field sweeping aft. Ionized particles are held in the regions of low magnetic field by the stronger fields before and behind, compressed to greater and greater densities until they fuse. At this point the magnetic fields to the rear open up into a rocket nozzle of forces.

The rear end cap slowly chews its way up the length of the ship, feeding fuel into the engine. The amount of lithium hydride before and behind the living quarters is chosen so the engine uses most of the rear fuel accelerating: then, as the ship nears its destination, the end caps are released and the ship reversed so the forward section (now needed more for fuel than shielding) docks into the engine. The umbrella shield is discarded as excess mass, and will be rebuilt during refueling.

Deceleration poses an interesting problem, since one can hardly put an umbrella shield *behind* the main engine. But the hot breath of an engine like this should sizzle nearly everything within a light-day of the nozzle into ionic vapors—and the engine's magnetic fields protect the ship from ions. An arriving ship appears as an enormous dim comet, with tail pointing along its path rather than away from the sun—and like comets of old, it can be an omen of change.

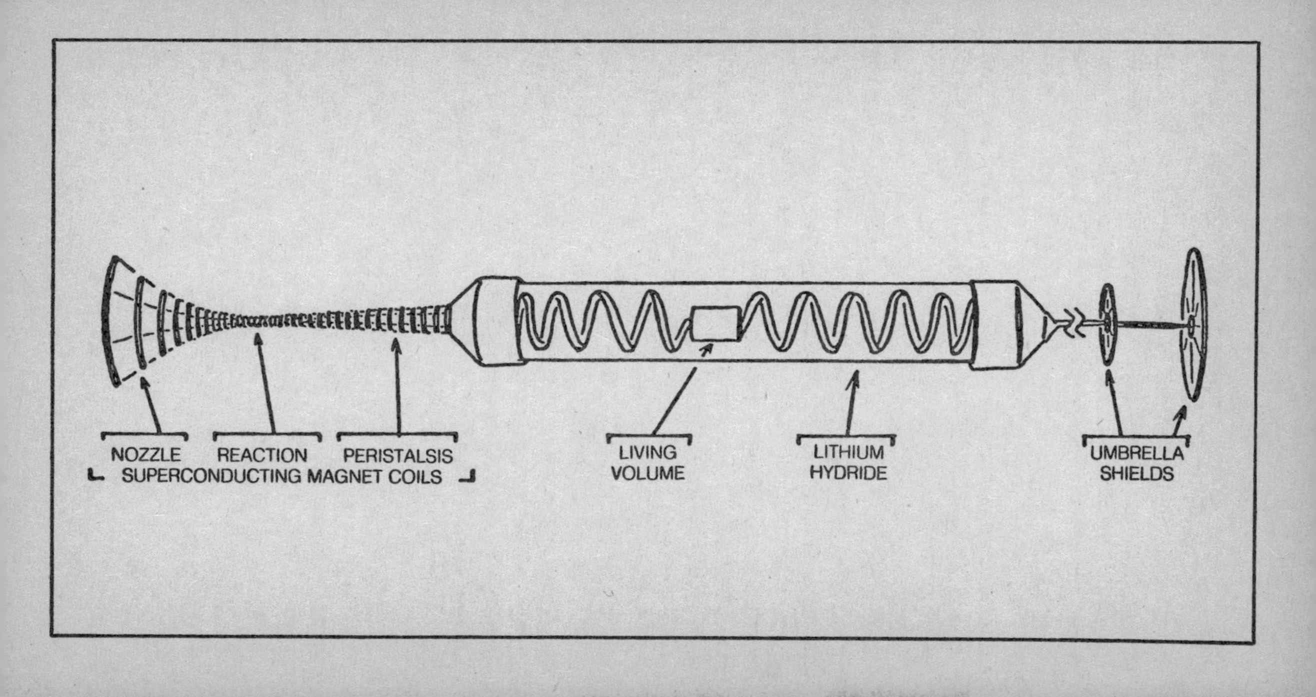
NOZZLE
REACTION
PERISTALSIS
SUPERCONDUCTING MAGNET COILS
LIVING VOLUME
LITHIUM HYDRIDE
UMBRELLA SHIELDS